Praise for

The Blanche Murninghan Mysteries

"It's Blanche alone who puts the bang in the book, and her debut should make readers sit up and take notice. A welcome newcomer to the South Florida genre."
—Kirkus Reviews

"Saving Tuna Street is more than just a murder mystery."
— Midwest Book Review

"A murder disrupts the perfect vacation in the Irish countryside. Cozily delightful."
—Marilyn Levinson aka Allison Brook,
author of the *Haunted Library Mystery Series*

"A delightful cozy filled with colorful characters and a captivating mystery. Cozy fans will enjoy the close bond between Bang and her cousin and their shared humor as they explore Ireland on the hunt for a killer."
—Michelle Hillen Klump,
author of the *Cocktails and Catering Mysteries*

"A fun mystery that takes you to an Irish castle where a cast of likeable characters weave you through the twists and turns of a captivating whodunit."
—Christina Romeril,
author of the *Killer Chocolate Mysteries*

Hot Tango in Argentina

Argentina

A Blanche Murninghan Mystery

The Blanche Murninghan Mysteries

Saving Tuna Street
Trouble Down Mexico Way
Mission Improbable: Vietnam
A Deathly Irish Secret
Hot Tango in Argentina

Hot Tango in Argentina

A Blanche Murninghan Mystery

Nancy Nau Sullivan

Torchflame Books

Vista, CA

ISBN: 978-1-61153-615-7 (paperback)
ISBN: 978-1-61153-616-4 (ebook)
ISBN: 978-1-61153-617-1 (large print)

Library of Congress Control Number: 2025903829

Hot Tango in Argentina is published by: Torchflame Books, an imprint of Top Reads Publishing, LLC, 1035 E. Vista Way, Suite 205, Vista, CA 92084, USA

Cover design: Jori Hanna
Book interior layout: Jori Hanna

The publisher is not responsible for websites or social media accounts (or their content) that are not owned by the publisher.

This is a work of fiction. All characters, organizations, and events portrayed in this novel are either products of the author's imagination or are used fictitiously.

To Charles John Nau, Jr.
primo mio, por siempre
(1947-2024)

What do you call it
Sadness and beauty's all you see
What do you call it
Another man's face is ropes and knives
The frown on his face been there for years ...

~from "Argentina" by Miles Sullivan
December, 2005

Prologue

BUENOS AIRES, ARGENTINA

February, 1978

THE MEN WORE DRAB GREEN, *much the same shade as their dusty Ford Falcon.*

The four of them got out of the car, as if on cue, and pounded up the walk to the house. They hammered on the door, and the maid opened it slowly. A hot wind swept through, moving the filmy white curtains, bringing ill fortune. The boy crouched near the entry, hardly able to breathe. He'd heard about these visits, and now they had come.

The men marched through the house, their boots making a hard, hollow sound on the slick yellow tile. All the way to the back of the house they went. They'd done this many times before. Who knew how many times? It didn't matter the number. It only mattered when it happened to you. Everybody was on edge, dreading that pounding on the door.

The boy didn't move from the corner; tears froze behind his eyes. He pressed his small body against the rough plaster and listened for sounds from the back of the house. Eduardo's shrill cries rose up, panicky, rebellious in

1

a crescendo of protest. Then his voice died away. The men dragged Eduardo through the entryway to the front door, shoes and boots and arms and legs scraping in resistance.

The boy crept to the window and peeked over the sill to see the last of his brother. The white shirt, the legs curled up to his chest, his body in a protective knot. The men slammed him into the back seat.

The car pulled away in a cloud of black smoke. The boy looked about frantically, up and down the street. All the windows and doors were shut tight. His chest heaving, he sank to the floor. Eduardo was gone.

Disappeared.

SANTA MARIA ISLAND, FLORIDA

February, 2005

One

A Hunka Burning Trouble

BLANCHE SAT UP IN the bed and ran her fingers over the angry red scar on Emilio's shoulder. She pressed on it gently.

Wish I could erase it.

But no such thing was ever going to happen. Just as the memory of how it got there could never be erased.

"They didn't do such a hot job of putting you back together." The flat tone of remorse crept into her voice.

"No, *mi Baquita.*"

That name. He'd started calling her that after they met in Mexico. She loved it. But then, there wasn't much she didn't love about Emilio Del Sierra.

"Sorry," she whispered.

"It is all right." He pulled her closer, the covers tangling around his legs. He tapped the bumpy scar. "This ..." he said, without looking at it.

"A very bad thing," she said.

"Maybe." He lifted her chin to meet his eyes. "I kinda like it. It reminds me of you. And it reminds me to be careful. The two things are not *separado.*"

They shifted on the mussed bed. The empty bottle of Veuve Clicquot clunked onto the floor.

"*Careful?* Why do you say that?"

"You know what I mean." He pulled the sheet up around them.

"I do regret it. The shooting, I mean. That guy could have *killed* you." Blanche curled against him. She traced the muscles of his chest with her fingers and watched the easy rise and fall of his breathing.

"I don't think you meant to get me shot ... did you?"

Blanche bolted upright, the sheet clutched in her fist. "*¡Qué cosa!*"

"Yes, *mi Baquita*. What a thing." One corner of his mouth tilted in a wry grin. He pulled her back down and rested his chin on the top of her head. "I'm just glad we made it out of there more or less intact."

"And now you're here. Finally." Her fingers trailed over the scar again. "I hope I can make it up to you, my love."

"Ah, but you have."

The late-morning sun slanted into the cabin off the beach. They'd drifted off to sleep again, but now Blanche was awake as Emilio slept on. She stretched lazily, propped herself on a pillow, and studied the line of his nose and lips. A clatter of parrots in the pines startled her, sending a shiver down her arms. The good kind. She was happier now than she'd ever been, and it was all because of him. Because of them. Together.

Two years had gone by since they met at a fiesta in Tepequito, a dusty, little town outside Mexico City. Blanche had walked in, past the rickety wood tables with blazing, fat white candles and the colorful flags fluttering across the rafters, right up to where Emilio was playing the guitar. She'd sat down and smiled and waited until he unfolded his long legs from that barstool and came over to talk with her. The connection was instantaneous.

But like so many things in her life, there were complications.

With Blanche, there were always complications. She'd only been in Mexico a few hours when she caused a fuss at the Palacio Nacional. A mummy in the exhibit hadn't looked quite real. In fact, this shriveled human looked *new*. Clearly, this was a case of foul play, but no one seemed to get the drift. Not until she raised the alarm.

Emilio didn't leave her side until the case was closed. He hadn't much choice; they were stuck together like goodies in a burrito. But then the bad guy had to go and shoot him, no thanks to Blanche.

Now he was here from Mexico—in Florida on Tuna Street at her cabin. She'd done nothing but smile since the slamming of that taxi door announced his arrival. She'd run off the porch and thrown herself into his arms, nearly knocking him and his guitar to the ground. Her heart had darn near stopped with joy.

The empty bottle of champagne glinted in a sunbeam on the rough wood floor. It was well worth the celebration. She lay back against the pillow and closed her eyes. Even the mild headache was worth it. The sun was high and hot. It promised to be another gorgeous day on Santa Maria Island.

Emilio's eyes were closed, and then he stirred and reached for her. She gave him a gentle poke in the ribs. "Hey! How's coffee sound?"

He opened one eye and rolled over. Smiling. Of course, he smiled. "Good morning, Sunshine."

They shrugged into their shorts and T-shirts and headed to the porch. Blanche flopped into a wicker chair.

"Bagels and coffee, coming up," he said, one hand on the screen door.

"Don't get lost," she said.

The door stuttered behind him as he stepped down onto the sand. He looked up at her. Hand on heart.

Oh, boy. Blanche curled up in the chair and wrapped her arms around her knees. She watched him speed away on her motorcycle, the crushed shell rocketing every which way beneath the rear tire. It wasn't far to Peach's Bakery, but even this short separation tugged at her.

The thought of him and that long, easy gait that was just the slightest bit pigeon-toed lingered. Charming and smart, he'd make such a fine doctor, saving sick children in the pediatric ward of a Mexican hospital. What an unlikely pair they were! She, a part-time journalist and reluctant sleuth, and he, a Mexican doctor.

How were they going to keep this going? Would she give up Santa Maria Island and hang out in a small Mexican town while he served two years of medical duty in a rural village? Blanche considered these complications and put them aside for now.

She looked up at the whine of the bike and leaned forward in the chair. He was back. Emilio crossed the short stretch of shaded beach toward the cabin, head down, his boots crunching the shell and pine needles. She swung her legs out from under her and stood up. His former happy expression was gone. Something in the set of his jaw kicked off her radar.

Blanche had excellent radar.

He balanced the large brown paper bag in the crook of his arm and held a sheet of notepaper at his side. It was slightly crumpled, but the large, black cursive was evident from where she stood on the porch. He quickly tucked the paper into his back pocket.

Worry lines deepened on that face she knew and loved.

She pushed open the screen door. "Hey. You."

He stepped inside and brushed her lips with a kiss. "Hungry?"

"Starving." Her eyes lingered on his back pocket. She had an inclination to grab at that paper and read it. But she wouldn't.

He draped an arm around her, and she leaned into him, forgetting momentarily his obvious concern.

He set the bag on the table. "Let's eat."

Out came two paper cups of coffee, several tubs of cream cheese, and a couple of bagels studded with blueberries and two sprinkled with "everything." The plastic knives and napkins lined up nicely.

"You operating?" She felt a rush of pleasure but failed to deliver a light tone.

"Mmmmm." He haphazardly smoothed cream cheese on half a bagel. In silence, they sat opposite, knees touching, sipping and chewing, and his worry lines faded. With the breeze and a golden sun on the beach, it was a shimmering Florida day. Low seventies, little chance of rain. A perfect day.

Whatever he's worrying about can wait. Blanche stole glances at him as he dissected a second bagel.

"This, *bueno*. Not so common in Mexico," he said, distractedly.

"They're easy to make, really. Just the right amount of water and dense dough. And technique."

"Is that right? Is that another of your talents? Besides sleuthing."

"Very funny."

He leaned over and offered her another half. "So, tell me."

"Bagels or sleuthing?"

He laughed. "We'll leave bagels to Peach's. What really made you start digging around? In the dirt, so to speak."

"You know it got dirty when Bob was killed. Those damn developers came to town." Blanche's gaze drifted away, out to the beach, back in time. She turned to Emilio. "One thing led to another. I just knew there was a connection between his death and the alarming business around here. I kept digging until we got them. Well, the sheriff and the DEA clamped down on that drug ring they were operating. But I did stir things up. I couldn't let it go. Guess I'm curious. And stubborn."

"Yes, you do have that about you." He smiled. "And other things."

Blanche wasn't hungry anymore. The curiosity had taken over. She wanted to know what Emilio was sitting on in that back pocket. He pushed the half-eaten bagel away and gripped the arms of his chair.

"Emilio? What's the matter? Is it the letter? The one in your pocket?" She often got to the point, but she kept her tone as casual as she could.

He laughed, this time uneasily. "Those eyes. They do not miss much. How you say, *ojo de águila?*"

"Eagle eye. Yup, that's me."

She was a snooper and a digger. After uncovering Bob's murder on Santa Maria Island, she'd stretched her dubious talents for solving murder as far away as Vietnam and Ireland. And, of course, Mexico, where she'd met Emilio. He reached over and crumbled the remnants of a bagel on to the waxed paper. The tense lines around the eyes returned.

"Your question ... It *is* a letter," he said. "From an aunt."

"Really? I thought you didn't have family, Emilio." She scooted her chair closer and put a hand on his knee.

"I didn't think so, either. Until recently. But I do. Tía Margarita. In Argentina." Then, as if the answer were floating on the sparkling Gulf of Mexico, he looked out across the beach.

"Wow." Blanche thumped back against the cushion.

"I did know of her." He stopped there, uncertainty darkening his expression. "She's the sister of my mother, but I thought she'd passed away."

"Argentina? You're not all from Mexico?"

"My parents moved to Mexico from Buenos Aires a long time ago. I was born outside Mexico City. They never said much about Argentina. In fact, I can't remember them talking about family there at all." He pulled the letter out of his back pocket and held it up. "Now this?"

"But that's so … so sad, Emilio. Your parents never talked about family there?"

"You have to understand. They didn't talk much at all about their past. They were hard-working farmers trying to start a new life. It wasn't easy."

"Oh."

"They were happy, and good. But they were quiet and kept to themselves." He flattened the letter on the table. "Margarita tells me she has a daughter. In Buenos Aires. My *cousin*. Now, I have a cousin, too," he said, the realization newly dawning on him.

"That's great. Right?" She was thrilled for him but she checked her enthusiasm. He seemed anxious—more stunned than thrilled. "Or is it? Emilio?"

Still, he was thoughtful, his lips pressed together. It sounded wonderful to Blanche. She'd always longed for family, especially after Gran died. Her few relations weren't around much, except for her peripatetic, always loyal and loving cousin, Haasi, who had taken to her charter boat and gone off to St. Croix. And sometimes, Cousin Jack would show up, but he was busy living the dream of a mega-entrepreneur in international freight. Then there were Liza and Cap, *like* family, but not.

"I think so." Emilio locked eyes with Blanche. "Yes. It is great."

She still sensed some hesitation. "Well, I'm glad she found you. Family is important. What does your aunt say? Is she coming here? Are they both coming here? That would be exciting!"

He grinned, a twisty, confused grin. "Uh. Afraid not. She wants me to go *there*." He studied the scrawl on the notepaper.

"What? Why?" Blanche wanted to reach for it. Read the large, messy handwriting for herself. She sat on her hands.

"It seems there's trouble, Blanche. She needs my help."

This news hit her. He was going off to Argentina? To help an aunt he didn't even know? The coffee burned like acid in her stomach. She was relieved she hadn't added much of a bagel to the mix. All she could think was that he didn't need a surprise like this: family trouble in a far-off place. Neither did she.

"Argentina isn't exactly around the corner," she said.

He nodded.

"Emilio, you can't just go. Your studies!" *And me.* "Besides you don't even know her." The sound of her own words made her cringe. After all, she was talking about *family.*

"She's not just anyone, Blanche. She is my Tía." He stood up and paced the floor.

Blanche closed her eyes. Selfish thoughts took up space in her brain and heart. She needed him to *need* to be here. With her. Not off somewhere in Argentina.

She wanted to tell him that he couldn't go. No, she couldn't do that, knowing that the question she was about to ask would open a Pandora's box that couldn't be closed. She had to ask. "What kind of trouble?"

"Her letter doesn't really say much. I need more information. But it's been hard to get through to her."

Oh, sweet relief. He didn't say he would go, for certain. But she was puzzled. When had the letter come? When had he tried to call his aunt? She took a deep breath and leaned over. His fingers were warm and strong—with a faint trembling.

"How long have you had the letter, Emilio? And you've spoken with your aunt? Why am I just finding this out now?"

"I did not want to worry you."

Blanche didn't let go of his hand. *Why would an estranged aunt wait until now?* She held back while she couldn't bear to see him hurt. Or used.

Maybe she was making more of the situation than necessary.

But something didn't feel right. She couldn't deny it. *Why does love have to be so complicated?*

Well, it had to be. Or, it wouldn't be worth it.

Love was in the air all right. But so was something else. And Blanche didn't like it.

Two

Call For Help

EMILIO PLEADED WITH BLANCHE to go with him to Buenos Aires. For once, she was at a loss for words. But not for long.

"Why, Emilio? And how would you even know where to begin once you got there? What would you do if you found your aunt? And your cousin?"

"You have a lot of questions, *Baquita*. That is not so unusual." He smiled and then shrugged.

"How did she ever even find *you*?"

"Through connections? Travel documents and newspaper obituaries? Maybe she made some phone calls. I'm sure it was difficult, and tedious, under the circumstances."

She was reluctant to discourage him even though the effort to rescue his aunt would require an enormous amount of follow-up to these desperate letters and phone calls. This was not a situation one could work out over the phone. It would require shoe leather. And time and resources. She wasn't sure they had enough of the latter to solve the problem.

His silence indicated agreement that running off to one of the largest cities in South America on the edge of the vast pampa required serious consideration, especially considering he'd never laid eyes on his aunt.

"If I went with you, Emilio, I'd just be in the way. What good would I be in the middle of your family trouble?"

"Trouble is your middle name!"

"And, what's *that* supposed to mean?!" She pursed her lips.

"Oh, no, no! I mean, the good kind."

"Ummm."

"Besides, I love you. I need you to be with me."

If she went with him to Argentina, she'd be as supportive as possible, but she shouldn't get directly involved in such a complicated family situation. Should she?

The answer to that was obvious: His problem was hers, like a weight on both their hearts.

They sat on the porch, the bagels and cream cheese forgotten. "Does trouble follow love? Like night follows day?"

"What do I know? All I know is that I want to do this with you. Just like you say, 'I have a feeling'."

Blanche cocked her head. "A feeling?"

Emilio stood up and thrust his arms out. "Yes! We need to do this together."

He'd never appeared to be so sure, and now here he was with this startling concentration and persuasion.

She tucked her legs under her. It was going to be a long day. "It's not cheap to fly to Argentina, you know. Has to be a thousand bucks, at least."

"*Tía* says there's money. Family money put away, and it's been growing." Emilio straightened his shoulders. "I will go, and you will go with me. *Por favor?*"

She smiled at him. "I don't need the money, Emilio. You know Gran was generous, and I spend practically nothing." Her wardrobe, ancient water-marked furniture, and time-scrubbed kitchen were proof of that. The old Taurus sat in the shed getting rustier by the day. She got around mostly on her feet or on her Honda Dream.

He touched her hand then flung himself into the opposite chair. The sun began to sink over the Gulf. Blanche went for the Coronas. Emilio was insistent, and Blanche's mood wavered. Her thoughts spun around in her head like clothes in the dryer. She couldn't deny one aspect of the situation. The excitement of another adventure began to intrigue her. But Argentina? It was troubling, for sure, and a curious challenge. His aunt lived in a country fraught with military coups, corruption, and on-going economic woes. All this would surely affect their effort, but, she had to admit, figuring out a solution to such a problem had enormous pull on her. It might knock her right off her feet. It had happened before, and she'd landed safely. Mostly.

"Want to take a walk?" She stood up and stretched.

They headed to the beach and shuffled along the hard-packed sand at the edge of the water. Hand in hand, they ended up at the point of the island where the Gulf and bay met in a confluence of turquoise and gray. Unseen sharks lazed in the turbulent water. Family trouble disappeared into the soft, humid air. As the evening deepened and the waves beat a rhythm, they lingered, sharing a compatible silence.

Trouble simmered to the surface.

"I need to call her," he said. "She's out on the pampa at an estancia."

"That sounds like another language."

"It is. Another world." He pulled her toward him. "We don't have to run off this minute ..." They watched a pair of dolphins arc out of the Gulf. Listened to the last call of terns as they headed to their nests.

"*We.* I do like that part." She leaned against his shoulder. "I've never been to the pampa."

"There's a first time for everything."

The pelicans circled over the water. Blanche hated to move off this beach, but the sun decided for them, disappearing in a flash and leaving them in the dark. She took his hand, and they started back toward the cabin, their empty stomachs rumbling.

What kind of trouble was his Aunt Margarita in? And how would they get her out of it? So many questions, and the only answers lay due South. About ten hours by air.

Emilio had known of the existence of his Aunt Margarita for only a short time. The complications and danger mounted with the last couple of letters, and it was nearly impossible to call her, mostly because of her employers.

Margarita Felipe Goyez worked for Nazis, Karl and Gerda Schemmer. Decades earlier, the young Schemmers had arrived in Buenos Aires with a flood of European immigrants from Germany after World War Two. At the time, they were just teenagers. They'd blended into the picaresque culture of Indigenous, Spanish, Italian, and German peoples, and then they'd set out to seize opportunity. They soon found their way to the estancia, La Palma, and into the hardscrabble employ of the Caudillo José Bartolo de Losada Iglesias.

It was the early seventies when Tía Margarita went to work at La Palma as a housekeeper. By then the caudillo was old, and the Schemmers were gaining control at La Palma, moving up from shoveling manure and cleaning and hauling to management of the property. It had taken decades, but they'd persisted.

The Schemmers' background wasn't clear to Margarita in her early years at La Palma. But details emerged. How they'd fled Germany, finagled their way into Bartolo's graces, and gradually taken over at the estancia. Margarita learned things about the

Schemmers that they preferred to remain hidden in the wilds of the pampa. Their background was sinister, and sketchy at best. And now the situation was boiling over.

Margarita was afraid for several reasons, and she had to get out. Leave Buenos Aires altogether. But she was stuck. This much Emilio knew. It was not a lot to go on. In fact, it was hardly anything to go on.

"Tía," he called her. He'd phoned her many times, and, finally, he managed to get through.

"I can't talk for long, *mijo*," she whispered. "Lately, they've been placating me, but then they find ways to keep me here. And it's getting worse."

"Worse?"

"They intimidate. Not only them. They have staff. Bullies, they are. They are afraid of the things I know—about where they came from and what they've done. There're secrets. I hear things about the wars. The one they came from, and the one here in Argentina. The Dirty War. I've heard the phone calls and the talking. People have shown up."

"*¿Qué?*"

"I'll tell you soon. When I see you."

"Tía, I don't know when that'll be …"

"You must try. I need you to come!" Her voice changed pitch. "They are frightful, dangerous people. I am so afraid."

He coaxed her for more, but her hesitation was palpable. He heard the catch in her voice. A door slammed in the background.

"You will come, won't you?" she urged.

"I'll figure out something," he said.

"I know about your studies, and I am happy for you. And don't worry. The money for the flight and the car, it's not important. There's money in the trust. You will share it."

Emilio was astounded at that revelation. *A family trust?* His family had left Argentina fifty years ago and made a life in Mexico. A hard life that took up all their energy just to survive. The past was buried to the Del Sierra family.

Now the past had caught up. How exactly was he going to get the last of his family out of this mess?

"I'll look into it. *Prontito*," he said.

"You are good, that I can tell. You'll do what you can, Emilio, I know, and I'm sorry to bother you, but I am desperate."

"You are no bother, Tía. *Por favor*."

"They need to accept my retirement, especially for the welfare of my daughter. I am due. It's time. But I worry, and they delay. My daughter must not get involved. I need to get to her and then we need to go far away from this place." Her words ran together.

"I didn't know I had ... you. And a cousin!"

"'There's much you don't know, Emilito." A muffled sound of voices. And then more doors slamming. "I need to go. Your cousin is Issie. You'll meet her ... She is the one good reason I have been so careful with the Schemmers. I don't want them going after *her*."

"Where is she?" He raked fingers through his hair.

"In the Capital. I'll get more directions to you later, and we'll leave this all behind. Be a family. I'm sorry it's taken so long."

"How do I get to you? And *kidnap* you?"

Her voice dropped. "No, no, *mijo*. That's a bad thought. Do not put that into the air. Especially here."

"*Lo siento*."

He remembered then. The *Proceso*, or Dirty War, of the '70s and '80s and the trail of kidnappings, torture, and death across Argentina. His family, a family he didn't know, had lived through that? Hundreds of detention centers had sprung up and at least thirty thousand disappeared. The thought of it sunk in like a dead weight on his soul. He'd been so young when his mother mentioned the Dirty War, murmuring and crossing herself to "pray for the poor souls." Now, here it was, 2005, and the ghost of the past had come to haunt his family.

"Argentina is a country on edge, *mijo*," Margarita said, woefully. "We have anxiety here. About the past, present, and future."

Her words struck him with a sense of foreboding. *What was he getting himself and Blanche into?*

"The Schemmers take in guests at the estancia," she whispered. "It is a type of hotel. *Muy bonito*. Come as a visitor, and then we'll leave together under circumstances we will create. I'm not sure how." Her voice trailed off. "Maybe you'll get a car? No. We can decide when you get here. I may know someone ..."

In the background a voice boomed. *"¡Margarita, ven!"*

"I must go," she said. "I'll send details, and I'll tell you about your cousin. Issie. She goes by the name, Isabel Goyez, and she lives in San Telmo at the center of the Capital. She is a student, and artist. You will love her. Oh, I am so happy to find you ..."

"¡Margarita!"

Click.

Emilio and Blanche lay in bed in the cabin, their fingers entwined. The waves pounded on this windy beach day, and his concern ripped through her like an electric charge. They were both thinking the same thing. *Argentina!*

"Do you know things about Argentina, *Baquita?*"

"Evita and Juan Perón? Gauchos and roast meat? Big beautiful open pampas." She'd mention the beauty, but the horror could not be ignored. "They had a terrible run-in with the military. Twenty years ago? It's over now."

"The Dirty War. It started in the mid-seventies and lasted about eight years."

"A horrible abuse of power. I studied South America. And the language."

"And you speak fine Spanish." He ran a finger over her lips.

"Very funny. I can barely order a cerveza. But I get along."

"You do." He stared at her intently then flopped onto his back and resumed staring at the ceiling. "Nazis fled to Argentina after World War Two. Do you know about that, too?"

"I do. The 'Ratline.' Connections in the governments, and even the Church, throughout Europe helped the Nazis and collaborators escape."

"Yeah, well, my aunt's employers might be involved in some of that. Margarita's at an estancia with a couple from Germany, and from what she tells me, it doesn't sound good."

Blanche sat up. "What did you find out?"

"Not much. She says the caretakers are Nazis. I have to get her out of there because of what she knows. And she's worried about her daughter—my cousin."

He tossed onto his side toward Blanche, propped his head in his hand, and stared into her eyes. "We'll make a plan, won't we?"

She leaned into Emilio and stroked his cheek.

The mission, such as it was, sounded precarious, if not ominous. They had to fly to Argentina and extract Margarita Goyez from an estancia out in the middle of nowhere. Blanche was pulled in two directions. She wanted him to stay out of it altogether, and she wanted to be with him if he went.

They had no plan, really. How could they, given all the unknowns? It didn't matter how many times they went round and round about it, the situation didn't become any clearer. Except for this: He'd been an only child, the last hope of aging parents, and now they were gone. Of his family, Margarita and Issie remained. Emilio had one objective now. He was determined to rescue his last living relatives.

How could she refuse to be part of that when she felt she was part of him?

Three

Bestia On Wheels

THE FLIGHT FROM MIAMI TO BUENOS AIRES lasted a little more than nine hours. Blanche passed the time with a tray of beef and rice, a Miller Lite, and one long nap. Flying often put her to sleep instantly, even now, with the prospect of trouble. She drifted in and out of dreams, then nightmares. They were dropping into a dark hole of the unknown, but they were determined to get Margarita out of trouble.

Emilio clutched her hand and the warm comfort of his long leg and arm brushing against her lulled her into a temporary peace.

She awoke to a view of the silvery brown Rio de la Plata, and this much she knew: Sixteenth-century conquerors named it for the promise of silver flowing from the faraway Andes. They didn't find any, but the name stuck. Buenos Aires grew into a great triangle around La Plata at the edge of the Atlantic Ocean, the city's barrios split into rich and poor, beautiful and miserable.

As the plane dipped over the edge of Buenos Aires, she thrilled at the expanse of parks and buildings and water. Then, as if she were looking at an obstacle course, her mind reeled over the hurdles they faced. She stole a glance at Emilio. Were his nerves strung as tight as hers?

"I hope it'll be right," he murmured. She squeezed his hand.

He craned his neck at the sprawling city, mostly white and green in the bright morning.

"It'll be *bueno*," she said.

"Buenos Aires. Good air," he said. "Yes, it will be. We will make it."

She loved his attitude. These bursts of optimism. She wouldn't let doubt get in the way. Even when it reared its ugly little head, she'd beat it down.

They'd traveled light, and the customs process was relatively smooth. They stopped at an ATM for pesos and then exited the airport to find a line of black and yellow taxis lined up like bees. Soon they headed toward the city center.

The driver raced out of the airport along parks lush with flowering shrubs and trees shading the wide walkways. The city's beauty reflected Paris, Madrid, and Rome with flair and abundance. The boulevards, parks, cafes, and French architecture of the city on La Plata rightfully bore the name, "Paris of South America."

"It's so *grand*," she said.

"Ah, *muy grande*," said the driver, smiling. Their official welcome committee.

"They invented the word," said Emilio, gazing at the vista. "So much space."

The boulevards teemed with cabs and lorries, tiny sputtering cars, and luxurious Mercedes Benzes. A striking row of palm trees rose into a cloudless sky. Only twenty minutes later, their spacious welcome at the airport turned into a tangle of congestion. It was slow going. The taxi wove through traffic in the inner city like an aimless bee in a net.

They cruised around the lovely, leafy Plaza San Martín. Palms and acacias shaded the afternoon crowd. The area seemed to be a favorite spot for relaxing and catching some sun. Children chased soccer balls. Working men and woman lounged on benches eating their lunches and chatting.

"*El General.*" The cab driver slowed past the bronze figure of the liberator, General José de San Martín, atop a marble pedestal pointing west toward the Andes. The driver pounded his chest with pride.

At the north end of the plaza a neo-classical palacio gleamed like a Parisian mansion, embellished with a slate mansard roof and colonnades, ornate stained glass, and wrought iron. On another corner across the wide green space, a basilica christened with white marble domes and turrets was reminiscent of Paris's Sacre Coeur.

The taxi stopped in front of a small hotel near the plaza. Blanche and Emilio thanked the driver and grabbed their small bags. They held hands as they walked into the spare lobby decked out with speckled mirrors on the walls and shiny mustard tiles on the floor. Once checked in, they boarded an elevator cage that creaked up to the fifth floor. A short narrow corridor led to a surprisingly bright corner room.

Blanche dropped her bag inside the door. "From spacious and grand to tiny. I like it." She did a quick turn around and flopped into an overstuffed chair.

"We don't need much space," said Emilio, grinning.

The room, washed in white, with only a bowl of fruit on a small corner table reminded Blanche of a minimalist painting. The creamy beige duvet on the bed offset all the white.

She jumped up and went to the window. "Come and look at this beautiful view of the plaza." She reached for Emilio. He put his arms around her. "The view's better in here."

She ran her fingers down the ridges of his lean back and looked up into his eyes. Way up. He was almost a foot taller.

He murmured, "Thank you for doing this. We will have fun, too. I promise."

"Like right now?"

He laughed. "Like right now." He guided her toward the bed.

She sighed and took his hand. "Emilio, if I lie down, I won't get up!"

"I think that's the idea." He curled a lock of hair over her ear.

She laced her fingers in his and edged him toward the door. A rush of excitement hit her. *Yes, the adventure!* "Let's see what's out there! It's barely noon, and the sun is shining on Buenos Aires. Then ..." She pointed in the direction of the bed.

"*Prontito.*"

They walked over to Calle Florida, a pedestrian street that pulsed with music and city noise. No wheels allowed. The area teemed with people, strolling and hurrying in and out of the restaurants and shops.

"Looks like 42nd Street," Blanche said.

"*¡Che!* In one very long block."

"Che? Guevara?"

"Uh-huh. The Argentine icon, born and educated here, but he ended up in Cuba. Che just means, hey, that's cool or whatever you want it to say. It's just a word."

"Now, how do you know that?"

"I'm kind of an Argentine, you know."

"You are!" She looked at him sideways. "What are we dealing with here?"

"You will see, Señorita."

A mime, painted gold from head to foot, stood on one leg, Minnie Mouse carried a sign advertising empanadas, the lights on the storefronts blinked off and on at the restaurants, La Chacra and Facundo. A man in tight black leather waved the crowd toward Club Pussy.

25

Blanche and Emilio moved out of the tide of walkers. The smell of roasted meat and bread, cologne, the screams of children, laughter and far-off strings of the tango excited Blanche.

"This is wonderful!" she said, stretching to look over the bobbing heads.

"Sí," said Emilio, absently peering into a shop window.

Blanche spotted a lone biker barreling down the *peotanal*. A *biker?* What was a bike doing on the pedestrian walkway? He sped closer, weaving in and out of the crowd. The knots of people came apart, casually, as if it were no big deal. The biker's head was down, hair whipping, as he gripped the handlebars.

Blanche locked eyes on his white knuckles, barely managing a look at his wild expression.

"What the hell?!" She needed to get out of his path, but she had nowhere to go. Blanche froze. The front wheel of the speeding bike aimed right at her. This guy was intent on mowing her down. No doubt in her mind.

It happened in a split second.

Out of nowhere, a pair of hands grabbed her and hurled her up into the air, out of the bike's way and flung her against the wall of a restaurant. She blinked in surprise and shock.

"*¡Che, boludo!*" Her savior stood protectively in front of her, waving a fist and shouting after the rider who disappeared into the sea of shopping bags and people. Blanche shook herself and looked into merry, brown eyes under a wide-brimmed hat. He was short and stocky and of an indeterminate age. It was hard to read that taut, leathery face. He wore pointy, tooled boots, and a tight, black jacket embroidered with white trim. She let out a breath and shot a glance from him to a startled Emilio who now hovered over her.

The man doffed his hat. "*Así, chica rica.* Are you all right? You almost purchase a ticket to the hospital."

Blanche straightened up, confused at first, which quickly turned to anger at the biker. But then she managed to smile at the little man. *"¿Gracias?"*

"¿Qué pasa?" Emilio's eyes swept over Blanche.

"Ruffians. Argentina, she has her fill. I am happy to say you escaped this one." As he spoke, he twirled his hat through his fingers. He bowed slightly. "Tomás Fernaní Abella. At your service."

"Señor Abella, thank you very much. If you hadn't ..." Blanche shuddered at what could have happened. "I am forever indebted to you."

He kept working the rim of his hat, round and round, his eyes flicking back and forth between Emilio and Blanche. "You must be *norteamericanos*? Visiting Buenos Aires?"

"Just arrived." She glanced around, warily.

"Pues, I am sorry for this introduction to our beautiful city. We *porteños* are normally more hospitable."

"Can we take you for a coffee, or something. *Anything*?" Blanche said.

Emilio nodded.

"It would be my great pleasure to join you," Tomás said, without hesitation. "We could use a little refreshment and a revival of the spirits, *sí*?" His sardonic tone was not to be missed. He pointed down the walkway. "There's a fine café a few blocks away."

"A coffee and ... lunch?" She had no idea what time it was. She wasn't hungry. Her stomach was still somewhere up in her throat. "It's the least we can do."

Blanche was considering a good stiff whiskey rather than coffee. *I should be getting used to disaster by now.* But it was something she never got used to, the weird feeling of wariness that always seemed to insinuate itself into the excitement of her every adventure. She already harbored questions about Emilio's troubled relatives in the back of her mind. This episode unsettled her further.

She looked at the concern on Emilio's face and at the constant smile on Tomás's. She blew out a breath of air.

Enough already.

This was a one-off, and she wasn't going to let it spoil the day. She'd enjoy it with Emilio and this adorable man who'd yanked her to safety.

"¡Qué bestia!" Tomás muttered, shaking his head and leading the way down the *peotanal*. "I'm truly sorry. We are not all bent on leaving our visitors with bad memories. We need to work on our manners!"

Four

Pillow Tango

BLANCHE AND EMILIO FOLLOWED Tomás into The Café Tortoni on the Avenida de Mayo. The cool, cavernous restaurant with grand columns and art deco mirrors and portraits on the dark wood walls was a welcome escape from the noisy walkway. Glass cases sparkled with treats in frilly paper cups stacked in pyramids. Baristas huddled over the espresso machines as they whooshed out their specialty coffees. The air was redolent of bread and sugar and coffee, and she was suddenly hungry. A white-coated waiter relaxed against a counter, tango music lilting in the background. Other waiters glided among the tables where Argentines were involved in the serious pastime of eating, reading, and murmuring amongst themselves, clearly making café life an art form.

They pulled up chairs to a round, marble-topped table. Blanche idly turned the pages of an abandoned *La Nación,* understanding little except for President Néstor Kirchner's dire announcement about the economy. *Malo* was a universal word.

Emilio ordered ham and cheese tostadas and raspberry-filled tarts. They hadn't eaten much since Florida. Tomás asked for coffee and *medialunas*—the Argentine version of the croissant. He seemed relaxed, in his element, and Blanche welcomed the mood. There

29

was something enchanting about him. As yet, though, Blanche couldn't figure what it was. She imagined him in a cottage in the forest with creatures frolicking about the door, the sound of a rivulet trickling by ...

"Blanche? You all right?" Emilio studied her with concern.

"Oh, yes, I'm fine. It's lovely here," she mused.

"Not like your McDonald's. In and out, you know," Tomás said, without a trace of judgement. "We like to sit awhile with our *cafecitos.*"

"Is it always so crowded for a workday morning?" said Blanche.

Tomás shrugged. The corner of his mouth lifted in a wry smile. "Eh?! Work! It is a cherished thing here, but good work is rare. And for only this we do not choose to live." His gaze wandered around the cafe. "Many are idle. Perhaps, accepting of it."

Blanche shot him a quizzical look. "Many?"

He hunched his shoulders and raised his hands as if in resignation. "There are not so many good jobs, and when you get the job, the inflation eats it all." She noticed the mottled skin on his arms, the curved fingernails, the callouses on his palms. They were the hands of hard work.

Blanche could see how their American dollar would stretch. Even a bottle of water cost a third of what she'd pay in the U.S.

"The economy," Tomás said, "what can I say? It takes one disastrous turn after another."

"You spared us one disaster, Tomás. Thanks, again," she said.

Emilio reached for Blanche with his free hand and ravenously attacked a tostada with the other. Blanche nibbled while Tomás had her full attention.

"It is indeed my pleasure," Tomás said. His English was exceptional, but she didn't ask how he came by it. She preferred to hear him speak Spanish. She loved the distinctive shushing sound of

Buenos Aires, an influence of Italian immigrants, in particular, who stamped their Mediterranean affect onto Argentine speech.

Blanche tilted her head. He seemed to read her mind: "I meet many tourists and immigrants through the years," he said. "I have learned the English and how to accommodate requests. I do this with my guitar and my songs. And my tango." He certainly was adept, switching easily from a formal, stilted speech to casual.

"Of course! You were playing the guitar in front of the restaurant. Is that how you happened to be right there?" It did seem odd to Blanche that Tomás instantly dropped his guitar—his livelihood—and jumped to rescue her. Agile, and adept. His clothing, a durable-looking, well-tailored black serge, suggested the entertainment field. *Was he a busker? Making his living for tips?*

"I play the guitar at the doorway of Facundo and places that will have me. And from time to time, I teach the tango in the plazas and salons." He looked quickly from Blanche to Emilio and clapped. "You must come to the *milonga* in San Telmo! Tomorrow. I will show you the steps."

"The *milonga*?"

"A dancing of the tango on the plaza."

Blanche smiled at Emilio. "We should do that."

Tomás snapped his fingers. He jumped up, kicked one leg behind in a circular fashion, then bounced back like a yoyo. "*¡Boleo!*" he shouted and resumed his seat. A heavy-set, white-haired man at the next table looked up from his newspaper, "*¡Olé!*"

This delighted Blanche and Emilio. "*¡Olé!*"

Tomás propped his fist under his chin. "The *boleo*. It is a special form in the dance. And there are more I will show you." He grinned. "You know, we've come a long way from the golden age of tango in the forties and fifties, and then, *alors*, the Beatles almost killed it. Now it comes alive again. In the dancing halls, on the stage—and the plaza. You will see." He looked at them under expressive, thick brows. "Come to the *milonga*, and we will dance."

"I know something of tango," Emilio said, somewhat tentatively. "I taught dance to earn money when I was in school." A blush spread across his forehead.

"Wow. You're a tango dancer? Emilio, you keep secrets." Blanche teased, but she was delighted. A gifted guitarist and singer plus tango dancer? The drama of the tango didn't seem to fit her shy, young Mexican doctor.

"I wasn't very good, but, yes. Not long ago." He leaned over and whispered. "*Baquita*, we should go to the plaza. I move very good."

"I know."

"*Bueno.*" Tomas coughed lightly.

She couldn't wait to see Emilio twirling about to the strains of guitars, violins, and bandoneons. She glanced at her sandals. They definitely were not tango material. She needed those pumps with straps, a tight black dress with a slit up the side, an enormous rose in her hair. *Oh, so not me!*

Tomás finished his coffee and fastidiously swept the crumbs onto his napkin. His squinty eyes did not reflect much about the life of a tango instructor. But one thing was clear. Hardship was etched on Tomás's face. Turning to talk of dance and music exhilarated him.

"We will meet then," he said. "Anna Godoy de Gamoure is my partner. She is *divina*. The light of the dance world. She will sweep your feet off."

"Oh, no!" Blanche said. *My feet*. But tango might be good, and fun. With Emilio? Even better.

Tomás looked at her, a finger in his cheek. "You will be a fine student. *Muy linda*," he said. "And, Señor Emilio, I would like to see your skills, *por favor*."

Emilio looked dubious. "Skills?"

"You have danced the tango. Tell me. Where?" He lowered his voice, his intense expression darting between Blanche and Emilio.

"At a studio in Mexico City," Emilio said. "But I lived outside the Capital in a rural village."

"And you, Señorita Blanche, where do you live?"

"In Florida. Emilio and I are visiting family here. We're sort of on a mission to find Emilio's aunt—" Emilio nudged her foot under the table while he smiled pleasantly. She read the hesitation in his eyes and remembered Gran's words: *Open yer mouth and tell all ye know.*

Tomás nodded as if deep in thought.

"Actually, we are … sightseeing," said Emilio. "Maybe with an aunt. A cousin."

"I'd like to visit Borges's haunts." Blanche thought it might be better to steer off to the tourist aspect of the visit. "And Recoletas Cemetery. Eva Perón's tomb." The graveyard of ornate above-ground burial places was a prime fascination.

"Ah, you *norteamericanos* and the 'Don't Cry for Me' business," said Tomás. "You will see Evita at the much-visited tomb, and you will recall such a sad case. Dying at thirty-three—after enduring a lobotomy and cancer—and that husband! She was popular, but I was not a fan of her Juan Perón. That dictator was a friend of Mussolini." He shook his head emphatically. "And your Borges. He was not a fan of the Peróns—and certainly not of the Italian fascist. But how Borges loved Buenos Aires! He would walk the streets of the Capital, one end to the other, even as he was going blind." Tomás paused, lost to another flight of exuberance. "You must go to Switzerland to see his grave."

"I love Borges. His language is so rich. Obscure…," Blanche mused.

"The Argentines, they love to go deep into the mind and play there. Like their beloved Borges does in his poetry." He folded his arms tightly. "Do you do that?"

"Well, yes. I suppose." Blanche was used to lying awake, staring at the ceiling and visiting the dark corners of her mind while the seagulls circled in the night. "Reading Borges is like getting lost in a maze—but isn't that the point? To let yourself go when reading his poetry? Every time I read *'La Luna'* I get a new meaning."

He cracked a smile. He seemed enchanted that she was a fan of Argentina's famed writer. "I must gift you a book of his poems!"

"That would be wonderful! And I will gift you Walt Whitman's, *The Leaves of Grass.*"

"That's settled. The great poet *del norte.* We have much grasses here, you will see." He rubbed his hands together. "Now. Your travels will take you to the house of Borges in Buenos Aires and to other sites?"

"We are going to La Palma, an estancia a few hours from here," Blanche said.

Again, Emilio nudged her under the table.

"Ah. I happen to know the place. Lovely setting." His tone changed from happy and eager to somber.

What a strange reaction. She waited, hoping he'd say something more about La Palma. Instead, he focused on the last of a croissant.

She said, casually, "So, have you visited the estancia?"

"It has a reputation. *Un tipo de hotel.* With an excellent chef," Tomás said.

Emilio waited a beat. "You recommend it?"

"Indeed." Tomás glanced around the café then leaned toward Emilio. "You would do wise—"

Blanche interrupted. "Would do wise to what?"

"Oh. You'll see what a beautiful place it is, lovely grounds and all. But you will not stay long." It wasn't a question but more of an assertion.

"No, we won't. We will visit and be on our way," said Emilio.

"As the Lord provides. But while you are here in the Capital, you must go to an *asado*," he said, quickly. "The choices are on every corner. You will have the finest meats, the best cuts, wherever you decide to dine. I guarantee that. The selection at the *parilla* is *delicioso*."

Blanche fiddled with a second *medialuna*. Tomás had smoothly changed the subject and added nothing further about La Palma and the local sites. *No lingering.* If she let herself be uneasy, she would be. She put the feeling aside. They would be on their way soon enough. The day had offered a blur of events, including the acquaintance of this interesting little man.

Emilio ordered beers, but Tomás declined, claiming he never touched the *agua del diablo* though he seemed to have the rheumy eyes and red nose of a heavy drinker. The tango dancer was a surprising mix of attitudes. And, perhaps, secrets?

"Do you like ice cream?" Tomás asked. No more somber talk of estancias and sad history. "All *norteamericanos* love the ice cream and the sweets. Especially the *dulce de leche*. But you must try the *leche merengada* at the Tortoni."

"We should be going," Emilio said.

"No, please, I insist!" Before they could say another word, he hustled off to the counter and returned with small paper cups of egg whites, cream, and cinnamon. He beamed with enjoyment as if he'd invented it. Blanche was delighted. The *merengada* was a sweet note to leave on. They said goodbye and promised to meet up at the milonga the next day.

Blanche watched Tomás hobble down the street, humming a tune. A bowlegged tango dancer? *What a strange little man. But something dear, and sad, about him ...*

She turned to Emilio. "What do you think?"

"What do I think? I don't know." Emilio scratched his head. "This Tomás. *Amable pero un poquito raro.*"

"Rare? I guess so. He seems to be a lovely old soul. There is something sad about him, too. But it's weird—his reaction to La Palma. He knew the location, and he seemed a bit grim at the mention of it."

"¿Cómo?"

"He didn't give us much, really. Only the suggestion that we not stay long. Sounded to me like he had a distaste for the place. You know, too, it seemed a bit strange that he happened to be right there when the guy on the bike nearly ran me down. Like it was choreographed."

Emilio gave her a funny look. "He is a dancer."

"I guess. Still …"

He drew Blanche close. "We are fortunate, no? I am glad he was there."

"Yes. I'm glad, too, and I do like him."

"I am sorry I didn't get you away from that *idiota* on the bike."

"It's okay. You only turned your head for an instant."

"That is all it takes, *Baquita*. An instant." He touched the curls above her ear. "We need to be careful. I've heard things about this place. Some of it bad." He took her arm, and they started walking back to the hotel down a leafy, shaded sidewalk. The air had cooled in the late afternoon, and a faint smell of nutmeg wafted from the trees with leaves the size of a man's hand.

"What do you mean? Some of it bad?" She knew his moods. He'd relaxed some, but she could tell he was worried again. She laced her fingers in his, giving into the soft reassuring pressure of his arm against hers. She felt secure, but it was true. They needed to be careful.

Emilio swung her around. "Nothing bad right now. Only good." They walked around the corner, sheltered under the jacaranda. She wished Emilio hadn't hinted at danger—but it couldn't be ignored. Besides her brush with the biker, and Aunt Margarita's trouble,

Blanche sensed trouble everywhere—and pain. Buenos Aires was beautiful, and grand and busy, but bruised. The country was in a constant state of flux and recovery. She'd read about it. She'd also seen it in Tomás's face. "Let's do what we have to do and get back home," said Blanche. "And let's stick close. OK?"

"Like this?" He lifted her up against his chest.

She smiled into his eyes. "Yes, just like this."

They slept late the next day. Blanche awoke to branches scratching at the window and the sun beaming in her face. Her eyes shot open. She clutched the covers and looked around, confused, her mouth dry as cotton from the Malbec.

Argentina!

She thought back to their first day. They'd had a rocky start on the *peotanal*, but they'd made a full recovery and celebrated their arrival in Buenos Aires in the evening. They'd walked along the park at San Martín and down a fancy street of Juliet balconies and potted roses and shiny windows with gold lettering, past packed restaurants of lolling patrons, and stores full of leather and tightly dressed mannequins. They went to a bistro and ate thin pieces of salty beef with fries and drank red house wine for about fifty pesos—less than twenty dollars—for the two of them. They'd picked through boots, bags, and jackets of exquisite *carpincho* leather. Emilio tried on boots, but Blanche didn't need leather boots and bags on Santa Maria Island. Besides, they weren't there to shop. They'd walked and walked, and gawked and gawked, and later stopped at a street vendor and split a *choripán*, a delicious, greasy thing of chopped chorizo on French bread. They sat on a bench and ate and watched the people, their pace less frenetic than earlier in the day. In fact, the leisurely pace was a whole lot different here altogether, compared to Santa Maria Island where the shops and many of the restaurants closed by six so everyone could get up early and fish or beat the heat.

Blanche fluffed the pillow under her head. Last night, the trouble awaiting them at La Palma had seemed so distant. Now, she lay in bed watching the shadows shift onto the wall with uneasy anticipation. She'd keep the feeling to herself for now. *Enjoy the trip.* They'd manage it, she told herself. They'd swoop in, pick up Margarita, and get back Florida.

Once back in Florida, Emilio would be off to Gainesville for his studies, and there would be miles between them again. Their times together were always short and as sweet as *merengada*. She set her mind to living in the moment and making the most of it, and at this very moment, it wasn't difficult at all. She snuggled up against Emilio under the dreamy duvet that smelled faintly of lavender and him.

"*Baquita?* Why do you have your face set like that?" He smoothed a worry line.

She laughed. Her mind whirling, she hadn't known he was looking at her. When Blanche got off in her world, she could be quite oblivious to her surroundings. She reached over and stroked his arm. "It's nothing. Just wondering."

"Stop thinking. You know what the sign on the door says. Do Not Disturb." He pulled her toward him and slid under the covers. Without opening his eyes, he said, "Hmmm, what do I have here? A small creature?"

"A starving one."

"We will take care of that."

"Not just yet." Blanche ran her fingertips down the side of his face.

Emilio lay there, eyes wide open. "That feels very good."

"I'm dizzling you." It was a trick of the fingertips Gran had done to get Blanche to calm down and go to sleep when she was little.

When she'd closed her eyes, she imagined the feet of fairies lightly skipping over her face.

"Blanche the Dizzler." He sat up and settled against the headboard, drawing her next to him. She mussed his spikey black hair. Softly, the branches of the jacaranda scratched at the window.

"I can see you're worried, Emilio. You can't hide it. Those lines around your eyes keep coming back." She dizzled his nose.

"You make me forget. *Un poquito.*"

"Not quite. It seems."

"Tía says not to call her at the estancia, that I should wait another day, but I don't think I can wait anymore."

"Maybe you should."

He frowned. "She says they may have tapped her phone."

"Oh boy." She slid back down and burrowed into the covers. "We should probably get hold of Issie."

"She's supposed to call or leave a note with the post downstairs." He didn't move. "I'd go look, but you're such a distraction."

"Sorry," she said, "well, not sorry." But then she nudged him. "We'll go see Issie."

"She's not too far from here. We can walk it. She will know more, I hope." He sighed. "Then we'll all go back to Florida. One big happy family."

"Exactly. Should we take Tomás up on his offer? He said he'd get us a driver. Didn't he?"

"He did."

"I think we can trust him," she said, mentally reinforcing her faith in the tango dancer. "He knows his way around, and he's earnest, and sweet. He means to help."

Emilio gave her a sideways look and laughed. "You sweet on him?"

"Are you jealous?" She planted a kiss on his cheek.

He got out of bed and started fidgeting with his clothes. "I owe the guy. I'm sweet on him, too." He grinned at her, standing in a pool of sunshine.

She'd jump up and hug him if she weren't so downright cozy. "He did save me, but there's only one guy I'm sweet on."

"Now who would that be?" He didn't wait for an answer as he hopped into the leg of his jeans. "You wait right there. Don't move. I'm going down to the desk and check the mail and see if there are any calls."

Blanche sank back and pulled up the duvet. "Oh, I'll be here."

He kissed her lightly. *"¡Baquita!"*

She put her arms around his neck.

"Yes, you are such a distraction." He tucked her in, then buttoned his shirt. "I'll be right back. Then we will go. Soon."

"And we'll go dancing—the milonga."

He took a step toward her.

"Go." She laughed.

Such a good easy plan. What can possibly go wrong?

Five

The Gift

THERE WERE NO MESSAGES for them at the hotel desk. They tried to call Margarita and Issie. Neither answered. That did not deter Blanche and Emilio, so they set out. Issie would be expecting them—Margarita had said she'd call ahead to make the arrangement.

The walk from the Plaza San Martín to Issie's apartment in San Telmo was a long one, but Blanche was glad they'd taken it. Parks everywhere, lush and green, were full of parents pushing strollers, couples walking hand-in-hand, and bench sitters. The trees were grander than she'd ever seen, with gnarled trunks and flickering leaves of gold, orange, and red on this bright autumn day.

All along the wide sidewalks, mimes, jugglers, artists, guitarists entertained for pesos. The vendors spoke softly or shouted their bargains, waving fists of wool shawls and tatted linen. A leather bag. Strings of hand-made jewelry. The passers-by gawked and lingered, including Blanche, who was an unapologetic people watcher. The tightly dressed women on the arms of tall, thin, self-assured men with mysterious dark eyes radiated international flair.

Magnífico. Buenos Aires certainly has a rhythm and sway all its own. It was an exotic dance. Like the tango.

"Where are you, Blanche? Come back to me."

She squeezed his hand. "I'm right here. And I *still* can't believe it."

They crossed a boulevard and took a short cut through a pedestrian walkway, her attention diverted at every turn. Blanche tried to focus, but her thoughts wandered. To Issie, cut off from her mother who was in trouble, worrying about her daughter alone in this big city.

And to Tomás ...

Of all the estancias, and all the guitar players, how did they happen to meet one who knew La Palma—plus, one who would be so willing to help two strangers? Maybe it had been a stroke of pure luck that she and Emilio had befriended a local historian and guide? *Pure luck?* She didn't put much store in that. A person made her own luck, and, basically speaking, Blanche didn't see anything lucky in how she met Tomás.

So far, they knew little about the estancia, except for what the frightened aunt had told Emilio. Blanche wasn't going to wallow in trouble before she knew what they were dealing with. Wasted energy. They'd take this thing one step at a time and finish up the trip and have something to dance about, for sure. She looked forward to that. "Sweep your feet off," as Tomás suggested.

They reached San Telmo, dodging a soccer rally with people in blue and yellow jerseys hanging off light poles. Argentinians took their soccer seriously. Then again, they seemed to take everything seriously; they were often charming and accommodating while a bit subdued. She had yet to see a crowd of tango dancers. She could only imagine how serious that could be.

Neat but tattered, San Telmo was a lively neighborhood of barking dogs and lines of wash flapping in the sunny breeze over a nearby alleyway. The meaty aroma of cooking, olive oil and garlic, wafted from the formerly grand doorway.

At the Plaza Dorrego, they stopped near a beautiful, yet decayed, neo-classical mansion divided up into apartments. "Is this Issie's?" Blanche murmured. Emilio checked his notes. The impressive gray stone building had clearly seen better days. Its exterior was patchy with city fumes, and the walkway was a crumbling length of broken tile. The weathered, heavy wooden door featured a pane of cracked, beveled glass. At the second-floor windows flower boxes added splashes of blue and white.

"I think she lives here. In a flat," said Emilio. They started toward the door. A woman parted the filmy curtains and stared out at them, her round face and dark eyes tense with anticipation.

Blanche waved. "I think we found her," she said. "Or she found us."

No sooner had she spoken than the face disappeared, and the door opened enough for a young woman to squeeze through. She flew down the stone steps, missing some errant rubble, her arms waving. She wrapped herself around Emilio. *"¡Primo mio!"*

Blanche's heart swelled. To see Emilio so happily startled was a thrill. *Family*.

He grinned and held her at arm's length. "I guess there's a resemblance?"

Blanche folded her arms. "Well, you both have black hair, and you're both beautiful and handsome!"

Issie's outfit was one of a kind: sheer paisley blouse, tight, ratty jeans, a wide glittery belt and silver boots to match. Her hair was as spiky as a porcupine, and one of her ears was pierced with half a dozen glitzy studs that enhanced her iridescent green eyes. She hugged Blanche and reached for Emilio, looping an arm in his. "Come! Come up, now." The filmy sleeves of her top scented the air with patchouli and citrus as they climbed the steps.

The dim entry hall had once been grand, but the threadbare carpet, dull wood, and chipped molding showed their age. A staircase separated two sitting rooms of former splendor. Issie waved at the empty space, bounding toward the steps.

"Sometimes we sit down here and solve the problems of Argentina. We go all night. And we play the guitar if the landlady isn't around!" The wallpaper of fruits and flowers in the stairwell peeled downward like the skin of fruit. Faded, red-flocked paper buckled on the far walls of the downstairs rooms. Two worn, sagging sofas sat in front of a fireplace, now dark and cold, no longer adding warmth.

Her corner apartment on the second floor was filled with light from the large windows looking out over the neighborhood. That seemed to be the only saving feature. The smell of cat, tobacco, and old cooking oil was pervasive. A poster of the Rolling Stones's "Bohemio Hot Lips" covered most of one wall while Jefferson Airplane warbled "White Rabbit" from a rickety record player.

"*Mi casa*," said Issie, flinging herself onto a sofa covered in an India print. "Sit. I am so glad you are here. Mamí told me about you. And here you are. Finally." She patted the cushion next to her and pointed at various faded bean bags randomly spaced around the living room.

Her English had the casual ease of a North American hippie, straight out of the East Village. And she seemed happy. Score one there. Blanche had been afraid Issie would be sad and shy, sunk in despair with her mother stuck on the estancia and her country enmeshed in trouble. Clearly, Issie had a hopeful, carefree side.

Blanche sank into a bean bag. Emilio, clearly delighted, sat close to Issie.

"Issie," said Emilio, "when did you come here? How are you getting along? Please, tell us about the estancia with Tía Margarita. Tell us everything."

"So many questions, *primo mio!* My life story?" She threw herself against a faded pillow. Her bright smile dimmed like the sun disappearing behind a cloud. "I grew up on the pampa. At the estancia with Mamí. Until the *witch* kicked me out." Issie's heavy eye make-up and patchy dyed hair added an edge to her expression.

"The witch?" Blanche leaned forward. "You mean Frau Schemmer?"

Issie nodded. "I had to get away from her, and, believe me, Mamí wanted me out of there. It's a toxic environment, you'll see. I came to Buenos Aires to study art and languages, and I'm safer away from that place. But I miss my mother. We talk—sometimes—but very little!"

"You didn't feel safe out there?" Emilio asked.

"No, I did not."

Blanche and Emilio exchanged a look.

This just gets more interesting by the minute. Blanche filed away this piece of news. "And your father? You couldn't go to him? He didn't live at the estancia?"

"No." She shifted around on the cushion. Picked up a glass globe and shook it nervously. "I didn't really know my father. My parents weren't together." She placed the globe back on the table with a click and watched the sparkles settle over the idyllic cottage scene.

Blanche started to ask further but dropped it.

"Issie, I am sorry," said Emilio.

"It's all right, I guess. I never knew him, and my mother did not talk about him."

"Why didn't you feel safe at La Palma?" Emilio asked, gently. "You say this woman, the Frau, is a witch?"

"*Mala.* They are all *malos.* There are secrets and cold, heartless people. And other things go on. Strange phone calls. Visitors late at night and at weird hours."

45

"What did you overhear?" Blanche asked.

"I wish I could say exactly, but I can't. Place was creepy. Frau Schemmer kept me away, separate from Mamí. She put me to work out of sight. She even sent meals to my room on the far side of the house. *¡Bruja!*"

"This must be so difficult," said Blanche. Issie's separation from Margarita—and talk of her father—tugged at Blanche who'd lost her mother in a car wreck and her father in Vietnam. She had a missing part in her even while she was eternally grateful for the love of her wonderful, eccentric, and now departed Gran who had raised her in that cabin on the beach.

Issie crossed her arms tightly to her chest and frowned. "Mamí did all she could. At least I had books to read and study." Blanche took in the wall of books teetering almost to the ceiling, one on top of another, without support of a bookcase.

"We both read much. There were many books at La Palma, and I learned to read and speak English from Mamí." Her gaze wandered off to better times. "She taught the Schemmers' children and she came up to my room and read to me and then I read back to her. She likes Hemingway and Twain, Dickens and Austen. All of them. I practice now with North American students."

Blanche raised her eyebrows. "Are their children still around? How many do they have?"

"Oh, no. The Schemmers' children—twins they had late in life—were sent away to boarding school in Europe. And then I was all alone. I don't know what happened to them." She paused. "*Por cierto*, they are glad to get away from their parents and La Palma."

Blanche sighed. Having to deal with the parents was one thing, but the children could've posed even more problems. "What are we getting into?"

"No. We have to get *out!*" Issie bounced off the sofa and down again, a plume of dust rising into a sunbeam. "These people. The

Schemmers. It did no good for Mamí to talk to the Frau about me. She just ignored anything Mamí asked." Issie turned to Blanche. "I've been gone years now. I try to visit. But it is never good. The witch sends me away. Mamí is too busy to be with me, or another thing."

She leaned toward Emilio. "We are afraid. Of what these people can—and will—do. We do not know how far is the reach." Issie stood up, her fists at her side. "My mother doesn't want me to worry, I know it. She is trying to protect me."

"Tell me what you do know, Issie." Blanche said.

"Mamí says these odd visitors come to La Palma. She overhears things, but she won't tell me what they say, these people in old, stiff clothes with their mean talk. They are *not* tourists. They sweep in like *la Zonda.*"

"The *Zonda?*" Blanche and Emilio asked at once.

She looked from Blanche to Emilio. "The evil wind. *La Zonda.* It blows the dust up and turns the sky black. Rattles the windows in the night and blinds the riders and animals in the fields. It's a blast that leaves people devastated, the land dry and lifeless as a desert in the pampa. The devil wind.

"Legend is that the hunter Gilanco mistreated Mother Earth and killed the birds and the animals with no mercy. So, the gods punished him. He disappeared. In his place the fierce, blinding winds came, and now we say the *Zonda* is the soul of Gilanco."

The *Zonda* sounded like a storm without the rain. Blanche loved storms when they blew up over the Gulf, the sky bright and sunny at one end of the horizon and black as night on the other. The ominous strength and power—the danger—mesmerized her. The waves, like mini tsunamis, and the torrents of sea water that swallowed up the beach, the whorls of stinging white sand swirling and scouring the beach were thrilling, and then it all blew away leaving a dip in temperature and clean air. Even so, Blanche respected the danger and got out of the way. She had shelter where she could ride out the storm with people she loved and trusted.

Issie and her mother were not in a safe place, and, in any case, weather was the least of their concerns. They faced the secrets of the Schemmers and possible disaster if these secrets came to light. It renewed a resolve in Blanche—to do *something*. She studied Issie. Emilio held Issie's hand and hung on every word. Issie's staunch nature could be her saving grace.

"Mamí, she says to be patient." Issie bit off the words in frustration.

Emilio exchanged a glance with Blanche. "We need to go. Tomorrow."

"Issie, why can't your mother just leave? What's holding her there?" Blanche pressed for more information.

"Bullies. They've insinuated—more like, insisted—she not leave, or else. The Frau denies it, of course." Issie shook her head. "The Schemmers have excuses. They tell her things, meant to delay. They have a rush of guests, or a catered party, or some other thing. Always an emergency. This week, they promised to set up a fund for her, but she must wait to sign papers. It is all *mierda*. Bullshit." Issie's eyes darted from one to the other. "*Lo siento*."

Blanche mulled this over. "Delay tactics. And bullies."

"She's afraid of what they might do to *me*." Issie jumped up and paced. "But I am sure she has a way to leave with you once you get to La Palma."

Blanche's mind was spinning. *But what if Margarita hasn't set up a way to elude the Germans?*

"We need wheels." Blanche looked at Emilio. He nodded. "We can set that up with Tomás. He's promised transportation."

"Be tourists exploring different parts of Buenos Aires," Issie said. "Act like you don't know Mamí, but when you find her, *leave*."

It sounded so easy.

"Issie, you stay here, and we will bring your mother to you," Emilio said. "We will keep our connection to you and Margarita a secret."

"Those snakes know everything." Issie stopped pacing and threw her hands up in the air. "They have spies. Do not trust anyone out there."

"Wish my Spanish was half as good as your English, Issie," said Blanche. "I try, but it's not so *bueno*."

"You will be fine. Many people speak English. So do the Schemmers. They're German, but with visitors from over the world, and being near the Capital, English is necessary."

"And the staff?"

"Yes." Issie shook her finger at them. "And don't let them fool you that they don't understand. They do understand so they can pass on things to the Frau."

"Oh, great," said Blanche. Some of the staff at La Palma might be in the same predicament as Margarita.

"We may not do so much talking at all. Actions speak *loud*," said Emilio.

Issie picked up a framed photo of her mother and handed it to Emilio. He studied the photo and handed it to Blanche. She noted Margarita's dark eyes so like Emilio's and Issie's. Her gray hair was pulled back severely, but her full red lips and bright expression were warm and serene.

"Lovely," Blanche said, replacing Margarita's photo carefully on the table.

Again, her heart filled with hope they could pull this off. And soon. Blanche felt a tie reinforce their resolve.

"Thank you, *primo mio*. And Blanche. For doing this," Issie said, her gaze soft with gratitude.

Emilio paced back and forth to the window.

Blanche watched him and waited a beat before making a gloomy prediction. "Issie, is it safe for you and your mother to stay here? The Schemmers will probably track down Margarita. And you." *What would they do?* Hiding out temporarily might not be the end of it. Issie was surely the major reason Margarita was being so careful about her exit.

"We'll be all right, I hope." Issie wrung her hands. "I have a plan. I have friends in Uruguay. They will help us get out of Buenos Aires." She looked around her apartment. "Believe it or not, I've already started to pack up some things."

Every surface of her table held a small tchotchke, paint brushes, books, candles, records, and vases of dried flowers. Blanche had never seen so many *things* in one small room. Then the cat appeared. Blanche, the cat whisperer, immediately found the orange calico curled up in her lap, purring her head off, her eyes slits of pleasure. She absently rubbed the small creature and looked up at Issie. "And this little friend? Don't forget her ... or him?"

"Her. MariLu. Loves chicken skin and chasing *cucarachas*." Issie sighed. "She'll fit in my pocket." Blanche nodded while thinking how far they were away from realizing safety for all of them.

Issie jumped up off the cushion and waved her arms. "Oh, I am sorry. What a hostess I am! We've had nothing to eat or drink. We must have *mate!*"

"¿Mate?" Blanche had heard of the herb drink but never tried it.

"You've not tried it? It's wonderful. Wait and see." Issie scurried off to the back of the apartment and returned promptly with a tray. In the center, she'd placed an old copper kettle. Steam rose from the spout. Next to it was a large gourd and a silver straw sticking out of it. A plate of cookies and small cakes.

She put the tray on a low table in front of them. "First, I pack the herb into the gourd. Like this." Then she lifted the kettle and poured the hot water in a slow trickle down the side of the metal straw, *la bombilla*, into the gourd. There followed a moment or two of steeping, then she took a sip and passed the gourd to Blanche. She paused, unsure, and looked up at Emilio.

Issie laughed. "We share same straw."

Emilio gestured for her to drink up.

Blanche drew on the straw. The *mate* was bitter, somewhat like tobacco but oddly appealing and stimulating, much like a strong drink of tea. The camaraderie among the three of them added to it. When she handed the gourd to Emilio, he didn't hesitate.

"How did *mate* ever become a custom? I see these gourds everywhere," said Blanche. At tables in the park, even on steps and curbs, people gathered and sipped *mate*. Vendors sold *bombillas* and gourds and other receptacles at the street markets and in the shops. Some were fancy filigreed metal cups; some more humble, like Issie's, of hollowed-out squash gourds.

Issie sat cross-legged on an enormous purple velvet pillow on the floor, cradling her cat. "*Mate* is common in many Latin American countries. It's for relaxing, quite like tea. It has caffeine but delivers more smoothly than coffee. We share *mate* with people we're close to. Those we trust. Know what I mean?"

Blanche nodded. She didn't like to drink with someone she didn't trust though she had done it for a lot of reasons. Mainly, when people drank alcohol, they talked. *Mate* was a ritual with much the same outcome, but different. More intimate. Taking a bottle off the shelf and pouring into a glass didn't create the same effect as the unique sharing of *mate*.

"Here we have stories for everything," said Issie. "Want to hear an old Guaraní myth about *mate*?"

"Of course!" Blanche was always up for a story.

Issie grinned and settled into the sofa. "Well, here's how it happened ... Maybe ..."

A young goddess with long, black hair and silvery skin lived in the heavens, but she spent much of her time pining for the humans on earth. She was drawn to their kindness and ingenuity and to the families safe in their hutches and well fed on maize and honey.

The goddess wanted to visit earth, but her father forbade it. "Child, you don't know the place, and it wouldn't be safe for you."

"For a short visit?"

"No. On earth you would be without the power of the gods."

She took another angle. "But I promise to be careful, father."

"Ah, you are as relentless as the winds and rain and tides." He softened and finally gave in. "You may go with my heavenly blessing but without support on earth," he said, sternly, as he put his hands lovingly on his daughter's shoulders. "Return soon."

Impetuous—and ecstatic—she descended to the plains and jungles as a young girl. She played in the rivers, ate the abundant fruit, and searched for her beloved humans.

Then one night in the shelter of a cave, she awoke to a dreadful roar. Terror swept through her. Eyes like hot coals burned in the darkness. A snarling jaguar bared its teeth and pawed the ground. Defenseless, she shut her eyes and steeled herself for the inevitable.

Nothing happened. She opened her eyes. "Don't be afraid," said a young man. He pulled at a long vine and dangled it at the jaguar. Distracted, the big cat purred and wandered away, and the young man bowed to the girl. "My name is Arami."

"I'm so grateful to you. I'm Jasy."

"You shouldn't be here alone. Come stay with my family," he said. "It's so dark tonight with no moon." At the sound of the word "moon," Jasy smiled and peered up into the sky. At last, she'd met a human, and he was as kind as she'd suspected. Jasy met his wife and admired the children. They gave her shelter.

They soon went off to sleep, and Arami dreamed he was floating over the trees. Jasy spoke to him in his sleep: "Thank you for your care. I'm going now, but I'm leaving you a gift. Tomorrow, you'll wake to find the *yerba mate* in your garden. Roast it and steep it for a comforting drink."

Arami awoke to find the herb, and that night he looked up into a sky filled with light. It was Jasy. He knew it. Her round, silvery face shined down, her hair flowed in endless black waves. He thanked her for watching over them and for the wonderful drink of *yerba mate*.

Six

Hot Tango Tonight

BLANCHE, EMILIO, AND ISSIE left the apartment and headed to the plaza to meet Tomás for the *milonga*—and to get directions for the ride out to La Palma. Blanche and Emilio had formed a plan to leave the next day; Issie would await word in Buenos Aires.

Emilio strode ahead, his boots pounding the sidewalk. "I'm calling Tía. *Ahorita*," he said. "Just as soon as we leave the dancing and get back to the hotel." Issie and Blanche fell in next to him.

"Hey!" Blanche hooked her arm in his. "Take it easy."

He turned toward Blanche, his expression softened.

"*Mira*," Issie interjected. "You two go out there to the estancia. Maybe you shouldn't do anything at first. Just look around and figure it out from there. Mamí may have some idea of what to do."

Emilio raked his fingers through his hair. Issie stared up into his eyes. "All these days, I never thought it a good idea for me to go—to just show up at La Palma. Me, saying, come on Mamí, let's go. I've told her I would do it, but she said it would never work to leave like that."

"You may have to move quickly, Issie," said Blanche, "so you need to be ready. With or without your mother."

54

"No! I will not go without my mother. We will leave the city. Together. Or, not at all." Issie cocked her head, her jaw set.

"Issie, the Schemmers may know where you live. Have you thought of that?" Blanche tried to think of every angle.

"For now, my friends will hide us, if necessary. I don't think the witch would come looking for us here." But Issie did not look convinced.

As they drew closer to the plaza, the tango music captured their attention with a cascade of notes, the dancers twirling past.

"Wow!" Blanche said. "Violins, guitars, and even a piano!"

"An *orquesta típica*," Issie said.

A loud and happy distraction, the music excited Blanche—and was a welcome diversion—as Issie pulled them along.

"Let the tango carry you away," Issie said dreamily. "I wish I could stay, but I must meet some students. I'll see you soon? With Mamí. Call me and let me know how things are working." She hugged them both.

By the time they entered the plaza, it was early evening. The dusky light softened the rough edges of the storefronts and cracked walkways but did not dim the colorful outfits of the locals. A tonic of citrusy cologne and cigarette smoke filled the air, the tango music pulsed, creating a frenzy in the crowd. Dancers of all ages and sizes paired off to the strains of Carlos Gardel's *"Mi Buenos Aires Querido."* They turned and lunged, some graceful, some bordering on violent, energetic lust. Gardel, this most famous composer of the tango, had been dead for seventy years, but his music still held Argentinians captive.

A woman with long, black hair pulled back in a sleek bun danced by. Rather, she dipped and twirled by. The red halter-top dress and scuffed black heels gave her a sultry look, but it was the dance that did it. She clutched her partner's hand and leaned into him, one leg extended behind her. The man was tall and handsome, his fedora pulled low over an aquiline nose, his legs whipping about in loose black trousers. He yanked her close, both their faces like stone.

Blanche murmured, "Do you think we can do that?"

Emilio hunched his shoulders and grinned. They made their way around the edge of the plaza. Blanche scanned the faces for Tomás.

"You have come!" A voice as loud as one of those horns startled Blanche. Tomás came toward them across the plaza, smiling. He wore the same, black-embroidered jacket and flat-brimmed hat as on the *peotanal*. He extended his arms and waved happily, his exuberance catchy.

"Tomás!" Blanche waved back.

He bowed. "*Encantado.*" They headed for a café nearby, dodging tango dancers spilling onto the sidewalk. A bottle of red wine and small stemless glasses graced the middle of a round, rickety table. Tomás pulled out one of the flimsy chairs with curly wrought-iron legs.

"*A tomar un chato de vino,*" he said.

Never one to turn down a glass of wine, especially in the middle of festivities, Blanche nodded as she perched herself on the chair and sipped Malbec.

The music reached a crescendo with a screech of strings and the energetic whoosh of the accordion. The dancers' heels clicked over the stone plaza like castanets. A dazzling pair swung past them. The young woman's expression was empty and serious as was her partner's, an older man in a tight suit and fine leather shoes. The violin and bandoneon, bass, and a clarinet blended together in waves of tango music, a sound that had a sway and dip all its own.

This tango business looked complicated with its show of quick feet and taut arms, clingy outfits and rousing music. Complicated yet spectacular. It was not her island style but certainly hypnotic.

She smiled at Tomás. "I'm not sure I'm cut out for the tango."

"Ah, indeed you are!" He winked at Emilio. "You will see, *chica rica.*"

Emilio moved to the music. They sipped the Malbec.

"*Un momentito.*" Tomás jumped up from the chair and turned on his heel, managing the uneven cobblestone deftly, and hurried off. *Oh, great.* She'd decided that the tango was fine to watch. For now. But they needed to talk about the major reason they were there. She wanted more information about La Palma and follow through on his promise of a driver. She looked for his return while Emilio, on his feet, one hand in his pocket, swayed to the tune of the festivities.

Tomás popped out of the crowd leading a dazzling, large-busted woman with intense dark eyes. He lifted her long slender arm and beamed. "Allow me to introduce Anna Godoy de Gamoure, my long time tango partner." Apparently, he'd stolen her from the tight-suited, older man. She was a good head taller than Tomás and the vision of every perfect tango dancer lunging about the plaza. Sultry. Bewitching. Her tight, shimmery red dress hugged every curve. Pinned in her hair, a large, black rose accented her dainty ear, and her eyes blazed under long, full lashes. She studied Emilio from head to toe. He bowed, his eyes lingering on her, lips to hips. Blanche swallowed hard. A tinge of jealousy burned her cheeks.

"As I said, *divina,*" said Tomás. He kissed the tips of Anna's fingers, and then, of all things, offered them to Emilio.

Oh glory. Blanche crossed over to another world. Tomás held out his arms to Blanche. "Shall we?"

"Shall we what?" Blanche clutched her wine glass and slid sideways on the wobbly chair. She righted herself just in time.

"We will have the tango now," he said.

She glanced at Anna. Her voice low and rumbly, and disturbingly inviting, she said, "And Señor Emilio? We will dance now?" Blanche twisted a curl at her neck into a knot. She wished Emilio didn't look so … interested. And, well, *eager.*

Anna dismissed Blanche with the look of a woman who has just stolen something. *Her man.* She adjusted the strap of her low-cut dress with those long, shiny red talons and took Emilio's hand. They headed toward the dancing crowd. He didn't look back.

"Wait ..." The words died on Blanche's lips.

The band broke into a stirring rendition, another pulsing chorus, a seductive blast of enchantment. Anna laid her hand on Emilio's shoulder and yanked his arm straight out. She pulled him in close. Very close. Blanche gripped her glass hard, swallowed the last bit of wine, and tapped it on the table.

"*Ahorita. Andamos,*" Señorita de Gamoure commanded.

"We walk?" Emilio searched Anna's eyes. Then he looked around at Blanche. For what? Help? Blanche didn't feel helpful at all.

"*Sí,* we walk." Anna took three steps backward, holding tight to Emilio. Then, as if Emilio's boots came to life, he fell in and they tangoed off into the crowd.

Tomás grinned at Blanche then led her out onto the plaza. The music was deafening, the smell of roses and sweat and dust choked her. But she walked the steps back and forth gamely, taking Tomás's lead. They were about the same height, the brim of his hat bumping her head. He smelled spicy, like peppery oregano, and his thick eyebrows worked up and down. "You see, it is the woman who holds the dance in her heart and gives passion and meaning to the tango, and the man who meets her with equal passion," he intoned, pointing to Señorita de Gamoure and Emilio with his chin. He patted Blanche's hand on his shoulder.

"Am I walking the right way?" Blanche asked.

"Yes, and you will be fluid. *Naturalmente.* You will concentrate now." Tomás jostled Blanche as she searched for Emilio. "You are the river, and I am the current."

"I don't feel like a river," Blanche said.

"The river, yes," Tomás murmured calmly, but firmly. "One ... two ... three." He picked up the tempo. Blanche checked her feet and hoped they behaved.

"Do not look down. Hold your head up. Like the *divina* that you are." He lifted her arm and stuck out his elbow. "And do not look at *them*."

Blanche tore her eyes away from Emilio and Anna who swept by as if they were the only two people in the world. Her long, sinewy neck turned this way and that as she twisted about. Her hips appeared to be on a swivel. She kicked with controlled and enviable abandon.

Blanche tried not to look, but how could she help it? The two stopped, abruptly, nearby. "Señor Emilio, you must find your middle," Anna growled, and then whipped him around in a circle. "Right here." She patted his stomach. Her lip curled, revealing perfect teeth.

The heat of anger threatened to overtake Blanche.

Now they were sharing a laugh. An intimate, knowing laugh. Blanche didn't remember ever hearing the like from Emilio, but she had hardly a second to stop and seethe. Tomás was working her in circles. Yet she caught Anna swinging her leg around Emilio's thigh. Such a mix of emotions coursed through Blanche, she wasn't sure where this would end, but it had to end soon before she exploded.

"Ah, that *eeez eeet!*" Anna yelled. And again, the two spun off down the edge of the plaza, wrapped in a frenzy of feet and legs, Emilio now in the lead.

"Where did he learn to do *that?*" Blanche hissed. She couldn't keep her head straight for keeping up.

"He is a natural, your Emilio. And so are you, Señorita Blanche. This is a contest of wills and love, strength and passion! *¡Ándele!*" Tomás nearly swept her off her feet. She'd stumbled, but now something switched, and she was just fired up enough to want to do it right. She would not look at Emilio and that woman.

Tomás said. "Let go yourself."

How many times have I done that? Enough to know she'd almost done herself in several times. Now she'd lost Emilio to an exotic tango dancer. There they were again, sailing around the plaza. Complicated and passionate, and disturbing.

Tomás's fingers dug into her back, his hand gripped hers. She hated this little interlude, but at the same time it was compelling. She blamed the enchantress, Anna, for casting a spell over the evening.

Blanche stared at Tomás. He was remarkably sure-footed and a good leader. She gave in and somehow followed the steps.

"Do not look at anyone but into yourself. Find your core."

"I thought I was the river or the stream, or something," she yelled over the music.

"You are all the things you wish to be." He smiled widely, the gap in his teeth adding to his charm.

Dammit, I'm going to enjoy it!

Suddenly, as in all things Blanche Murninghan, the dance took over. She could feel the music from her fingers to her toes, her core relaxed, her feet obeyed. She stretched out her arms to meet Tomás, and she *tangoed*.

"*Bueno*," he announced. It wasn't an A-plus rating, but she'd take it.

She smiled into his dark eyes. "At least I haven't stepped on your feet."

"That is *muy bueno*. I have the gout."

Seven

Little Greenie

TOMÁS LED BLANCHE BACK to the café table. She snatched the bottle of wine and filled her glass. Let the lovely spirits wash over her senses. *Delicioso. But I'm still totally pissed.* She searched for the dancers, but Emilio was nowhere to be seen. Tomás pulled up a chair. He took out a small notebook and tore out a page.

"Señorita, here's the name of the driver. Ramón Garcia." He slid the scrap of paper across the table. "He will take you to the estancia. And here is my phone number, in case."

She grabbed the paper. At the moment she was thinking she might ask the driver to take her to the airport. She was fuming, but she managed to remember her manners. "Thank you, Tomás," she mumbled.

Tomás cocked his head at her with a gentle look. "Is something wrong?"

"Sorry, just a bit out of sorts." She averted her eyes and concentrated on the small beetle plodding across the wrought iron surface of the table. For a moment, she envied that bug. Not a care in the world.

"Maybe you go easy on the grape of the devil? It makes your mood not so good."

She slumped in the chair and checked the tight feeling in her throat. "You're right."

Then she spied Emilio. Blanche narrowed her eyes as he hugged Anna's waist and dipped her backwards. She gulped the wine. Such a contorted slithery thing in that dress. How much mileage and places they'd been.

It would be a shame if she sprained her ankle.

Anna's lips were close to Emilio's. They paused in close, animated conversation. She threw her head back and laughed. Emilio looked like a little kid with a new toy.

Blanche pushed away from the table and stood up, fists at her side. The two dancers swayed, hands clasped, supposedly reviewing the basics. Making goo-goo eyes.

Blanche could not stop the little green monster that threatened to take over. If Emilio didn't knock it off with Señorita Dancing Queen, she knew she'd do something she'd regret. Of course, it wouldn't be the first time for shoot-from-the-lip "Bang" Murninghan.

She stopped, uncharacteristically, and checked herself. Maybe she and Emilio weren't such a great pair after all. She'd assumed that he belonged to her. The truth was he didn't belong to her any more than she belonged to him. No one was anybody's. Gran, on her deathbed, had told Blanche: "We're alone when we come into this world, and we're alone when we go out." This was her grandmother's way of framing life at both ends. As soon as you are born, you're on the way to dying. *Well, that's a sober thought.* Blanche sighed. She needed a good dose of sobriety, and reality.

One thing she could not deny, no matter how annoyed she was, she loved Emilio.

She plopped back down at the table and twisted around for another look at the plaza. *Get a grip, Blanche.* It wasn't working. Emilio was having too good a time. La Gamoure was doing most of the laughing, but he didn't have to appear to enjoy it so much. Blanche ignored Tomás's advice about the grape of the devil and drank the rest of the Malbec.

Tomás sat, busily running his fingers over the guitar strings, murmuring to himself in Spanish. She'd been totally lost in her thoughts of murdering Anna and hadn't paid any attention to Tomás. *So rude.* She forced a smile, crossed her arms, and tried to be nice while she couldn't help glowering.

Tomás glanced across the plaza and then back at Blanche.

"Señorita Blanche?"

"I'm here, barely."

He shook his head and laughed softly. "*Olé tu padre.* Do not worry. It is simply the dance, and like always, the dance, it ends." He laid the beat-up Martin in a tattered case, closed it, and bounced to his feet. He patted her hand. She looked up at him, hopefully, and went back to gazing at Emilio.

"I must go," he said. "If you have questions about Ramón, the driver, you will call me. Yes? You have the details about where to meet, and how much it will cost and all that business."

She listened with half an ear. Tomás was a little blurry through the haze of wine.

"He drives a small white Renault. You can't miss it." He put a finger to his lips. "Now that I think, you can miss it. There are thousands of these small cars."

"Thanks, Tomás," said Blanche, embarrassed at her lack of appreciation. Irritation was so close to the surface. "You are kind. We'll sort it out. I'll just have a word with Emilio." She clapped her glass onto the table.

Tomás shook his head and shouldered the hefty guitar case. "*Ahorita.* I am late for my performance, but *bueno.* You will talk with Emilio and settle things." His eyes twinkled. "You will give him directions. I wish you much luck." Tomás, the philosopher of the guitar and tango and life, explained things in more ways than one.

"*Gracias*, Tomás. Wait! When will we see you?"

He touched the brim of his hat and rolled his eyes toward heaven. "We will meet again, but only God knows. No doubt about it. Right on the money, or peso, so to speak."

She called after him. "And this Ramón, he's reliable?"

He waved his hand, walking off in that funny, tilted gait, hat squarely on his head, and shoulders back. *Damn. I forgot to ask him about the return trip from La Palma.* She'd also wanted to pick his brain for more information about the estancia, but the wine and that witch de Gamoure had gotten in the way. It would have to do. They'd just have to arrange their transportation with this Ramón. She'd think about it later.

Right now, she was intent on getting Emilio back. She got up from the table and stood on the edge of the plaza. Zeroed in on Anna, those possessive dark, heavily mascaraed slits for eyes. *Horrors.* What if Emilio didn't want to get away from her? Blanche wouldn't believe it. She wanted him, all of him. To herself.

The two dancers were gone again, but it sure as hell wasn't hard to find them. He was tall, and Anna was, well, obvious.

Blanche stomped toward them, gritting her teeth behind that smile. "Hi! Hola!" Emilio clearly was startled. Blanche gave La-La Gamoure a curt nod. *I'd like to strangle this woman.*

Blanche had interrupted ... something. Emilio was suddenly aware of his surroundings. He dropped Anna's hand and reached for Blanche, but she backed away. "I'm ready to go. You?" He hesitated. She turned and walked but didn't get far. Without a word, there he was, his hand on her shoulder. "*Baquita*—"

"Don't call me that." She walked faster. Emilio hurried to keep up.

"Blanche, please ... I ..."

She stopped. Seething. All she managed to say was, "I have the name of the driver from Tomás. We're all set. He had to leave. Since you were so *busy*, he said he was sorry he couldn't say good-bye." The heat rose up her neck. She had to get away before things got even uglier.

Emilio grabbed her arm, tilted his head at her. Pleading. "Don't you want to stay and dance? I'd like to show you what I learned."

"Oh, I bet you would." Too late to take that one back.

"*Baquita*. Please," he begged.

"I've already done enough dancing. With Tomás. He was kind enough ... We went out for a spin."

Now her lip was quivering. *How mortifying! Am I going to start blubbering right here in the middle of a milonga?* Blanche glared. "Of all the—"

The woman had followed them. Managing a bored—and sultry—look, Señorita Gamoure poked at that pile of hair. "Emilio?!"

Blanche stepped in front of her and clenched her fists. "Excuse me. We are having a conversation here."

Anna airily ignored Blanche and stood her ground. She was very sure of her ground. Anna threw her shoulders back, casting her cleavage into the conversation. Her talons lightly traced Emilio's arm. "*Un hombre delicioso*," she growled.

"Yes, he is." Blanche was furious. Anna had just said he was *delicious*. "*Why don't you go away?*" Something snapped. Blanche had had enough tango for the night, and quite enough of Anna de Gamoure. Blanche peeled Anna's fingers off Emilio and pushed her, none too gently, while fighting an irrepressible urge to clock her a good one. Emilio's eyes were big as shiny moons. If Blanche hadn't been so angry, she would have laughed.

Anna tossed her head and had the good sense to step back. It was hard to read the moves of this person except for the fact that she could tango and drive Blanche to the edge. She gave Anna a killer look. One that could not be misinterpreted.

Anna twiddled her fingers at Emilio, then cocked a hip. "Now … you two. You will dance. I think." She batted those spider-like lashes and languidly offered her hand to a tall, thin man, who tapped one fine-leather toe. He drew Anna into the dance, and as simple as walking or breathing, they tangoed away.

Blanche deflated with relief.

Emilio called after Anna. "It's been a pleasure, Señorita. I had no idea—"

Blanche rounded on Emilio and crossed her arms. "Of what?" The little green monster took over. She brushed past Emilio. "I … am … leaving."

"¡Baquita!" He chased after her. "The music …"

"I told you not to call me that."

"I am … we got carried away. Por favor." His hands up in a beseeching way. "Will you dance with me? Por favor?"

"Uh, I don't think so," she said. Her size fives felt like they were encased in concrete.

Emilio reached for her. "Baquita," he said softly. He wrapped his arms around her and nuzzled her neck.

"Why … ?"

He didn't answer.

She couldn't deny this ambivalence, the anger and the love all at once. She fought with herself and tried to breathe. Breathing was winning out, and so was love. Be sensible, she told herself. Don't walk away. Communicate.

It was hard to stay angry with Emilio, especially with those warm, strong arms around her. A burst of tango music startled her. She closed her eyes and gave in to the music. His face close to hers, he murmured, "Allow me?"

Emilio spun her around, his hand pressing into the small of her back. They took a few steps. He really knew what he was doing ... the *perrito*.

Backwards ... forwards, they twirled. Blanche ignored Anna, but she couldn't help catch a glimpse of one more wry, painted smile.

It didn't matter. Emilio only had eyes for Blanche.

"*Mira.*" He held her at arm's length but kept a tight hold on her. "Look at us! I had a good teacher. But ..." He grinned down at Blanche and squeezed her fingers. She looked up at him and bit her tongue. "But better than that, I have the best partner. In everything."

It was eleven o'clock, and La Brigada was getting crowded for the dinner hours. There was no such thing as *hour*; midday and night, the Argentines made a drawn-out ceremony of eating.

"*¿Achuras?*" Emilio studied the menu skeptically. "Appetizers?"

"*What?* Goat sweetbreads. Pickled tongue. Beef testicles?" Blanche slapped the menu on the table and sat back against the banquette and crossed her arms. The memory of their evening of tango still stung. The white-coated waiter carried a tray of grilled meat past her head. Blanche had been hungry, but now her stomach was a jumble. "Ugh."

"Blanche." Emilio leaned forward across the booth, his eyes dark and earnest. "It was only a dance lesson."

"Hmmm. Some lesson." She gulped the Malbec, then pushed it away. *Should listen to Tomás.*

"Now, come on. Let's get some of this *lomo* with *chimichurri* and *papas a la provenzal*. It looks *riquísimo.*"

"Don't distract me." They had stopped in for dinner at a *parilla*. It was their first visit to a typical Argentine grill and their first argument. Blanche's insides burned. After they'd finished their tango, the annoying Anna had returned to Emilio with some rat-a-tat

Spanish that Blanche had a hard time following. "That woman was all googly over you. And you certainly looked like you were having a time of it. And what was that she said to you?"

"That I'm a good dancer. But it doesn't matter what she said." He smiled, tentative and charming. "It was all about the music. You know how I love music. It takes over. And, please, believe me, it was only that."

She softened remembering the first time she laid eyes on him. *Music.* He was playing the guitar at that fiesta in the farmhouse, his voice passionate, his long fingers running over the strings. Yes, she knew how he was with music. She loved that about him.

He walked his fingers across the tabletop to hers and squeezed, the menu shoved aside. She didn't return the squeeze, and certainly didn't trust herself to talk, so she again concentrated on the disgusting menu of appetizers. Sometimes silence was the best talk.

"*Baquita.* Your eyes. *Ventanas del alma.* I see right in there to that soul, and I love what I see."

She withdrew her fingers, gently, and sipped the Malbec. Just a tiny sip. "Well, I do, too. *You.*"

She locked eyes with him, and it struck her: This moment, that particular look of love on Emilio's face, would it always be like this?

The endless uncertainty, and everything else in the world, faded. She wanted the moment to last forever. The waiters gliding with trays balanced overhead, the conversation, the bursts of laughter, the grilled meat delivered on swords. Outside the wide windows, Buenos Aires glittered in the night.

They ordered the *lomo.* She took a bite of the tenderloin, salty and juicy, and murmured approval. They were suddenly hungry, and nothing had ever tasted so good. A waiter rolled up with a dessert cart. Custard puffs, cakes covered in chocolate and *dulce de leche,* mounds of whipped cream and coconut. *"¿Qué le gusta, señorita?"* the waiter asked. She smiled at him. Emilio took her hand, and she squeezed back.

"I think we're good," she said. "Very good."

It was well past midnight by the time they finished dinner and left the restaurant. They found a side street to their hotel where the streetlights glowed in and out of the canopy of trees, softening the night. Instead of talking about La Palma and Margarita and Issie—and all the other worrisome distractions—they talked about each other. The humor they shared, and their fascination with the beach and birds, the quiet before the rain hit the roof of the cabin. They wanted to stay together, no matter what. She admitted that seeing him dance with Anna had opened up some new feelings. Anger and jealously, and she didn't like it. "I was afraid of losing something ... No, I was afraid of losing you."

He drew her tightly against his chest and draped his jacket around her. "That, well, that is never going to happen." His arm around her shoulders, Blanche thrilled at the realization and at how they fit together.

They walked fast toward the hotel, a sense of urgency drawing them closer. Blanche shut out the world. They hurried through the lobby and into their room. Crashed into each other's arms. The streetlight shined in and made a silhouette of him. She couldn't see his eyes, but she could feel him all around her, his heart beating fast. Just like hers.

Laughter and the sounds of a far-off guitar floated up from the street below. Music filled the air.

Eight
Who Was That Gihost?

THE RUSTY WHITE RENAULT pulled up at the curb near the Plaza San Martín. Emilio bent down into the car window and talked to the driver. "Ramón?" His long hair nearly covered his face. He clutched the steering wheel and stared directly out front. His only acknowledgment to Emilio was a curt nod.

"*Vamos a La Palma. Ahorita.*"

"*¿Habla inglés?*"

"*Nada.*" Brusque and final.

Emilio and Blanche settled into the back seat. The soiled cloth upholstery had seen better days, and the air, even with the windows open, smelled of stale tobacco. *Típico.* Everyone in Buenos Aires smoked.

Blanche stuck her head out the window for a breath of fresh air but got a lung-full of fumes from a truck unloading cases of beer. She scooted forward to talk to the driver but stopped. Her Spanish wasn't so hot, and the man didn't seem so happy—in any language. She would chat him up later, perhaps.

Bicycles and scooters whizzed by. The cars were a furious assortment of small, backfiring demons, spewing exhaust and weaving in and out of traffic with little regard for stop signs and pedestrians.

Blanche was eager to get out of the city and into the country of fresh grasslands and wide-open spaces. The driver pulled a cap down over his face and sped off into traffic. He seemed oblivious that they were even in the car. Still, she kept her voice low. "What did the Schemmers say?"

Emilio put his arm around her. "Told the Frau we'd be out today."

She could feel how tense he was. "And? What did she sound like?"

"Like talking to an iceberg? 'All zee arrangements are made,' she say."

"Did you call your aunt?"

"No, no. It's difficult for her to talk. She knows we're coming." Emilio craned his neck at a field of very small soccer players in striped jerseys, bounding about like scampering rabbits. He fidgeted, his fingers tapping her arm.

"She doesn't know exactly when, though?"

"No, but she promised to find us. In private."

She reached up and touched Emilio' cheek. "We'll get her out of there, and everything will be *great*." If she said it enough and wished it enough, it had to come true.

Blanche caught Ramón's eye in the rearview mirror. Something in his expression made her wary. Did he know any English? Was he listening? He fiddled with the radio to adjust the sound of a string of classical Latin songs.

"*¿Está bien, la música?*"

She nodded. She liked the music. In fact, she loved it.

Soon, they were out of the city. The day was bright, and the sun reflected off the vast sea of grass that stretched as far as the eye could see. The air was heavy but clean. They bumped along the badly paved roads. It didn't matter. With each jolt, they were closer to getting this done instead of talking and worrying about it.

71

Ramón seemed competent. It wouldn't be good to have an incident out here. She and Emilio were rocketing toward the middle of nowhere. She slumped further into the seat.

Soon the road narrowed further, and they trundled past grasses taller than the car. Thick and impenetrable stalks. It was hard to call this grass; it was more like a dense forest of sticks. There was nothing around, not a house or another car. And it was eerily silent. They'd only been out of the city for an hour.

"¿Ramón, cuántas horas, el viaje?" Blanche leaned forward in her seat, her hand on the high back in front of her. The man shrunk further into his seat.

He shrugged, and grunted. *"Dos horas y media. Mas o menos, señorita."*

"Listo," said Emilio. "Trip's about two hours."

"¿Listo? I hear people saying that all the time here. It means?"

"Ready? OK? I'm here?" He mused as they sped through the tunnel of grass. "They say it for everything."

"So different than Mexico. In many ways."

"Sí."

Blanche waved her hand at the landscape. "The sky and land go on forever. So much space. A thousand miles at its widest and two and half times that, north to south. Nothing for miles. It's unnerving, and mysterious, isn't it? Feels like we're the only ones out here. Cut off like this." Her voice fell off wistfully. "It's a little like Mexico, but not really. Mexico has miles and miles of sunflowers. And black hills and blue, blue sky. So lovely, lots of space, but open."

"Baquita."

"What?"

"I love you for that."

"For what?" Sometimes she wondered what it was, exactly, he loved about her. What exactly did she see in him? They were *exact* opposites, really. He was tall and reserved and sure. She was short, impulsive, and talked. A lot. Some would say too much. She was often blunt, but Emilio didn't complain. He'd smile, thoughtfully, almost methodical and careful in his replies. Then there were times he would say something that totally threw her.

"I love you—for you." He leaned down and kissed her. "And Mexico. Two things very wonderful. What is it you say? *La variedad es la sal de la vida.*"

She laughed. "Variety is the salt of life. Yes, it is." She buried her nose in his shirt. He smelled of something undefinable, a combination of soap and clean air.

They settled into the lumpy seat. The wind ruffled her hair, and the dusty dry pampa made her sneeze. The late morning wrapped around them like a blanket. A shot of uneasiness raced through Blanche. She wasn't sure why, pressed against Emilio, comfy and secure, but the emptiness of the pampa did nothing to reassure her.

"There must be gauchos out here. Can you imagine living outside, riding and camping? Your whole life. How do they get through this stuff?"

"They're out there. It's a hard life on the pampa. Many work alone or on the ranches. Sometimes they roam together in small bands. And they live by their own code," he said.

"What code is that?"

"Freedom, at all costs, and their tradition is strong. They don't tolerate limits, or government, or institutions. To them, the Capital is a symbol of restriction. Most gauchos are staunchly Christian, but they have their own way with the commandments. They respect the Indigenous, but they'll take their women and land—and kill—if necessary. They answer to no one."

"Where did you hear this?"

"Margarita, my parents. And I read about it. You know Martín Fierro?"

"Yes. *Song of the Gaucho.*"

"The former owner of La Palma was the spirit of Martín Fierro. A respected caudillo among gauchos."

"And now the Schemmers have taken over. Mysteriously."

Emilio frowned. "From what I can tell, that transition, it wasn't so smooth."

Blanche's eyes cut to Ramón again to see if he seemed to be listening. She whispered to Emilio. "Wonder if the Schemmers actually own the place? How would that work? They arrive from Germany and become the owners of an estancia? Why would the owner sell to them?"

"They've been there a long time, but it is curious. So is the history." He leaned close to her ear. "The caudillo of La Palma was Bartolo Losada de Iglesias. He died of old age, a stroke, perhaps, while riding his horse. Out of respect for him, his gauchos did not let him fall to the ground. They kept him upright in his saddle for the ride back to the estancia, and from there, they carried him standing to his bed. He eventually succumbed to the horizontal in a tomb on the grounds of La Palma."

"How odd."

"Yes, but legends such as he die in such a way. Margarita says he was generous and well loved. He, too, lived by his own set of rules. And he must have been good to the Schemmers because they were close to him, and he accepted them. Let them in," Emilio said. "He had made La Palma a fortress of independence, but things change. Maybe the Schemmers changed. I don't know. I do know that his way and the way of the gaucho are dying out."

"When did he die?"

"The seventies, before the horror of the *Proceso.*"

"And the Schemmers took over then?"

He seemed thoughtful. "Not sure when the transition was. They came to La Palma after a short time in Buenos Aires. Margarita knew Bartolo and then the Schemmers. She knows much, maybe too much."

"Emilio, there must be secrets, and that's why they want to control your aunt. She knows things." Blanche didn't say it, but she felt it. *Secrets have a way of taking root, but sooner or later, the truth comes out. You just can't keep a good secret down.*

The driver didn't look their way, his gaze implacable. He tended to business, yet still he made her uneasy. Maybe it was his stony demeanor, his robotic attitude. In any event, they'd whispered, and the wind blowing through the open windows swallowed the rest of their conversation.

They came to a break in the grasslands and swung around a clearing of low, stucco houses lined with rusted cars and equipment and small hutches for animals. Still, not a soul in sight. She'd never felt so alienated. She shivered in the late-morning heat. From nerves. Blanche was anxious to meet the aunt. More than anything, though, she was just plain anxious. They needed to get out of this car and rejoin civilization, whatever that turned out to be.

The car jolted over a pothole, and they were tossed sideways. The ride was bumpy, but the waves of grass were hypnotizing. Emilio dozed off, his chin on chest. She resisted the rhythm of the pampa, but finally she closed her eyes and gave in to the overwhelming land and sky and the comforting weight of his arm around her.

"*Estamos cerca,*" said the driver.

"Close?" Blanche's eyes shot open to the vista of a neglected, dusty plaza. A small, sad church dominated the square of broken pavers. The thin steeple on the church, Baroque in miniature, reached to a cloudless, blue sky. The few other buildings were even paler versions—a non-descript grocer with bins offering a spare assortment of produce, a cantina, and a house. At least there were signs of life. A stout woman in a full, colorful red, orange, and green skirt carried a baby on her hip. Several men sat on wooden chairs smoking in front of the bar. *"¿Dondé estamos?"*

"El pueblo de San Antonio de Padua." His hands, ten and two, negotiated the potholes with ease.

He drove around the plaza and down a road past a grape arbor. The dust subsided and a stretch of hedges, oaks, and palm trees came into view. In the distance, the estancia of La Palma rose out of a sweeping stretch of green—a grand, bright pink palace with crenelated roofline on the main house, a separate tower, and a long white fence enclosing a stone patio. The tall, flowering shrubs surrounding the main house looked like a moat of green instead of water. Was it to keep people out? Or in?

Blanche gasped. It was quite a sight. *"Pink?"*

"Muy pink," said Emilio. *"¿Rosada?"*

"Sí," said the driver, still slouched behind the wheel. *"Muy famoso. Por el color y otras cosas."*

Here we go again with the … *other things.* She had a weird flashback to her adventure in Ireland, and the day she'd heard about "other things." She was lucky to have gotten back home to Santa Maria Island intact, thanks to her Irish pluck and the support of her Irish family and friends. But first she'd had to deal with secrets and *things.*

Ramón accelerated suddenly around a curved drive and stopped at the wide portal. Emilio jumped out, bag in hand, and reached for Blanche. She gaped at the abundant roses, the highly polished door with brass knob and trim, the twin manicured topiaries on either side of the slate entry.

Ramón climbed out of the driver's seat. He pulled his hat even lower and mumbled, *"Un momento, por favor."* This was a man of few words, and in a hurry. He bounded around the side of the house, presumably to seek a back entrance and use the toilet? Or a bush? Emilio and Blanche exchanged looks.

"Man on a mission," said Blanche.

Emilio shrugged. "When a man's gotta go …"

"Well, probably. But doesn't he seem strange to you? Turning away, and now he's running off?"

They looked up as Ramón came back around the corner, his head down. Without a word, he jumped into the car. He revved the engine as Emilio handed him some bills.

"*Gracias por todo.*" Ramón grabbed the money, and in the distraction of the moment that dinero can create, he turned toward Blanche. They locked eyes. She knew that face. *But how and where? Where have I seen him?*

They watched the rear end of the Renault as it disappeared down the road in a crunch of gravel and dust. She swallowed and tried to still the trembling in her knees and the paralysis that gripped her.

"Blanche? What's wrong?" Emilio put his hands on her shoulders. "Your face. You are so … pale."

"Oh, Emilio. Something is very wrong here." She gasped. A hand flew to her cheek. "I'm sure that was the guy who tried to run me down with his bike on the *peotanal*. I swear it was him."

Nine

Out In The Cold

"BLANCHE! YOU AREN'T SERIOUS!" Emilio bent down and looked into her eyes. "Are you?"

"Serious," she whispered, thumping her chest to make it stop fluttering.

"But Tomás set us up with Ramón. He arranged it for us!"

Stunned, she said, "Exactly. And now we're way the hell out here!"

"I had a strange feeling about Tomás. And that driver. *Por Dios.*" Emilio clenched his jaw.

Blanche looked around quickly. "He did deliver us though. At least he didn't kill us or anything. But it's all very weird."

"I'm going to call Tomás."

"And say what? The Attacker of the *Peotanal* is on the loose? Thanks to you?"

Emilio didn't respond.

Just then the door to the pink palace opened dramatically. At ten feet tall or so and carved of heavy, dark wood, this was not the kind of door that burst open. Instead, it creaked a solemn welcome. Blanche promptly forgot about Ramón when a tall, thin woman with strong features stood framed in the doorway, her startling blond hair contrasting sharply with the dark interior behind her. Her deadpan expression was like a mannequin's. Given the fright after recognizing Ramón, Blanche was not entirely receptive to this odd figure.

They all locked eyes, and the woman finally spoke. "Good afternoon. I'm Gerda Schemmer. And you must be Señorita Blanche and Señor Emilio. *Bienvenido a La Palma.*" Her voice was as hard as her looks.

Blanche smiled, tentatively, and murmured a greeting. They were in it now. *Murderous driver. Cold eccentric host.*

Emilio stepped forward. He nodded at Frau Schemmer and extended his hand. She joined them on the portico and offered him slim, white fingers, immediately warming to him. She smiled, stiffly, at Blanche.

Blanche's gaze swept over the immaculate surroundings, the high polish on the door and windows. The scent of roses and a fresh lemony smell. Gerda Schemmer was certainly set in a beautiful frame. Blanche pulled herself together. "This is wonderful!"

The Frau nodded. Her expression stayed fixed, ageless and smooth. The conservative, tight-fitting white sweater and gray pencil skirt hid nothing. She looked like she belonged in a Forties movie with Humphrey Bogart and a whole lot of intrigue.

"It was a good drive out?" She didn't wait for an answer but waved them into the house. They carried little luggage. Their stay would not be long, and Blanche was glad of that.

The hall entry was heavy with gold-framed pictures, a tall settee lined with carvings of gargoyles, and a series of long, thick, dark red rugs. The Frau led a quick tour, briefly commenting, her heels clicking the parquet—to a library with couches and books, a dining room with a long table, glass doors with triple panes at the back and a view of a lush garden and the courtyard in back. She pointed off to the kitchen in a far corner. Blanche took it all in, eagerly, eyes averted from the Frau's scrutiny. This map of La Palma, set to memory, would come in handy; it secured her snooping skills. She followed along, marveling at the warren of comfortable, airy rooms. The estancia with its grounds and luxury were like one big jewel dropped into a barren, dusty bowl.

They followed her mincing steps to a living room with high narrow windows hung with red-striped drapery against cement block and exposed brick walls. A fortress. Couches in front of a fireplace faced a blue glass coffee table with an array of porcelain figures and a letter opener. The table sat on a splendid chevron-patterned rug. Blanche stifled a chuckle at the thought of her shabby, sweet, cozy cabin on the beach. *Well, I sure do get around.*

Emilio set the bag down next to the doorway. "*Bonito.*"

"I'm sure you'll be comfortable here in the salon while I finalize your room preparation," Frau Schemmer said. She moved around with not a ripple in her expression.

"Yes, thank you," Blanche said. "It's lovely!"

"We think so." Her tone wasn't boastful, just factual and accommodating. "Lusita will bring you tea. Herr Schemmer—Karl—is at the stable, but he will be back soon. I know he will like to meet you." She put her hands together and turned without waiting for a reply. Like Ramón, she seemed to be in a hurry as she disappeared through the doorway.

"Tea? Perfect," Blanche murmured. She sat down on the edge of the sofa and smoothed her hand over the fine brocade. "It is quite the spot, don't you think?" She stood up abruptly and poked her head into the hallway, wondering where Margarita was.

"Quite." Emilio came up behind her and whispered. "Not exactly *amable*, and, how do you say, peppy?"

"No, she's not. But she seemed to warm up to you!"

"That is because of my Latin charm?"

Blanche gave him a look. "She hasn't seen much of your Latin charm."

"But you have." He leaned over and kissed her forehead.

Blanche's thoughts returned to Ramón. "Oh, Emilio. What about that driver?"

"And his lack of Latin charm? I don't know."

"This does not add up." Emilio pounded his fist into the palm of his hand. "Tomás had to know the driver was that guy on the bike. And out of all the people on the *peotanal* Tomás happened to be the one to save you? Too strange for words." He took Blanche by her shoulders and looked into her eyes. "I'm sorry I ever got you into this. I'll make it up to you. I will talk to him."

"Not yet. Please. We're here, and we're safe. Right?" She looked around. "We certainly can get another ride back. Once we find Margarita." She started pacing the floor. There had to be a reason for all these strange occurrences. There were always reasons, or excuses. She had the eerie feeling the situation didn't bode well, but it was too late now.

Emilio put his arm around her. "It will be all right." They walked to a doorway on the other side of the room and peered out. "I wonder where she is. She must know we've arrived. We gave her warning, and so did Issie."

"We'll have a peek around. Wait until later, once we know we're more or less alone."

She wished they were both somewhere else—even though the estancia and its view of the pampa were inviting. She'd have loved to grab Emilio and run across the lawn, sit among the roses, and sniff the fresh open air. "We're gonna have to be really cool," she murmured.

"Like the ice queen?"

Blanche gave him a gentle poke. "Yeah."

"*Soy Lusita.*" A small woman hurried into the room, soundless on the thick rug. *"Bienvenido a La Palma. Un poco de té y dulce y empana-das."* She shyly placed the clinking cups and plates onto the low table and bowed. *"Por favor. Disfrute."*

Blanche smiled at Lusita in her crisply ironed navy dress and white apron. Suddenly Blanche was starving. *"Gracias, Lusita! Soy Blanche, y Emilio."*

Lusita dipped her head in a funny little bow and turned to leave.

"Gracias, Lusita." Emilio hesitated, clearly searching for words. *"Un momentito, por favor.* We're guests for a few days."

"Sí," she said, smiling. *"Mucho gusto.* I am happy to meet you." Clear and precise. "Do you need something?"

"Well, no, but *gracias!"* Emilio looked at her with a wry expression.

"These treats are lovely … and this place! Must take a lot to do all this." Blanche waved at the room full of bibelots, sparkling windows, and rugs with precise marks from a vacuum.

"Take a lot? What is this?"

"It must take a lot of effort and work from many people. The staff, I mean," said Blanche. Friendly and casual, striking just the right tone.

"Pues." Lusita put a finger to her cheek. "I am in the kitchen with Pablo and Bruno. Maria is in the bed chambers, and many work in the garden and the stables. Yes, there are many."

"All young? Any older?"

"Lusita!" A tall silver-haired man stepped into the room. His face was flushed, and he wore a tight, gray serge sports jacket and high leather boots. Blanche supposed he'd been out for a good gallop with the horses. "Why all this chatting?" he demanded. But then he turned to Blanche and Emilio, and his expression changed instantly. He laughed. "Chatting! That's what you *norteamericanos* call it, don't you? Hello there!" He took two long steps, nodded at Blanche, graciously, and extended his hand to Emilio.

Lusita didn't hang around. She fled into the dark of the house like a wisp, leaving this imposing man rocking slightly in his boots. "Karl Schemmer here. And you are, Señor Emilio and Señorita Blanche, I presume. So good of you to visit La Palma." His effusive warmth contrasted with Gerda's cool greeting.

Blanche relaxed. Here was a warm welcome. She'd take it, for now, but the unsettled feeling did not go away. First, the driver, then Gerda, and, finally, Lusita, who'd clearly been on edge and not eager to talk with them. She might have led them directly to Margarita. Now they were sidelined with this person who was bent on being host with the most.

Blanche sensed opportunity. She glanced up at Emilio. His eyes were reassuring and relaxed. There was that.

"May I join you?" Herr Schemmer didn't wait for an answer. He sat down next to the fireplace and swung a long leg over one knee. His gold ring began tapping the carved wooden arm of the chair.

"Tea?" Blanche poured him a cup. "One lump or two?" She didn't wait for an answer. She dropped the sugar in the cup and handed it to him with a smile.

"Americans! So generous in all things." He bowed slightly. "*Danke.*" The last word he murmured into his cup. The pleasant look on his face remained; however, the smile didn't quite reach his eyes. Blanche wondered if the patina of ruddy good cheer was for show. He seemed a man adept at hiding his thoughts and feelings. She sat back, sipped her tea, and nibbled on the empanada.

"Tell me. How did you come to visit La Palma? We are some distance from the Capital," said Herr Schemmer.

"That's an understatement!" Blanche laughed lightly. "What a drive! Enchanting! Through the pampa and all. Couldn't believe the *immensity!*" She scooted to the edge of the sofa, empanada flakes all over her lap.

"It is incredible territory. We are cut off from the world." Herr

Schemmer continued swinging his leg, his eyes focused like lasers, first at Blanche then Emilio. He didn't have to remind her. She swallowed hard and returned his stare.

"But, please, how did you find us?" There was something crisp and robotic about his question. It set Blanche on edge, but she partied on.

"We're visitors to Buenos Aires, you know. We happened to meet a tango dancer." She felt the slightest pressure on her shoulder. Emilio's signal. She smiled and shrugged. "And she mentioned excursions out of Buenos Aires. Such as to this lovely place."

"We are a fine destination indeed. You'll be happy here." He tilted his large head, which Blanche guessed was whirling with thoughts she wished she could read. She tried to put this conversation into context with the other weird events of the day.

Emilio walked casually to the fireplace. He put one hand on the polished mantel. "It's fortunate we're here," he said. "My family is originally from a farm in Argentina. Many years ago. I've always wanted to visit."

"Is that so?" Schemmer seemed genuinely interested. "Where was that?"

"Oh, it's so long ago. I'm not quite sure. Perhaps near Cordoba."

"Great farming territory. Cattle and wheat." The man was a good ambassador. His paunch hinted at one who enjoyed the pleasures of life, and his cheerful air showed the world his self-satisfaction. Blanche did her best to mask her thoughts. She couldn't help but remember Margarita's fears and desperation to get away from here—and him. She should not be fooled.

Blanche sipped her tea. It was obvious that Herr Schemmer didn't miss much.

"We celebrate your arrival!" Herr boomed. He jumped up, walked over to a serving cabinet that held a silver tray with an array of liquor decanters. He filled three glasses with a generous hand and gave one to Blanche, another to Emilio. He lifted his own with hearty good cheer.

"Thank you." Blanche took a tiny sip and replaced the glass carefully. She'd definitely keep her wits about her. Or try to.

Herr Schemmler was a drinker who seemed to take pleasure in that first jolt of the day. At least they had that in common. Blanche liked the burn of the whiskey that went right to her toes. It occasionally gave her Dutch-Irish courage.

"Mister ... Herr."

"Karl, please."

Blanche picked up her glass and said, "Karl. La Palma must need an *army* to keep it in such beautiful condition!" Army. Probably an unfortunate word in view of the Dirty War, not to mention World War Two and World War One. She cleared her throat and took a sip.

His expression reflected mild surprise, or amusement?

"The estancia does require many hands. But my wife Gerda is a marvel. Yes, she is." The glass clicked onto the tabletop. He tented his fingers thoughtfully. "She keeps the staff on the up and up and our visitors happy." There was that smile again. He had remarkable huge, white teeth.

"Frau Gerda? She does all this by herself?" Emilio's arm swept the room and its pristine contents. "And Lusita? What about the others?" He probed gently as he glanced around the room. Blanche suppressed a smile. His mellifluous pitch was perfect, probably from all that singing and guitar-playing.

"Lusita did mention the staff. I overheard," said the Herr. He got up and poured himself another whiskey, this time setting the crystal decanter on the table between them. "Couldn't get along without them."

"And—" Blanche pressed.

"And?" His forehead creased in mild affront. "Why are you so interested in our staff? I assure you, we are prepared here. We take exceptionally good care of our guests. Please, do not worry."

"I do not doubt that. But surely it can't be easy," Blanche said quickly. "Everything is perfect. Seems so effortless and comfortable." She dusted bits of pastry into a tiny pile and deposited them on her saucer.

The compliment mollified him. She'd leave the business about staff and cleaning and such for now and get back to Margarita soon enough. *Time to pivot.* Blanche pounced, softly, like a cat landing on a cushion. "How did you happen to come to La Palma? From Germany, is it?"

"Quite true, we did. By way of Italy we arrived. I was born in a little town some kilometers from Frankfurt. Do you know Frankfurt?" His eyes opened wide as he leaned forward. Blanche guessed it was her cue to launch into details about her visits to Germany, land of sport and *gemütlichkeit,* but she must disappoint him.

"No," she said. "I can't say that I've had the opportunity or pleasure. But maybe someday."

"Ah, you will love Germany. The Eagle's Nest. The mountains of Bavaria. The clear, crisp days, the beer and schnitzel, and many wide-open spaces. I do miss it all."

"You have quite a bit of that here in Buenos Aires province, don't you? Except for the mountains," she pressed. "How did you happen to come to Argentina?" She hoped she didn't sound nosey, but she probably did. Sometimes it was impossible to rein it in.

"The war. It was a horror." His voice dropped away. He stood up and went to the window. "But you wouldn't know that. You are so young."

"I've seen a horror, or two," Blanche murmured. She wasn't proud of the dead bodies she'd come across in her sleuthing. She was not always willingly dragged into solving the crime. But her dogged stubbornness pushed her. Like now. "You left Germany during World War Two?"

Emilio was gritting his teeth, she could tell, and his posture was a bit rigid. He hadn't touched the whiskey.

Schemmer rocked back and forth, heel to toe, in his heavy boots. The heels made light, rhythmic taps on the floorboards. Reminiscent of marching. "We left just after the war. We were fortunate to come to La Palma and start this little hotel, so it is." He turned to them suddenly. "Out in the middle of nowhere! I am happy you made your way here." He laughed easily and swung the stemmed crystal around in an arc as if to take in all the pampa and surroundings.

"So fortunate." Blanche agreed, concealing her thoughts about the turn of events that brought him here. "Did you purchase it?" She couldn't imagine coming across this place in the real estate listings.

Emilio sat down beside her. Blanche felt the tension of his leg pressed against hers. He squeezed her hand. She squeezed back.

"Oh, now we're getting into complicated territory." The Herr turned to them. His tone took on an edge of haughtiness. "Let us just say we are fortunate." He poured another drink and threw it back in one swallow, then clinked the glass onto the tray. He clasped his hands behind his back. "You must be tired. Why don't you be off to your room?" Now his haughtiness took on an edge of impatience.

He seemed to be in a hurry, too. Here they were, out in the middle of nowhere, and *everyone* seemed to be in a hurry. First that driver, and then Gerda the Frau. Even Lusita had scurried away. *Why?* When people hurried—unnecessarily, it would seem—they wanted to leave their present circumstances and hurry on to something else, probably something equally undesirable, or unsettling. At least, that was Blanche's impression. They reminded her of a bunch of hamsters on a huge wheel on the pampa. An undercurrent of anxiety mixed into all this glorious luxury and relaxation. She tried to make sense of it, and so far, she was having a hard time. Emilio was perplexed. She could see it in his eyes.

Herr Schemmer reached for a narrow tapestry pull on the wall and yanked. Lusita appeared in the doorway. She wrung her hands in her apron. The tendrils of her black curly hair framed startled eyes, like a deer encountering the hunter.

"Lusita! Please show our guests to their room, won't you? They must be fatigued." He smiled widely, but he definitely wanted them gone. The whiskey and perhaps the exercise had made him start to wilt. "Staff will ring the bell for lunch. About two thirty then? Is that agreeable?"

"Thank you. For everything," said Blanche. She felt the gentle pressure of Emilio's hand on her back. "That's just ... great."

Ten

Don't Tell Me

"*BAQUITA!* WORLD WAR ONE? And Two?" Emilio lay on his back, hugging Blanche close. He turned on his side and propped on his elbow. Stared down into her face. "Really? Do you want to start World War Three?"

"Oh, geez, Emilio." She ran a finger lightly down his cheek. "Sometimes you have to push a little." Now she was sitting up, slightly wired from meeting the Schemmers. "You know, they live in a bubble out here, and that's to our advantage. Don't you think? I can work around that with my little interrogations and investigations and such. They are just a little bit oblivious. Out of practice, so to speak?"

"Why ever would you say that?"

"They're an elderly couple running a fancy B and B."

"Blanche, they're Nazis."

"Oh, God, Emilio. I know, I know. I'm trying to think how to deal with this."

He flopped back on the pillow. "Not now, Blanche. Get some sleep." He was exhausted, his arm falling off the bed. "It's probably not a good idea to get them all stirred up. Let's find Margarita and get the hell out of here."

"That's what we're going to do. But, in case you didn't notice, they're not offering her up on a platter."

"I have to think about this. I'll close my eyes for a minute. Then we go." He snuggled her next to him.

"Go *where*, exactly?"

"To find my aunt in this place. This huge place," he said, but he was already nodding off. She rested her head on his chest. His breathing slowed to a regular heartbeat. So reassuring, and normal.

"All right," she murmured.

She stared up into the magnificent red silk canopy over the four-poster bed, counting the gold swirls of embroidery. *Round and round I go, where I stop nobody knows.* Emilio lay completely still, already dead asleep. She put her hand up to his nose to feel his breathing. She was getting paranoid about *everything*.

He didn't move. He didn't even snore. Never did. Slept like a baby—the sleep of the innocent. They'd only sporadically gotten a wink since they arrived in Argentina, which was normal for Blanche. She ran on boundless energy and ideas, sometimes anger, and lately, love.

She gazed at Emilio and restrained herself from leaning over and waking him up. It was time to concentrate. Get on track. Her only thought right now was that this mission end well, and that it end soon.

Her mind would not stop spinning. She glanced at the windows and the drapery of red damask. The whole room was red—blood red—which fed her unsettled feeling of not knowing what the hell was going on at La Palma, where Margarita was, that driver who nearly ran her down, and their creepy hosts. *Nazis.*

A beam of sunlight slanted into the room. A view of the wide green lawn stretched to the edge of the pampa. It was a beautiful place, this pink palace of luxury. Lovely. And ominous. She lay back down and closed her eyes. For just a minute. With the love of her life at her side.

It wasn't working. She couldn't relax or give in to sleep. She'd purchased a burner phone at a kiosk in Buenos Aires. But what good was it out here? Who would she call? And who would come? Certainly not Tomás and his yahoo driver. Did this place even have an address? Now was a great time to wonder about that. It wouldn't be easy to find one small American and the Mexican doctor, like needles in an endless stack of pampa grass.

Maybe she was making more of it than need be. They would find Margarita and get out. She prayed Margarita had a driver lined up. The element of surprise would be the clincher. Fast and without preamble, like the Prussian General von Clausewitz. Herr Schemmer probably knew all about that, and so they would borrow from his playbook. *Surprise!*

Enough already. She inched slowly away from Emilio toward the edge of the bed, glad he hadn't woken up with all her fidgeting. "Time for a little exploring," she murmured.

She took one more peek at him. If Margarita didn't surface by lunch, he'd whispered on their way to the room, they'd go looking for her. But Blanche couldn't wait. When did she ever?

She rolled off the bed and opted for bare feet as she crept out into the hallway. Faint chatter from below rose to the top floor. The aroma of delicious baking and cooking. *Meat? Soup?* Her appetite stirred, but adrenalin replaced the pangs in her stomach. She took a deep breath and checked the long, carpeted hallway from one end to the other. Dim but for the triangle of light cast from the window at the far end.

The upstairs included rooms sprawled across a U-shaped hallway in the back. Some of them overlooked a courtyard; she'd gotten a good glimpse of the layout of the house and grounds during the Frau's short tour. The drawing room with large windows and glass doors were near the front entry on the first floor; the dining, kitchen, den, and another drawing room flowed to the other side of the house.

She left the hallway and took a few steps down the sweeping staircase they'd ascended and hesitated. She sank down on the carpeted tread. The open banister and high archway afforded a good view of an ivy-covered patio of herringbone brick. The round linen-covered tables were set for lunch. Very quiet, except for the clinking of silver and china coming from the direction of the kitchen.

She crept down another step. The light fell on a Baroque fire-place mantel, one of several in the house. The room boasted two-foot brass candleholders, large Delft ginger jars, and tables with carved legs; chinoises plates, red silk pillows, and vases full of pink lilies added splashes of color. The entire house was well apportioned with a patina of good taste only money could buy.

This stuff hadn't come from the Sears catalogue. Probably imports from England and France, China, and India. How? And who had purchased all this beauty? The gold and red. Spice and flowers. Had the Schemmers done all this? If so, they'd done a fine job of it. Or did the old caudillo have a hand in it? Once again, she wondered about ownership.

She shook off the distraction and strained to fit herself into the bones of the house. *Think, Blanche.* The coast was clear in the rooms up front; no one was buzzing around. From a far corner, the hum of industry in the kitchen clinked on. Someone was singing softly. She wanted to go down and sit in that living room, enticing with the smell of roses from that open window. Now was not the time. She had fish to fry, as Gran would say. And she was looking for one particular fish.

Margarita wouldn't be lounging about down here. Blanche crouched on the steps. She needed to visit the servants' quarters. Margarita must be resting in one of those upstairs rooms in the back as a result of all the managing and arranging. She wasn't a cook, so she wouldn't be in the kitchen. Emilio had indicated that his aunt was a housekeeper, and the house certainly was kept in tip-top order.

She remembered from her brief visit to Dunfaedan castle in Ireland that the servants' quarters were conveniently situated over the kitchen, a common design. At La Palma, those rooms would be in the far corner of the house, so she retraced her steps back up the stairs and headed in that direction.

A row of half a dozen paneled doors closed off the rooms in the servants' quarters. She walked along the wall, avoiding the creaky boards in the middle and reached for the handle of the first door. It was unlocked and opened easily without a sound. The bedroom was dim and basic with a quilt and pillows, a small brass lamp, and a chamber pot. On to the next, her bold curiosity threatened to overwhelm her. Or was it lack of sleep and little food? A sip of whiskey did her no good. The second and third rooms were almost identical, but the odd thing was that none of these rooms looked like they'd been occupied for quite some time. Dusty with no personal items in view. Not a book, a flower, or a brush.

She went on. The fourth door was cracked open, and so she nudged it. It squealed and so she grabbed hold of the edge and slowly pushed. She glanced around in the low light from a small window. This space was unlike the rest; it was larger, a bedroom, for sure, but also a sitting room with a small table, a couple of upholstered chairs, and a daybed. Her eyes adjusted to the light.

Feet protruded from beneath the border of the daybed. It appeared that the owner of the feet was looking for something under the bed. Blanche started to make a hasty retreat but then froze. The feet wore clunky, black, lace-up shoes. The legs were bluish, and none of it, leg, feet, or the rest, was moving.

Blanche gripped the glass doorknob and stared down at the

floor. *Please tell me this is not what I think it is.* Immediately, she wanted to run. But this was not the time for flight. Instead, like in other times of dire encounters, a buzzer went off. She swallowed hard, then scanned the room and soaked in every detail—along with a horrible sense of what was in store.

She inched closer. Here was an elderly woman. Tortoise-shell pins held her bun tight against her head. A tendril of hair lay across the pale nape of her neck. Only a quarter of her face exposed a smooth cheek of mottled complexion, a strong aquiline nose, and full lips.

"No," she whispered. Chills ran down her arms. She confirmed the worst. Without disturbing a hair, she touched the woman's neck. She jerked her fingers back. *Cold. Definitely dead.* Margarita was beyond help.

She pressed her hands to her roiling stomach and backed away to the doorway. Trying to regain her composure, she grabbed at the door frame and stared down at the floor, unable to drag herself away. She had to do *something.* Get help. Emilio. Oh God. She had to get to Emilio. He had to know.

She ran back to the bedroom where Emilio lay, still sleeping peacefully. She hated to wake him up to this terrible news, but she didn't have any choice. All their choices had been ripped away, rearranged and shattered into broken, unrecognizable pieces. Drastically. Margarita was dead.

Blanche leapt onto the bed. She shook Emilio, gently at first and then urgently.

"*Emilio!*"

He rolled over. Dead asleep, but she kept after him. He finally awoke with a start.

"What?" Irritation crept into his expression. Blanche drew back.

Focus, Blanche! She clutched his arm and shook him.

"Oh, Emilio." The tremor in her hands would not stop, her voice shook. "You have to come and see this!"

"See what?" Emilio clutched a fistful of the linen and pulled himself up. "You look like you see a ghost!"

"I do. I have." Blanche covered her face and rocked back on her heels.

"You are white as this sheet, *Baquita*." He ran his fingers down her arm, soothingly. He pulled himself up. "What is going on?"

"Come with me. *Now*."

"Blanche! I'm not dressed!"

"Forget the pants!" She looked him over. Boxers and a T-shirt. "You're fine." *OMG, nothing is fine.* She grabbed his pants and flung them at him.

Emilio stumbled into the jeans and followed Blanche down the hall. She put a finger to her lips. Thankfully, the upstairs was deserted as they made their way in silence. Blanche glanced at Emilio. He seemed only half awake and totally confused and numb, which was probably a good thing. Dread washed over her as they approached the bedroom door.

Before she pushed it open, she said, "I'm so sorry, Emilio."

He looked around the room. "For what?"

Except for the day bed, the table, and a small brass lamp, the room was empty. Clean as you please.

"What the ... ?" Blanche sucked in a breath. She held Emilio's hand and dragged him out into the hallway and counted the rooms. Sure enough, this was where she'd seen Margarita. Dead.

"What is going on?" He looked at her quizzically.

No more than fifteen minutes had passed. And now the space next to the bed ... nothing. Nobody. *No body.*

Blanche choked out the bad news. "Margarita. I'm sure it was her. On the floor next to the bed. I was just in here and found her there!"

"Found her! What did she say? Where is she?"

"Oh, Emilio. She didn't say anything. She was ... *dead.*"

Emilio darted around the bedroom, his eyes wide. He pulled Blanche with him as he rushed over to the other side of the bed. "There's no one here. Dead or alive."

"I tell you, Emilio, she was here. Right here!" Blanche dropped his hand and knelt down on the rug next to the daybed. She peered along the floor. No sign of her. Margarita was gone—as gone as she could be.

"But, Blanche, this is impossible. Maybe whoever you saw was looking for something and now this person left?"

"I felt her neck, Emilio. She was cold," Blanche said gently. She had a hard time repeating "dead" as she fixed on Emilio's frantic expression.

Disbelief spread across his face, but the terrible words hit him. He crouched down next to her on the floor. *"Por Dios.* Are you sure?"

"Emilio, I'm sure. I've seen her picture. Remember? In Florida? And at Issie's apartment." She sat up on her knees and scanned the room, searching for some clue that death had happened here. *A suspicious death.* She crouched down again near the daybed. Patted the rug. Sniffed it. For something, anything—the scent of a person, a blood stain, anything tangible. She had no idea what she was looking for, but there had to be something. Whether Emilio believed her or not, a dead body had been here minutes ago.

Blanche stood and shook her head. "How could they have taken her away? So *quickly?*"

Emilio leapt up and ran into the hallway. Desperately looking around. Aimlessly. The lone window threw weak light across the carpet. He wrung his hands, pacing, and Blanche followed. They peered out the window. Off in the distance, a tall man carried a bundle near the tower, the gardening equipment strewn about. Other than that, the lawn and gardens—all of it was clear and didn't offer a single clue.

"We need to find out where they took her," she said.

Emilio raked both hands through his hair.

They ended up back in that ill-fated bedroom. "Blanche, what are you doing?"

She'd resumed her search on the floor around the bed. "Time is short. You know this place will be picked over if it's a crime scene. Closed off. We won't be able to get back in here, for sure."

"But there's no one here. There is no crime scene."

Blanche sat back on her heels, totally befuddled. "She may have dropped dead. But then, why not an alarm? Or an ambulance? *Some authority?* Why—and how—does she suddenly disappear?"

"Uh-huh. Why the secrecy?" His eyes grew darker. "Tía was afraid of them, and she was about to expose them."

"Is anyone even going to believe that? Or this? That I saw her dead on the floor? Someone moved her. She didn't get up and walk away."

"If what you say is true, there has to be something here."

A tray with a saucer, a sugar bowl, and a small empty pitcher sat on a table near the window. She picked up the china. It was dry with a faint odor of something herbal. She couldn't place it. A strange, woodsy smell.

"The small bloodhound, *mi Baquita*," murmured Emilio. "What have you found there?"

"Funny smells," she said, holding the saucer out to Emilio. "What do you think it is?"

"I don't smell anything, except you, soap and something nice."

He reached for her, and she caught his fingers. "Don't you smell it? Could be poison."

"Poison?"

"Hmmm. Maybe not. Herbal tea? The cup is missing." She replaced the saucer. It wouldn't be good to remove evidence if, in fact, this service had poison in it. The herbal smell could have been potpourri, but she just couldn't tell. Her heart sank.

Blanche looked around the room. Bookcases. Statues. Pillows. Someone had been here from the look of the dishes and personal items. But the room was stuffy.

Then she spied it. A small ball of crumpled paper on the floor under the table. She retrieved it and smoothed it out. The writing was a hasty scrawl: *"No más. Por fin, no más."*

Blanche handed the paper to Emilio. "What's it mean? No more? Finally?"

He shrugged. "Depends on the context. Could mean enough. Just. No longer. Different things."

Blanche digested his words like she was eating a mouth full of gravel. Emilio's explanation seemed useless.

"Pretty straightforward." He scratched his head. "But not really."

Blanche threw up her hands.

"It kind of goes along with what your aunt was telling you—with a lot of pieces missing. She didn't want to deal with this business anymore."

"So, we're back to that."

She paced the room. "I hate to say it, but I think she was murdered."

"You really think the Schemmers killed her?" His voice raspy.

"Oh, Emilio, I don't know. But whoever did this, whoever moved her, must be around here. And must know."

"And you are absolutely certain it was my aunt you saw under that bed?"

"I'm certain," she whispered.

He folded his arms tight around his middle. *"No puede ser, no lo creo."*

"I am sorry." What else could she say? She wanted to believe it wasn't Margarita, but it was the aunt. She didn't doubt it for a minute; it would be a waste of time to think otherwise.

Emilio and Blanche stood over the spot where Margarita had lain on the carpet. Blanche took one more look around the room. They drifted into the hall. She broke from Emilio's grasp and dashed to the window again, desperately. "We already looked ..." he said, faintly. "At nothing." The landscape was empty and sprawling, like a vast green lid holding down a mystery. The house was still as they crept back to their bedroom.

Blanche shut the door quietly. "We have to find out where they took her, and it's not going to be easy in this place. They won't be open to our snooping. We're just young tourists, come and gone. They're counting on that." She looked up into his eyes, the small bit of paper she'd found, grasped in her fist.

"How will we find her?" His tone was wistful, lost.

"I don't know."

"We need to call the police."

"No, not yet. What proof is there? We don't have *anything*."

He snapped his fingers. "The letters Margarita wrote. How she wanted out of here, how afraid she was, and that she knew things about the Schemmers."

"Where're those letters?"

He threw himself on the bed. "In Florida?"

"Great. Well, at least Issie will back up Margarita's complaint."

Emilio squinted with worry. "No! I don't want to call Issie yet. She'll only come out here and maybe go crazy that her mother is dead. The Schemmers will deny it ever happened."

"You're right, of course."

She sank into a chair near the window. The afternoon light slanted into the room, leaving the corners in dim, dark red shadow.

"We should go down there," he said. Still only half-dressed, his hair on end. "Lunch is the last thing I care about, but we have to get on with it. Face those people."

"See if we can't get something out of them? They have to drop a clue. You can't hide a body—much less kill someone—and go out to the kitchen and make soup." Blanche leaned back, her arms crossed tight against her chest. "We have to bring up Margarita somehow while acting like we don't know her. Hopefully, they'll let something slip. They might mention her, or more likely they'll deflect."

"Uh-huh. The Herr might talk. His wife seems awfully … cold."

"I can't see how he'd miss an opportunity to put on a show with that hardy *gemütlichkeit*. But I don't trust either one of them. Not after all Margarita said in her letters. And certainly not after this."

"Blanche, we don't even know for sure that they did anything."

She shook off the vision of Margarita's dead body and got up from her chair. "If they didn't do it, you can bet they know about it and know where she is."

Emilio leaned over Blanche and held her gently by the shoulders. "Let's not talk *too* much when we go down there."

Blanche opened her mouth to protest and grabbed his arm as if in shock. "What?! Are you saying I talk too much?" She let him go and went to her suitcase, pulled out a flouncy, cotton dress and snapped out the wrinkles before slipping it over her head.

He glanced sideways at Blanche and buttoned his shirt slowly. "You know what I mean. You like to talk."

"Who me?"

"Yes. You. And I like to hear you talk. But let the Schemmers talk this time." He kissed her lightly. They stood, hands together, their faces inches apart.

Blanche pulled away and sighed. "Seems I'm cursed with weird 'adventures' everywhere I go."

He drew her back in his arms. "I promise we'll get out of this and never do it again."

"That's a fine idea. Promise?"

"Promise."

"I'm going to hold you to that. But right now, let's find Margarita."

Blanche should have known better than to even think this would be the last time she'd find herself in the middle of a mess. Her history seemed to repeat itself. Like a reel, the troubles raced through her head: Santa Maria Island, Mexico, Vietnam, Ireland. Yes, she managed to get into a tangle everywhere she went. Blanche fastened a sandal and stood up. "Really, Emilio, this isn't your fault. But now that we're here, we *will* fix this."

"It's on me." Confusion reflected in Emilio's eyes. It came right back at her. They were in this together, and they would get out of it together.

"On us," she said.

Emilio bounced his fist off the palm of his hand as if this would help him figure things out. "How could they have moved her in *minutes?*"

"Weird." She drew a complete blank. "But then ... whoever did this had to know we were upstairs. Wouldn't you think? They probably hurried to get her out of there."

She reached for a brush and yanked it through her tangled curls as Emilio walked in a tight circle in front of the window. "Blanche. Do you think someone's watching?"

"Do you?"

"Did you hear anything?"

She closed her eyes and put herself back in the room with Margarita. "Nope. Not a sound."

"One thing for sure. She has to be somewhere."

"Let's go see what we can get out of Herr and Frau. We'll be cagey. And I'll let them talk. I promise."

He held her hand as they headed out the door. "Cagey. Yes."

If they allowed fear to take over, it would be worse for them. "We need sharp focus, Emilio," said Blanche. They walked hand in hand toward the stairs, and in step. It struck her that they needed to shift from getting Aunt Margarita out of the house and away from the Schemmers to finding her dead body and exposing the circumstances of her death. But she was pretty sure Emilio would not want to hang around to solve the murder. He wanted them gone. She couldn't think of letting it go. If Margarita had been murdered—and Blanche was pretty darn sure that she was—*who* was the culprit?

Eleven

The Search Is On

"I HOPE YOU ENJOY the pasta *rosada*. It is a specialty of the house." Frau Schemmer smiled down at the plate, obviously pleased with the large swirl of noodles covered in a pink sauce.

Blanche could not even look at it. *Am I sitting here listening to a murderer talk about noodles?* The more she thought about it, she couldn't come to any other conclusion. No one acted as if a dead body had been left in the drawing room upstairs.

Hands together and quite unperturbed, the Frau stood at the table, the sunlight streaming through the latticed canopy onto her blond-white head. Her face was as pale as her hair. Here was a woman secure in her ways and as immoveable as a mountain. Blanche shivered but kept her composure. It was hard to deal with, but there had to be a way to move around that mountain. Yes, they'd get to know the Schemmers, and the more they both knew, the better off they'd be. What was that saying? Better the devil you know ... Or, keep your friends close and your enemies closer? Well, she hoped it were true. All those annoying questions she asked made a pest of her but barely scratched the surface.

Blanche glanced down at the pasta. Ground pepper and parmesan plunked on top of the creamy sauce. It would have been tempting if it weren't competing with the roiling in her stomach. Emilio seemed to sense her tension, leaned her way, and smiled up at the Frau.

"*Delicioso*," he said. "Compliments to the chef." Blanche looked at his plate. He hadn't even tasted it.

"I am so glad you approve," said the Frau, biting off each word in precise English. "A sauce of tomatoes from the garden and cream from the farm." Her long fingers clutched a gleaming locket dangling from her neck.

"You are fortunate to have such a great cook," Blanche said. She picked up her fork as if it weighed a ton and dove into the dish. Swirling the pasta onto a fork, she held the dripping mess over her plate and managed a bite. It was delicious. She relaxed. For a second. "So nice—just the right amount of basil and garlic."

"I will pass along the compliment. A superior talent."

Blanche chewed slowly. Now might be a good time to engage the Frau. "Who is your cook—by the way? And other staff? Besides the cook. On the ranch, the estancia, I mean."

"Ranch? How delightful!" The Frau's laugh was a shocker, like the tinkle of a small bell.

"We say *ranch* back in the states, you know, for a large tract with lovely buildings and animals and such, especially horses and cows and pigs. But they are not pink. Like this *estancia*. And the sauce. All matching pink—" Blanche stopped before she made a complete fool of herself. Emilio was the picture of calm. He twirled his pasta slowly into something resembling a small volcano.

"I'm sorry, you were about to tell us about your chef," said Blanche.

"Donnella comes from Catamarca. She was here today. Only briefly. Her grandmother was Italian and taught her well on how to use seasonings and the special blend of vegetables and cream. We usually have Bruno in the kitchen."

"How did you ever decide on a pink house?" Blanche asked.

"Ox blood." The woman seemed to take pleasure in the bit of information. "That was the traditional tinting process. Pretty, isn't it?"

"Oh, yes," Blanche replied. "Houses coated in blood. They don't come along too often, do they?"

"True." The woman arched her eyebrows and started to turn toward the door. The conversation had not gone as Blanche planned.

She tried again. "You really must tell the cook—You mentioned Bruno before. Is he your regular chef?"

"Ah, yes, Bruno." The Frau was not forthcoming.

"No other helpers?"

The Frau pursed her lips. "No."

Dead end. Blanche stabbed the pasta. "Well, you have a fabulous ranch, or house. *Estancia.* Nothing like it in Germany. Right? You are from Germany, yes?"

"Yah."

"When did you come over?" Blanche leaned back in the chair, her head at a friendly tilt. When she reached for her glass, she splashed red wine onto the tablecloth. Emilio squeezed her knee gently.

"It's all right, *Baquita*," he whispered.

The Frau fussed with a pile of napkins on a side table. "Many years ago," she murmured. "We came here. Yes."

Nothing more. So that was it? She didn't warm to Blanche's questions. And why would she? This woman was a glacier. *But glaciers melt, eventually.*

"Again, my compliments to Donnella," Blanche said.

The Frau peered down at Blanche's plate and snapped, "Perhaps you should try more than one bite. Enjoy." Then she was gone, soundlessly, in her narrow, fine leather pumps.

Blanche watched her go. Strong legs and a broad back but on the lean side. Was she capable of moving a dead body? Quickly? In a matter of minutes? Margarita had been a small woman, not plump but far from thin. She was short, however. She would fit into a trunk or small closet. Or a freezer? Blanche gulped. She wondered how her mind could go so easily from pasta *rosada* to imagining how her host might hide a body in myriad ways. The depravity! But that was Blanche's mind. It whirled from one horrific detail to the next, and she couldn't stop it.

Emilio moved the pasta around while his gaze followed the retreating Frau. His smile painted on, his lips hardly moved. "That did not go well."

"Difficult to crack that one, for sure. But we will," she said in a low voice.

He gave her a crooked grin and whispered through gritted teeth. "We have to find Margarita. We have to call the police. We must get out of here."

"How are we going to do that? I mean, call the police? How will it look?" She put her head down. Lusita was bustling around and the other staff were outside the patio fiddling with a bundle of lawn tools. She leaned into Emilio. "We can't call the authorities. They'll just laugh at us. There's no *body*!" Then the obvious hit her: "We have to find one."

They were the only guests at lunch, in fact, in the whole house. Several other round tables covered in linen were set, but no one else appeared. They'd managed to eat some of the pasta, the bread, and a tossed salad. Lusita hovered near them and refilled their wine glasses before they were even empty. With no trouble at all, they'd drunk a carafe of Malbec that went down smooth as water.

Emilio laid his napkin on the table and took Blanche's hand. "I am going to explore," he said, looking around. More desperate than determined.

They still didn't have a plan, and Blanche's conversation to extort clues from the Frau hadn't gone well. She had talked too much.

Emilio stood up and pulled Blanche close to him. "I *will* find her."

"Where will you look? We can't go poking around in the house—the Schemmers and staff are around."

His eyes darted about the landscape. "The outbuildings. I think I'll look out there first. You've done your exploration, unfortunately with disastrous results, and now I'll do mine." He set his lips in a thin line. "We'll meet back in the room ... say, in about an hour?"

"You don't want me to go with you?"

"It'll be better by myself. I'll make it look like I'm interested in the work of a farm. I'll open some doors. And lids ... I know enough about plowing and hay to sound informed." He frowned. "Or get myself into more trouble."

"You come and get me if you find anything?" She was hesitant for him to leave. But if they split up, they could cover more area.

"Of course."

"Careful," she said. His ace was his charm, not his snooping skills. "Make it look real nice and casual if you get stopped? They should expect curiosity from their visitors." Blanche still held tightly to his arm.

Second thoughts threw her. She pouted, or tried to. She wanted to go. He laughed, then looked at her soberly. "What will you do?"

"I'll sit out there with a book," she said, pointing to a chaise lounge on the lawn. "Got a good one right here." She patted her bag. "Maybe take a short walk around the house. Listen in. That sort of thing."

Emilio gave her a sly glance. He was skeptical, for good reason. She was not the type to sit one out while he stumbled around looking for his dead aunt. It was a waste of time to bring it up. Blanche would sit and think. For one burning minute.

"Make a note if you think of something," he said.

"If I think of something?"

"On second thought. Make a note of who's coming and going. Anyone suspicious."

"That'll be a short list," she said. The Schemmers took the top spot as the culprits, in her mind. But the thought nagged her. She couldn't imagine Herr Schemmer in his jodhpurs and the silvery Frau Schemmer dragging off the dead nanny in the blink of an eye. There had to be an accomplice.

They hugged. "If you don't find her, we'll figure something out," she said, assuredly.

They walked across the lawn. Blanche glanced back at the house, and her gaze shifted from the main building to a far round tower. Frau Schemmer had told them it had extra rooms for an overflow of guests, especially at holiday time and in the summer. Right now it was autumn in Argentina—the opposite of springtime in Florida—and she supposed it was not high time for celebration at the estancia. The kids were in school, and it was months away from the holiday season. They'd hit a down time, which should have been a good thing, but obviously it wasn't. Not with a murder on the ranch.

They could not leave this place and go back to Florida without solving it. How would Emilio be able to concentrate on his medical studies, thinking about his murdered aunt carted away into oblivion?

Blanche stretched out on the chaise and looked up at him. "By the way ..."

"Yes?" The skeptical look on his face returned.

"That paper we found. The one in the room where I saw Margarita. Remember? 'No más'."

"No more?"

"Yes, but in context ..."

"When combined with *por fin*. Spanish is a language of subtleties."

Blanche was of the opinion that all languages had subtleties. And figuring them out was a game. A puzzle. Like now. "Give me an example?"

"The word 'just.' It is your funny word. It means so many things. A short word for justice, or *justicia* ... or enough. Or finally? *No más, por fin*, it could mean ..."

"What?"

"I don't know. But it might have implications."

"It's occurred to me, Emilio, the handwriting on that note. Is it really your aunt's?" Blanche didn't have the paper with her, but the terse bit of scrawl made her wonder.

"Now that you say it. No. I don't think so."

"Hmmm. Well, I wish you had her letters. We need to do a little comparing. Whoever wrote that note may have killed her." She spoke bluntly but there was no other way to say it. Someone else had been in Margarita's room or near enough to hand her the note if she hadn't written it. Here was one more reason to get into the main house and look through the Schemmers' papers and compare the handwriting.

Emilio looked off in the distance. "After all Tía and I talked about and wanted for each other. To get her out of here. To be together. Now this. And what about Issie? We have to tell her that her mother's been murdered."

"Oh, Issie," said Blanche.

Emilio bit his lip.

Blanche slipped her hand in his. "We have to wait, Emilio. You know that." They locked eyes. "There's no point in telling Issie now when we don't know anything."

A hot little stone of anger burned in Blanche's gut. She was angry at the unfairness of it all. Emilio had longed for this reunion, and it had been taken from him. He'd lost his aunt ... *to murder?* If Blanche was acutely aware of one thing, it was the importance of family—the precious randomness and closeness of it. He hadn't asked for family, and she hadn't either, but to have one was a gift. She had so few members of her own, and she was thankful for them. Half the time they were rolling their eyes at her or reining her in, but what would she do without them?

"Blanche! What if it wasn't murder?"

"We talked about that. I know you have doubts. But, then, why all the secrecy? Whisking her away like that? Why not just say that one of their beloved staff, Aunt Margarita, died? It's all too odd. Plus, the smell of something herbal, bitter on that saucer. The note. *No more. Finally.* It's bad."

"*Malísimo.*"

"Go. I'll meet you back upstairs in about an hour. It'll be light for a few more hours, won't it? We've got time. Dinner's ten-ish." She was anxious for him to start. Her wheels were spinning.

He lifted her chin and gave her a red-winey kiss. "Thank you."

"For what?"

"Your spirit."

"My spirit? My patience? And my expertise at the tango?"

Emilio laughed. "Yes, your expertise. In all things." She leaned close to him at the foot of the chaise, so close she could read the stubble on his chin and smell his lemon soap. She forgot for a moment the dread of what they might learn.

She pressed her face against his chest, her words muffled. "See you soon."

"You be careful," he said. "Whatever happens."

Blanche put her hands on his chest and looked in his eyes. "Oh, don't say that, Emilio!"

Whatever happened had better be something good that would fix this mess.

Blanche stretched out on the lounge chair and watched Emilio disappear behind the big house. She opened her book, but she had no intention of reading it. *Think, Blanche.* She laid her head back on the headrest and closed her eyes, trying to get her thoughts together. She breathed in the sweet-smelling pampa. Despite her anxiety, peace settled over her.

She'd only meant to shut her eyes for a minute. Twenty minutes later, she opened them to a ray of sun slanting through the trees. The sound of horse hooves shook her completely awake. A couple of horse riders pounded across her line of sight, bantering loudly in Spanish. They wore baggy trousers, neckerchiefs, and tight black hats. Gauchos.

Thankfully they ignored her, but she was glad to see others about the place. Life on the estancia went on with some normalcy even though somewhere lay a dead body. She swung her legs around. *Where the hell could Margarita be?* The possibilities of hiding her at La Palma were endless.

She checked her watch and tossed the book in her bag. Emilio had been gone about half an hour. There wasn't much time to explore if she were to be on schedule and meet him back at the room. But first, she needed water. The wine was great, the food salty, and mixed with the dry pampa and constant winds, she ended up in a world of thirst. She drew out a bottle of water from her bag and drank off half of it. Her ears tuned into the retreating gauchos and their curious whoops.

She should go after them. They'd made their way around a stand of trees when they set off in a full gallop. Clearly, they were headed to the outbuildings. To where Emilio had gone to look for

Margarita. He might talk to them, but it was her job to get the story. Who better to tell her a thing or two about La Palma—and about the nanny/housekeeper, Margarita Goyez?

She started off in their direction and glanced toward the patio where they'd had lunch. The sun-dappled, linen-covered tables awaited the next meal. The grounds were empty except for a yard-man lazily dragging a rake. *Where is everyone? And where is Emilio?*

The tower captured her attention. The oddly spaced windows in the rounded wall were dark except for one. Blanche blinked several times as, unbelievably, a silhouette moved about in the window frame. Was it a man? A woman? Or was it just the fading sunlight playing a trick on her eyes? She could only make out the shape of a hatless head, narrow shoulders, and medium stature. Then, he, or she, backed away out of sight.

Who was up there? The Frau had said the tower was closed up now, used only for the overflow of guests. In any case, Blanche was having a hard time believing anything the Frau said. She adjusted her bag, her eyes darting over the grounds, casually. A tourist taking a short walk—that was Blanche. She set off for the tower at a slow pace.

It would be good if whoever was in that window was a friendly Argentine. She'd welcome meeting another guest and learning something more about this place. A bit of history and background. It might even help to dispel her growing paranoia. The creep factor at La Palma was overwhelming.

She strolled up to the base of the tower and searched for a door. Like a proper guest, she would knock first though a warning bell in her head was telling her to turn around and leave at once. A tangle of orange bougainvillea grew in abandon all around the stucco wall. Surprisingly, the tower was not as well cared for as the gardens at the main house. She walked around looking for a door. There had to be one. Her curiosity prodded her as she fumbled through the weeds and pulled at vines, in vain, looking for an access.

She backed off to a row of bushes and peeked up at the window. No one was around, except that person in her mind's eye: a shape that prompted more questions. Not one answer came for any of them.

Twelve

I'll Drink To That

BLANCHE CONTINUED THE SEARCH of the tower. She poked about the base even as her heart pounded. She argued that her doubt was unreasonable; it was a person she'd seen, and there would be a reasonable explanation. It could have been a visitor—or maybe staff, despite the Frau's insistence otherwise. After all, La Palma needed an *army* to run it.

Most of the windows were dark; the grounds were empty, but she felt eyes on her. She was right. Far up the rounded wall of the tower, a shadow leaned against the glass. There, again, a figure in the window. It shifted in the frame and quickly dropped away. Her heart fluttered. She'd been spotted. Snooping.

Blanche flattened herself against the wall and almost fell into a recess hidden in the tangle of growth. The door was made of hewn slats fitted tightly together set deep in a stucco arch. On the right side, there was a latch and a keyhole of unpolished, black-metal iron that most likely was a fit for one of those old-time skeleton keys. She held back, then knocked, tentatively, and tried the latch. It was locked.

The door hadn't been opened in some time. A seam ran along the top, veined with cobwebs, and the arch was clogged with bugs, grass, and pods. Evidently, the entry hadn't been used for—months? Years?

Yet, someone was in the tower. So how did he, or she, get in there?

Blanche headed around the back, stepping carefully over the brambles. Unlike the main house, there were no fancy borders or flowers. A neat stack of garden tools leaned against the wall.

For now, she was stumped. Hands on hips, she took in the landscape. Farther away, at the end of a gravel path, the top of a low squat building protruded above the high patches of tall grasses. The growth would have buried it, but the way had been cleared. Fresh cuts on the shrubs and grasses bore the marks of shears. Blanche's curiosity triggered like a machine flipping into high gear. It was getting late, but she had time to have a quick look before meeting Emilio.

Her sneakers crunched on the gravel. Faint sounds of animals nickered in the woods as she picked her way along. The building wasn't a barn; it was a pink chapel faded to an extraordinary, aged patina. Above the door in an ornamental inset was a crucifix. A small cupola on top, now empty, possibly had housed a bell. The gothic windows on either side of the front door, once resplendent with intricate panes of multi-color glass, were dusted over and laced with cobwebs.

Under other circumstances, she might have enjoyed the pleasant afternoon. Today, there was no enjoyment. Just uneasiness. Again, that close feeling, the sensation of being cut off from the world in this strange place, made Blanche shiver. A gust of wind blew the leaves up frantically, then there followed a gentle breeze. She pushed at the door, but it didn't budge.

She made her way around the side of the chapel to the back. No windows here. She stopped abruptly and stared in disbelief. Puzzled, at first. Her arms and legs felt disconnected. Again, the same out-of-body experience she'd had when she found Margarita seized her.

The wall at the back of the chapel was riddled with holes. She closed her eyes, unable to move. The discovery sank in. Bullet holes.

She stared at the random arrangement—hundreds of them. Some four to six feet off the ground. The remains of horror. She drew closer through the thick fringe of weeds and buzzing insects and traced a finger over the holes. They were deep and varied in size, some flaking and filled with dust. Target practice of an awful sort. Her throat caught as she probed the rough, dry surface. Hundreds and hundreds of bullet holes.

Blanche stumbled backward through the growth, the vines catching her ankles. She turned away, bent over and pressed her stomach to stop the waves of revulsion. These lush grasslands were deceptive cover, the gentle lawn and rose bushes, the pink house and pink chapel. The past was in clear view. So strange that they didn't even try to hide it.

Blanche ran.

She couldn't get away fast enough. Far off the beaten path, she stopped, hands on her knees to catch her breath. She rejected the strange pull to return and examine that wall and the rest of it. She didn't want to be in Argentina, much less here, or have anything to do with any part of La Palma or the Schemmers.

As she ran, the jasmine wafted on the breeze, but the pleasant surroundings of La Palma did not distract her. It was not a pleasant place. Nothing would ever erase what had happened here. She couldn't block it out. The Dirty War. She was running in a killing field.

She dodged the clumps of wildflowers and fought the welling behind her eyes. The situation reached beyond Emilio's aunt, but she'd surely been a part of it. She'd been deeply involved here. She'd known things.

Blanche was no closer to finding her or unraveling any of the ugly secrets of La Palma. In fact, she was coming up with more unanswered questions, and she wondered about the extent of these dreadful secrets. The place was haunted.

Blanche reached the main house. The ox-blood-painted house, this godforsaken place. They needed a *real* plan to get away.

It was after six o'clock, and she was late to meet Emilio. She raced around the front of the house and burst through the door past Lusita. The maid was carrying a tray and stopped abruptly, holding on desperately to prevent the crystal and barware from crashing to the floor. Blanche lifted her hands and dashed up the stairs. "So sorry, Lusita."

"Emilio!" she yelled, stumbling into the bedroom. He wasn't there.

The room had been straightened, the covers neat and tidy, and the window thrown open to let in the early evening breeze. It was a welcoming sight, and she wished she could leave it all behind, immediately. Blanche glanced at her watch. The time was six-thirty. *Where is he?*

The mirror over the vanity stared back at her. Her hair was a fright of springy curls, and her eyes were like throbbing green lights. She jabbed at the tangle with a hairbrush and applied a mess of lip gloss. She went to the window, then out into the hall to look around for Emilio. Nothing.

"Okay, get a hold of yourself." She took a deep breath and dove into her suitcase. The outfit she chose was suitable, she supposed, but it didn't matter how she looked. She felt terrible. She chose a plain mid-length skirt and a loose peasant blouse and tied a silk scarf around her neck, then whipped it off, this light constriction too much. She adjusted the skirt and knotted the bottom of her blouse at the waist. *I look like a frantic hippie.*

Some yoga stretches and breathing exercises seemed to help, and so she did some more, deeply, until her fingertips and toes tingled. She squared her shoulders and started pacing. It wouldn't do any good to hang around in this room and wait for Emilio, so she headed out. Faint clinking sounds came from the kitchen. She clutched the polished banister. The living room was dim and shadowy, except for weak sunlight playing on the plush silk rug and crystal glasses on a butler's tray.

First things first, she made a beeline for the booze. Poured liquor into an etched glass, whiskey of some sort. The sip made her feel better instantly—with her dead Irish grandmother's nagging caution in her head. "There's no future in the *uisce beatha*," she always said. Right now, though, Blanche threw future to the wind. She was very much in the present. A drink, or two, would tune up her senses. Make her the very picture of sociability. It was quiet now, but no quiet moment ever lasted. It was unsettling how one after another exploded with alarming regularity.

Her eye on the front entry, she willed Emilio to appear. It had better be soon. She was ready to pop.

She took another sip. The liquor burned her throat, untightening her limbs, and she melted into the downy armchair. She closed her eyes. Took in the moment and tried to figure out her next move.

Footsteps sounded in the hall. Or was it boot steps?

Herr Schemmer stood in the door, a whip in his hand and cheeks flaming red from exertion.

"Ahhh! If it isn't the *americana del norte!*" he boomed.

She hesitated a beat, gathering her thoughts. Here was opportunity; she needed to plumb the depths of this blustering bozo.

"Yes! The girl from the north country." Blanche's lips were

numb, and she feared she looked like a wild-eyed, springy-haired zombie. She straightened up. "That would be me. You know Bob Dylan?"

"Who does not know the great balladeer of flowers in the wind and freedom, and don't think twice it's all right." He waved the whip in a tight little motion and tossed it on a chair. He headed for the decanter. "Señor Dylan is known far and wide. I must say, I admire all things *norteamericano*."

"Well, how did you end up here then? Why didn't you go to North America?" Too late. Diving right in. She needed to slow down and ease into this conversation. Blanche held off while her mind roamed the continents—Germany to Argentina to the USA. She considered the high drama that must have played out at the time of the Schemmers' arrival at La Palma.

Herr Schemmer seated himself in front of the fireplace with a generous pour of whiskey. His lips were pursed in thought, his gaze lingering at the cold, empty grate. A sudden breeze from the open window stirred the drapery and snapped him out of his reverie.

"It is complicated," he said, finally.

"A lot of things are." She bit her tongue. They'd only been in Argentina a few days, and the situation was becoming more complicated by the hour. She hoped he'd expand on those complications. She swirled her drink, then set it down with a click on the glass coffee table.

He raised an eyebrow. "All of *life* is complicated."

"Especially at La Palma?" She'd save the discussion of death and war and the discovery of the bullet holes.

"I suppose you're right. We've had many challenges through the years." He sipped his whiskey. "And I am a long way from the *Fatherland*"

"You know, that's always been an interesting concept," Blanche mused. "The Fatherland. Why not the Motherland? Or just the land?"

He had a piercing gaze. She didn't look away. "The father is the leader. In this circumstance, of the *vorld*," he said. "You must know of Germany's power ..."

Warm and charming, Blanche. "Please, won't you tell me how you and the Frau came to La Palma? And not, say, to the United States?"

He took a long draught of the whiskey. "Your country was not so welcoming to us after the war. But Argentina was."

"War? Which war? There've been so many," she said evenly. The word weighed heavily. Like a lead weight dropped right into the middle of the room. Blanche had only sad recollections for the concept of war. Mostly because she'd lost her father in Vietnam.

"Hmmm." He emptied his glass.

"Please allow me to get you a refill," Blanche said. She hoped— wanted—him to drink more. She didn't wait for an answer but reached for his glass. He handed it over, his eyes pinned on her. *"Danke, fraulein."*

When she sat back down, she picked up her drink and pretend- ed to sip. She would listen to his stories, poised and ready, if it took all damn night. "You were saying? About war?"

"World War Two," he said. "We were young."

She nodded, making a fresh calculation. He'd have to be in his mid-seventies now, a teenager at the end of World War Two. More than fifty years ago.

"The United States did have a troubled relationship with Germany at that time." *Troubled? Was that the right word?* She was having trouble keeping a level tone. Should she mention concen- tration camps, Hitler, and the horrors perpetrated by the Third Reich? The bullet holes in the chapel wall were another iteration altogether.

"That we did. Germany and the United States. But we are good friends now." He lifted his fleshy chin and studied her. "And you and I?"

"Oh, indeed, we are. Friends. It is lovely to meet you and the Frau. Thank you for your warm hospitality." *And for killing my boyfriend's aunt?*

"It's grand to have you. We enjoy our guests." He smiled. "And we very much like living here."

"Must be very different than your home. In Germany, I mean. Where exactly in Germany?"

"Schweinfurt, little town some ninety kilometers from Frankfurt," he said, softly. "So *schön*. You know it?"

She knew just enough German to know the name of the town meant "pig crossing."

"Ah, no, can't say that I do. Did you grow up there? What did you do there? Your family?"

"My family worked in the ball bearings factory in support of the war effort. I was a member of a youth group. I can say now, it is a matter of history."

The notorious Hitler Jugend? Blanche steadied her glass. A mild disorientation—lack of food, a lot of disgust—swept over her. Visions of the jack-booting young ones, loyal to the cause, marched through her brain. Nearly ninety percent of German youth had belonged to the nation-wide movement, some as young as eight and nine, at the start of the war. Nearly every single young person, boys and girls alike, was a member of the *Jugend*. "Youth group? What did you do in the youth group?"

"We trained. We worked." He looked at her sternly. "In work there is freedom."

Arbeit macht frei: Work sets one free. The sign hung over the entrance to Auschwitz and other concentration camps, the phrase borrowed from a nineteenth century writer and adopted by the

Nazis. Blanche nearly choked. What little she'd drunk boiled in her stomach. It was revolting to sit here with him, all cozy in the lap of luxury, and he, getting drunk as hell. Her mind raced. What had he done? What had the Schemmers done together? Why were they here and not in jail?

She refrained from getting up and running out of the room. It was all she could do not to yell at him. *How could you? What were you thinking? What were you all thinking?* Her teeth clinked the rim of the glass, a stupid, nervous habit she thought she'd kicked.

Blanche calmed herself before she spoke. "And then you arrived in Argentina. From your work in the *Jugend*?"

He looked at her sharply. "Yes. Are you a student of history? *Jugend fraulein?*"

She wanted to smack his fat, red face. "Oh, yes, certainly. But it doesn't take much of a history lesson to know what the *Jugend* did." She couldn't help herself. "They were active in the military ... and in all the war effort." She managed to state the fact pleasantly, but it took much effort. She could not risk antagonizing the Schemmers. Her questions and comments annoyed them, at times, but they had seemed accommodating.

"Yes, I suppose. I escaped the military, per se, but not the work of the war. Gerda was a member of the force in later years. We both escaped the aftermath." He dismissed the times with a wave of his sausage-like fingers.

"With no consequences."

"There are always consequences, Miss Blanche." His measured words shook her. "As I said, it is complicated and too boring to relate in polite conversation."

"You never tried to go to the United States?"

"No. Much easier here," he said, holding up the glass, twinkling amber in the light. "The escape route ... the route ... from Germany through Italy was well planned."

"Easier?" She sipped, careful not to spill her drink all over the front of her blouse.

"Yes, Argentina welcomed us. Left us be."

Too bad. "How did you find this place? Who was the owner when you came here?"

"Oh, now, I can't give away our real estate secrets." His condescending tone grated on her. "Let me say that the caudillo lived here, and he was persuaded to take us in. He was leery of the government, but he knew certain people, and it was *arranged*." The R's came out like a gargle. While his English was impeccable, every so often the German accent emphasized his point. "Much later, he was persuaded to hand us the reins, so to speak."

She tried to imagine how the "complicated" real estate transaction spelled out the transfer of property—if indeed it was transferred, or stolen. Were the Schemmers rightful owners? From teenagers in war-torn Europe to proprietors of an estancia in Argentina. "So, you bought La Palma?"

"Did I say that?"

"Oh, I guess not." She struck a tone of awe and deference. "But, really, you were fortunate to land in such a beautiful place. As luck would have it."

"There is no such thing, this falling into luck. One makes one's own luck."

This was probably the only bit of the human condition they could agree on.

"It is fine property, isn't it?" He unbuttoned his jacket and shifted comfortably. "You like it? We did much of the decoration over the years. Imports and such. Left over from—" He stopped himself. "We've made good connections along the way." The liquor was giving his speech sloppy edges, but he kept at it.

Oh, whiskey. The water of life, the Irish call it. They should call it the greaser of the tongue.

Blanche was intent on making her brain cells cooperate, so she watched those sips. "Please. Tell me how you managed the connections. I'm interested in investments and real estate and such. In Argentina. *How do you do it?*" She was such a liar. She hoped it didn't show and that she came across as charming though she was seething inside.

"Gerda and I came here to La Palma when we were very young. It was a difficult journey, from Bavaria down through the mountains to Italy and on to Buenos Aires by ship. The holy mother church and the monks, they helped us. You can imagine." He peered at her under those bushy eyebrows. Asking for empathy? She couldn't feel it. "We met the caudillo through an agent in Buenos Aires. He made the arrangements, and we worked. Hard. We helped in the farming here. There was much to do. Kitchen duties, cattle to care for, these massive grounds." He swept a hand over the room taking in all of La Palma.

"And staff? You must have lots of help."

"Yah." He tilted his head as if to question her remark.

"By the way, do you happen to know a Margarita Goyez?" Margarita was the elephant lingering in every nook and cranny, visible only to Blanche. Once again, she wondered: *Where the hell is her body, and where the hell is Emilio?*

The Herr blinked. "Margarita was a nanny to our children, and then she had other duties as housekeeper. She retired. I'm curious, how would you know Señora Felipe Goyez?"

Blanche deflected. She'd let herself walk right into it. She needed to keep calm. "We met a young student in Buenos Aires who knew of Margarita."

"Is that so?"

"Yes, isn't that a coincidence?" She twisted around in the chair and wiggled her foot.

The Herr sipped his whiskey slowly and smiled at her. His thick lips shined with the wet liquor. It was quite disgusting.

She picked up her drink, and now she put it down. She'd had enough.

"By the way, Herr Schemmer, have you seen Emilio?"

He gazed at her over the rim of his glass. "I have not seen your young man. Is he napping?"

"No, he said he wanted to take a walk on the grounds. After lunch. But that is some time ago. A couple of hours now." She could feel a good sweat working its way down her back.

"He could hardly be lost. Maybe he met the gauchos, and they are having a campfire or a drink. You know men."

"I know Emilio, and he said he'd be back here to meet me." Her voice rose, and she tamped down the heat and worry. "I suppose you're right. He'll be back soon."

They sat in less than companionable silence. Blanche was at the point of leaving, but she didn't know where to go. Back to her room? To stew some more? It was getting late, and there was still dinner. She worried about Emilio. Plus, she hadn't gotten far enough with Herr Schemmer, except to travel backwards to his involvement with the Third Reich. Now she knew for sure when they'd arrived and that they'd been at the estancia during the Dirty War of the 1970s and 1980s. At a time when thousands of Argentinians who disagreed with the military regime disappeared into the pampa and were tortured and shot. *Yes, things are complicated around here.*

"This student you met in Buenos Aires ... What does she have to do with Margarita?" Schemmer surprised Blanche by circling back to the mention of Emilio's aunt.

Crap. She didn't want even a hint at Issie. "We met this girl at a milonga. She was quite entertaining and mentioned Margarita when we told her we were coming out this way. To visit. A real estancia. In Argentina."

She took a deep breath. *Breathe diaphragmatically*, the choir director had told her in high school. She was not about to burst into song right now, but the exercise did help.

"Margarita is the type who keeps to herself." It was Frau Schemmer standing in the doorway to the living room, soundlessly appearing like a ghost. Blanche was beginning to wonder if she floated around inches off the ground. Her words were always perfunctory. Now, her movement was one long glide over to the butler's tray. She poured herself a good jot of whiskey and sipped carefully, wrinkling her upper lip and planting herself on the couch, her back ramrod straight. Every hair in place, the skirt taut and smooth across her thighs. "Why do you ask, *chérie?*"

"*Mais, je pense que … .*" Now she was speaking in tongues? Blanche had had only two years of high school French, so where did that come from? She hoped she didn't sound as weird as she felt, her stomach empty and rumbling. That trickle of sweat reminded her how truly uncomfortable she was. Fortunately, she was quite sober; she vowed to keep a clear head and not stir up the Schemmers—not too much. *How much is too much with these people?*

Blanche held her glass tightly, her fingertips cutting into the grooves of the crystal. She smiled at Frau Schemmer. "As I mentioned to Herr Schemmer, we met a lovely group of students." She switched from one student to a group, steering further away from thought of Issie. Maybe it was too late for that. She stole a look at Herr Schemmer, but he did not appear to be paying attention to Blanche; he was smiling at his wife.

"Students? Where was this?" the Frau asked, crisply.

"In Bueno Aires."

"The Capital is a large place. Where, exactly?" The woman's tone was more off hand than demanding.

"The tango dancing in a plaza. The name of the place escapes me now. We walked so much. All over. All day and all night." She took a tiny sip of her drink, her eyes locked on the Frau. The woman was unreadable.

"Karl and I enjoy the tango."

Blanche stammered. "What?! Really?!"

"You seem so surprised. We enjoy the music and the passion of the dance." Her head bobbled at Blanche's apparent disbelief. Blanche stifled a laugh at Gerda's righteous reaction as if she owned the tango, and Blanche was out of line. Herr Schemmer grinned.

It was hard to imagine Gerda and the passion of tango in the same sentence, but Blanche enthused. "That's wonderful! I love tango! Emilio and I had a few lessons. Had a lovely evening of it." She recalled wanting to kill the *divina* Gamoure.

The Frau stood up abruptly. She smoothed her skirt, still clutching the whiskey glass. "I must see about dinner." She smiled stiffly. "We will talk of tango later."

"Oh, certainly."

"By the way," she said, standing in front of Blanche. "I saw you walking the grounds earlier." Her inflection carried an accusatory edge. That stoney gaze again.

"Yes. I decided to take a little stroll and explore the grounds after lunch." Blanche put a hand on her chest to quiet the tremor and clear her throat. What was it about this woman that set her off? Blanche was fascinated but wary. "I didn't realize anyone was around. So quiet. And peaceful." The shadowy figure in the tower and the bullet holes popped into her head, but she kept smiling.

"Yes, it is peaceful. I am glad you are enjoying it."

"No one in the tower?" Blanche blurted. *Damn!*

"No," she said, flatly, and clearly peeved. Frau Schemmer stared down into her whiskey glass, sipped the rest, and set it down on the table. "I did see you strolling, as you say. You liked your little walk about, I see."

"Immensely."

Oh, goodie, she's spying on us? What else did she see?

"Frau Schemmer," Blanche called after her as she turned toward the door. "Since you do have an eye on what's going on around here—Have you seen Emilio? He was supposed to be back here at six."

"Why, no, I haven't. Haven't seen him since lunch. I'm sure he'll be back soon. For our lovely dinner."

The Herr had not said a word, his gaze settled pleasantly on his wife. He'd hardly peeped at Blanche since the Frau appeared. They were both on their feet now, towering over Blanche. He picked up the whip and tapped it against the palm of his hand.

"Dinner will be at ten o'clock," said the Frau. "Enjoy your cocktail, and do not hesitate to call if you need anything." She tilted her head and hurried off.

The Herr chuckled. He walked over to the window. "She is quite the lady, no? My queen of La Palma!"

"Oh, yes, quite."

"I've enjoyed our little chat, girl from the north country. We will see you and your fine young man at dinner perhaps?" He straightened up and clicked his heels.

Blanche winced.

He headed after his wife. These people were a mystery inside an enigma. Where had Blanche heard that one? Winston Churchill—talking about the time the Nazis invaded Poland. They'd also invaded Argentina. The Schemmers were definitely a puzzle. They didn't know the whereabouts of Emilio—or Margarita? Blanche didn't believe either one of them. About hardly anything.

She walked over to the window and stared into the dusk. So many stars pricked the blue-black sky and gave out so little light.

Herr Schemmer had left Blanche in the living room with a hearty goodbye. Probably off to whip some gauchos into shape, or someone else. Blanche gazed out at the lawn. At nothing. *Where are you, Emilio?*

She clutched her skirt and raced up the stairs to her room, hoping Emilio had gotten past her and the Schemmers while they talked over drinks. She doubted it. Her glance had zipped repeatedly to the doorway while the Herr carried on, lost in history but not revealing quite enough about him and his wife—and Margarita and the staff. At least, he'd volunteered some of their German background, his comments mostly evasive puffery and dismal historical reminders. The banter left a disappointing taste.

Emilio wasn't in the room, or in the bathroom, or down the hall. The room where they'd found Margarita was nice and tidy—and creepy. Blanche stared at the spot where the body had lain and stepped back slowly out the door and closed it. She went to her room to figure out the next step.

A beautiful mauve-orange sky had settled over the landscape, but the peaceful view did nothing to tamp down a certain desperation. If she could out-think the negative feelings, she could dispel them. But it wasn't working, and time was running out. A sickening sensation washed over her. It had been hours now since she'd seen Emilio. *What if he, too, is dead?*

She'd never felt so alone. Not even looking at the vast Gulf of Mexico in front of her cabin or at the endless ocean from the Irish shore could compare. This was different. She wasn't just alone. She was cut off—*they* were cut off—from civilization out here on the pampa.

She grabbed her bag and fished around for the phone they'd purchased at the kiosk in Buenos Aires. It was loaded with minutes but needed a charge. She plugged it in and hid it under the bed. Just in case. Who would she call to get them out of here? Maybe a sympathetic staff member would help. But who would that be? It was too risky to start asking around, but it might become a dire necessity.

The memory of those bullet holes in the chapel wall, of running her fingers over them, and the dust, swept her like a rogue wave. The horror those people must have felt. Blanche shuddered. She had no idea. How could she? She lived a lovely beach life in Florida. And, aside from the occasional scrapes while sleuthing and the misadventures with the weirdos she'd encountered on her travels, she was fortunate. She was not about to meet her end with something as terrible as a firing squad—she hoped—but the unknown of what was behind the happenings at La Palma was fearsome. Disturbing. Journalists, teachers, and artists had disappeared into the pampa, some tortured and killed and buried where no one would ever find them. *Where? Here? At La Palma?*

La Palma was one place where they'd surely waged their Dirty War. Thousands had died at the detention centers. Some were dropped from helicopters into the Rio de la Plata. At least thirty thousand people, by some counts, disappeared. The fact that murder might have happened here made her more anxious than ever. What had the Schemmers seen? Done? What were the two of them capable of?

And what had Margarita known?

Blanche was at the point of calling the police, but she still hesitated. Of course, she could report Emilio's disappearance. The police would help find him. And Margarita. She wanted to report the Schemmers, too, but for what? She had nothing on her hosts even though she suspected they were hiding terrible things. All she could tell the authorities was a whole lot of *nothing*. What would they say about the bullet holes? *Nothing.* The Dirty War was more than twenty years in the past, and the Schemmers' involvement in World War Two was sketchy at best. Lots of Germans fled during and after the war. At this point, the police might come out here and talk to her and then drive off into the pampa shaking their official heads over the ramblings of a crazed American.

There had to be a better way to tie this thing up.

Or, as in all things Blanche, the direct way.

She stopped pacing. Staying in this room, waiting, was not an option. She slipped out the door and headed toward the back stairs. No telling what she might learn from staff, especially Lusita. Blanche had to make the effort and move forward, no matter the risk.

The back hall over the kitchen was dim. Blanche fumbled for a light at the top of the stairs and listened to the clinking of dishes and silverware and conversation. Something savory was roasting. Her belly growled. Slowly, she crept down the steep stairs, moving carefully. When she reached the final step, her toe caught on a gap in the carpeting, and she pitched headlong through the kitchen door into a large basket of potatoes.

Lusita let out a yelp and dropped the knife on the chopping block.

Blanche stood up and tugged at her skirt. "Always like to make an entrance."

Everyone turned at once, all conversation stopped. A very large man at the stove raised his spoon, and red sauce dripped onto the floor. Blanche stared back at them, blinking. Trying to look respectable.

"*Muy buenas, Señorita,*" said Lusita, her round cheeks flaming. The tendrils of her curly hair escaped the tight kerchief. "What will I do for you?"

Blanche put on her best smile. She didn't want to cause them trouble, but she needed help. If she could get her business done, they could all get on with it, and she wouldn't bother them again.

They had little to do with her trouble. She was certain of that. Well, as certain as she could be.

"I'm sorry to drop in ... like this, Lusita. I'm looking for Emilio. Have you seen him? Or would you have any idea where I could look for him? You know the grounds, and maybe you'd give me an idea?" Her words rushed together as her eyes darted around the kitchen.

"Oh. No—no idea about the señor." Lusita patted the onions into a pile and wrung her hands on her apron. "I know nothing."

Which suddenly made it clear that she did know something. Blanche looked at everyone in the room. The two young helpers had turned back to the sink. They continued washing dishes and speaking to each other in whispered Spanish. The cook, too, returned to his bubbling saucepan. Blanche stood perfectly still. It struck her, right then and there, they *all* knew something.

"Lusita ..." Blanche hesitated before plunging forward. "I don't think I believe you." Silence filled the room. No one turned to look at her.

Blanche persisted. "You know nothing about where visitors might wander off to? Are you sure?"

Lusita, her mouth open, shook her head aggressively. "Oh, nothing. Nothing. Except ..."

"Except what?" Blanche sighed, loudly.

"There are places. The barn, perhaps? The ... the ... especially the chapel. It is an interesting place to explore."

Blanche's temper flared. "Lusita, I'm not going off to pray he comes back ... though it might be a good idea."

"No, no, I do not mean to pray for his return." She walked over to Blanche, her words barely audible. "Señorita, I mean for you to perhaps *explore* the chapel, is all. Do it ... how you say ... *rigurosamente*?"

"Huh?" Blanche was exasperated.

"You know. You must do with *rigor*. Thorough." Lusita's demeanor changed as she spat each word and resumed chopping.

"Well, all right then. I will. Thank you, Lusita." Now more confused than ever, a chill in the pit of her stomach, Blanche stared at the girl and waited. But she went on attacking peppers and did not meet Blanche's gaze. Was there nothing more? The chapel certainly was the scene of some speculation, but Emilio could not be in there, sitting in the dark. Praying? Or was there something else?

"Please, Lusita. You have to understand, I am not only looking for Emilio." She lowered her voice conspiratorially. "Can you tell me about Margarita Goyez?"

Startled, Lusita stepped back. She carefully placed the knife next to the peppers. Her lips moved but nothing came out as she glanced toward the door.

"Lusita? Please. Tell me."

"Señor Emilio, I do not know where he is. I tell you, for certain. And, the Señora Margarita, she is retired. I don't see her. No more. She has a cottage in the village, and she lives there." The information escaped Lusita in disjointed sound bites. She leaned over the board once again. Chop, chop, chop.

She lives there? "Did she ever live here? In the main house?"

"Oh, I think, many years ago, but, no. Señora Margarita does not live here."

Then what was she doing here lying dead on the floor in the upstairs bedroom?

"And the rest of the staff? In the tower, perhaps?" Blanche was still confounded by that person she'd seen in the tower.

"We don't live here," she said, "except some times in the rooms off the kitchen. But that is all." She moved quickly to the other end of the kitchen. Away from Blanche.

"What is happening in here?" Frau Schemmer's shrill, haughty voice cut into the conversation. She glowered at Blanche. "More questions, frauline? *Always* the questions." She walked into the kitchen and peered at the stove. The cook stepped aside. Blanche couldn't see his face, but the slump of his shoulders told her he was cowering—or protecting himself from a lashing. The Frau seemed capable of a lash or two. And why was she always appearing like she'd been hovering around a corner?

Blanche gritted her teeth. This was not going well. Maybe she should back off. *No, I will not.* Emilio could turn up soon, but if he didn't, she wasn't going to sit around and do nothing. Not anymore. If she didn't meet this head on, Margarita—and Emilio—might never turn up. Now or ever. The Frau's demeanor, and her continual stonewalling, grated on Blanche.

She walked toward the Frau as she lifted the cover of a pot and tasted the sauce. Her spoon clacked loudly onto the porcelain stovetop. She turned to Blanche, impatiently.

"Well, yes, I do have a question, or two, Frau Schemmer. I was asking about Emilio. He hasn't turned up, and I can't find him. We were to meet up back in our room at six o'clock."

"Meet up?"

"He was going to look at the farm operation. He is from farm country in Mexico, you know, and he is curious how things are done here. While he was walking around, I sat on the chaise on the lawn to relax. Now he's missing."

"I haven't seen him and surely have no idea where he is. He must be on the grounds."

She stepped closer to Blanche, the lines in her face relaxed slightly. What was under that tentative smile? "Why don't you have a drink in the salon? Or take a nice bath? Read a book?" Her eyes grew large, wickedly dark and opaque against that icy, white skin. "It's only been a few hours. Let the man be."

"The light's gone!" Blanche shouted. "Why would he be out on the *grounds?*"

"I don't know what to tell you. Curiosity? Seems to be a lot of that going around. He is *your* friend? You must have some idea about where he'd go."

She spoke at a clip, so precisely, Blanche wanted to scream.

"Are there other guests here? Salons? A library or game room?" Emilio wouldn't be off reading or knocking balls around a table by himself, but she had to put something out there.

"No other guests. And no other rooms."

This was going nowhere.

"I do have another question."

The Frau gave her a blank expression.

"Margarita?" Blanche waited for the woman to respond. When she didn't, Blanche continued. "Whenever I've asked about her, it seems I'm continually put off." Blanche crossed her arms in defiance. "It's happening again."

The Frau whirled around toward Blanche.

"I do not know what you mean. I do not see the business you have with Margarita."

"I've told you ..." Blanche was not going to accomplish anything with vinegar. She toned it down. "I'm sorry. I mentioned that we met a group of students, and one of them talked about Margarita and encouraged us to connect with her at La Palma." Blanche gazed directly at the Frau.

"No need to apologize." The Frau waved dismissively. "The nanny—Margarita—is no longer with us. I believe Lusita just told you that."

So, she had been listening. Heat rose up Blanche's neck and took over her brain. The constant evasiveness was maddening, but the lie about Margarita was the worst.

"We *need* to see Margarita."

135

Frau Schemmer turned to inspect the other pots. Her back to Blanche, she said, "I'm afraid I can't help you. Margarita is *retired.*"

"Retired you say? Actually, Frau, I think Margarita is *dead!*"

There. She'd said it. *Now what?* She had no filter, no matter what, and she was tired of being reminded of it. Whatever lumps she took, her big mouth certainly brought things to a head.

Lusita's chopping became frantic. The two young dishwashers looked from Lusita to the Frau to Blanche and quickly dipped their heads to their chests and resumed washing the dishes. The cook backed up against the cabinets. *Did he flinch?*

The Frau turned slowly. "Whatever would make you say such a thing. Margarita was just here ... visiting, but she left." Her voice rose an octave, near screech, but it was oddly under control.

"I don't know about that. I saw her. In one of the upstairs bedrooms. On the floor. It sure looked like Margarita."

"Someone you saw in the upstairs rooms, you say? Ridiculous."

A strange trill escaped the woman's lips and died away. "Margarita does not live here. Like I told you, she is no longer with us. Hasn't been for some time." Unyielding, and sure of herself. "It was someone dusting or arranging things, no doubt. We do have staff take care of those rooms."

How can I get through to her? I'm not even sure an icepick would do.

Blanche shifted gears. "All right. Perhaps I was mistaken. But I did see a woman on the floor ... She was quite cold." Blanche took a deep breath and smiled as pleasantly as she could under the circumstances.

The Frau waggled a finger at her as if Blanche were an obstinate child.

She fought off the urge to argue further. "Your powers of deflection are admirable, Frau Schemmer."

Frau Schemmer's eyebrows shot up. She turned away from Blanche and glared at Lusita.

Lusita backed up against a cupboard, her eyes round as moons. The dishwashers had skittered out of the room. The cook, however, crossed his arms and watched the conversation. *Licking his lips? Ugh.* Blanche figured if it came to blows, there would be hell to pay. She'd already done some of that, and she could be quite scrappy in a fight. The kitchen would need one damn good cleaning. For sure.

Lusita spoke up. "I am sorry, Frau Schemmer. I should not say anything." Her voice tremulous, the knife suspended.

Tension boiled over, but the Frau played it cool. She pointed a shimmery, white-tipped finger at the chopping block. "Lusita, I want those onions and peppers finely minced, the sauce must be smooth, all the flavors blended well." Then she turned to the cook. "And do not add too much of that bouquet sauce. It muddies the color, disguises the flavor of the tomatoes." Lusita went after a pile of tomatoes in front of her with vigor and a deep sigh. The cook turned and grunted.

The Frau finished upbraiding the cook and Lusita and glanced at a large clock high on the wall. "Dinner will be ready by ten. I hope you enjoy, Frauline Blanche. The *el diablo* sauce is exquisite." She smiled a tight little smile, turned and waved, and sailed out the door. "Carry on."

Fourteen

Shine A Light

ANGER BURNED IN BLANCHE'S CHEST. But right now, she couldn't do anything except watch that silvery-headed witch disappear into the dark hallway.

Blanche stormed back up the stairs to her room talking to herself all the way. Loudly. She was not going to take a bath or read a book as the Frau had suggested, nor was she going to let Emilio *be*. Maybe she would have that drink. But then she thought better of it. She needed a clear head.

Where would he have gone?

How am I going to find him out there? In the damn dark?

She peered out the window. It was dark, all right, but not pitch black. A faint white cloud stretched across the sky over a landscape of bumpy shapes. She counted on these wide-open spaces away from city lights. The stars and moon shined brighter out here in the open. Even so, she needed a flashlight. She'd had a penlight somewhere ... *where?* She searched the room and came up with nothing. Their clothes sat, crumpled in the corner, unpacked as yet. Their planned short visit was not short enough. It hadn't taken long to get into this mess. *What else is new?*

She wrung her hands. The more she paced, the worse she felt.

138

Emilio would not walk away and leave her alone here. He had to be in some kind of trouble. He'd been protective and concerned, and she knew better than to think he'd let her worry. He would surely have shown up by now, if he could.

All the while, Blanche kept thinking how Margarita would want them to get out of this creepy place. And she didn't even know Margarita! But Margarita, dead or alive, remained pivotal to this situation. They could not—would not—leave until they found her. They'd eventually get the police involved and finally press the Schemmers for answers.

And if Emilio still didn't turn up—God forbid—well, the police would have to search for him and find him. No choice but to follow her nose and keep looking. She certainly couldn't rely on the Schemmers. They were no help at all. In fact, they were an obstruction.

Blanche tore open the door and raced back downstairs to the kitchen in search of a flashlight. Lusita was still at it with those vegetables mincing away. The cook was fussing in the cabinets.

"Sorry to bother you." *Again.* Her eyes darted around the kitchen. She hoped she didn't look as frantic as she felt, and she prayed the Frau didn't show up. "Do you have a flashlight?"

Lusita shook her head and chucked a multi-colored pile of vegetables into a bowl. The cook wordlessly put down his spoon, went to a cupboard, and withdrew a heavy black flashlight. He solemnly handed it to Blanche. "*Viel glück,*" he said and went back to the cabinet.

"What's that mean?"

He turned half way toward Blanche. "Good luck."

She tried to see his face, but no luck there. "Thank you," she murmured. She hefted the clunky flashlight, slapping it against the palm of her hand. Clicked it on; it worked fine. She walked up close to him. He was hard to gauge, but she'd try. "Tell me, please, where do you think a visitor would go on the grounds at this hour?"

He raised his eyebrows, his face impassive. "No one walk there now, for sure. He'll come back. Maybe." He began stirring the pot of lumpy red sauce.

"Maybe? Why do you say that?"

"Many questions. I do not get paid to answer questions. You have the flashlight. Now you go look. I have cooking."

Blanche pressed ahead, exasperated. "Why 'good luck'? What do you mean by that?"

"Not one thing," he said. "It is, what? An expression? *Goodbye.* Also an expression."

She went out the back door. The flashlight cast a triangle of feeble light over the expanse of lush grass. It was well after eight o'clock, and quite a bit brighter than it had looked from her room. The lawn was flat, and the path across the property was clear. She kept walking farther from the house, not thinking about where she was going. She was just going. As the flashlight swept the area, she tried to pick up any sign of Emilio. Or anybody who might know *anything.*

Walking eased her frustration. At least she was doing something as she clomped purposely through the grass. The beach was her usual go-to place, but now, here she was in the pampa, in the dark. The space alone was something so foreign to her after growing up on a small island where some of the cottages were a mere twenty feet apart. Again, the vastness of Argentina hit her, and along with it, the impossibility of what lay ahead.

The farm buildings were some distance from the main house. Emilio had said he was going to pose as a curious visitor, a farmer by occupation. That alone seemed so ludicrous, Blanche laughed out loud. He looked more like an Aztec prince than a farmer. But it was a good cover since he did know a thing or two about farming. He'd grown up in the *bahio*, the breadbasket outside Mexico City, and he'd worked with his family there.

Animals rustled in the bushes. What kind of animals would those be? Lions and tigers? *Of course not, Blanche.* But in the near dark, and in her imagination, *in Argentina,* all kinds of creatures surrounded her with their cries and chittering, and, thank God, no roaring. She didn't have any idea what was out here and had no idea what was inside the building she was approaching. She crept on. The lawn was spongey under her feet, and the air had turned eerily quiet except for the whinny of a horse.

A powerful odor of manure mixed with hay blasted her as she pried the door open. The barn accommodated half a dozen stalls on each side. Fresh straw was piled on the wood floor, and tack gear was scattered about. The building was dismal, but neat and comfy if you were a horse. The snort of the animals and the scampering of mice looking for a meal were the only sounds.

"Emilio?" she croaked. She hoped she didn't find him here, knocked out or tied up, or worse. She swung the light all around the tight space. No one here, only the beautiful creatures. They shied from the light, and neighed and bobbed their heads, and then turned away.

The next building, the barn next to a pasture, was nearly empty. Out in the field she could see cows in various poses. Blanche hated to disturb cows. They were so peaceful and sweet, and they worked so hard on that milk production.

She called out in the barn and got no response.

The sturdy wood buildings stood outlined against a sky bleeding the last of fluorescent pink and red in the west. There were no other places to look here. Blanche stumbled around and went back in the direction of the tower and the chapel. She'd not had any luck getting into the tower, and the door to the chapel had been locked. Or stuck? Lusita had urged her to search there. But now it was getting late, and Emilio wasn't anywhere. *Dammit, Emilio, where are you?*

She hoped he'd returned to the house. It was nine o'clock and time to have a look. Get some dinner. It would be an opportunity to put the Schemmers on the spot, maybe, but she anticipated being all by herself. *How unpleasant!*

She headed back across the lawn, the flashlight leading the way. She'd decided to keep it as she would go out again and search later if he wasn't back. And she wouldn't stop until she found him.

Blanche ate dinner alone. Emilio still had not appeared, and neither did the Schemmers. So much for a showdown with the hosts. The elegant dining room was far from unpleasant. It looked wonderful with the roses and candles and white linen. The aroma of bread and meat wafted her way, but she was doubtful she'd be able to get any food down. Her muscles were taut as stretched wire. Shadows wavered in the dim corners, and the faces of Argentines frowned down at her out of gold Baroque frames. She'd jump start her appetite with a little of that Malbec. She poured herself a large goblet.

I've got to relax.

She walked over to the window. Every shape on the lawn and every object in the dining room, including those portraits, seemed to mock her. She wandered into the den and library and sighed. No Emilio. Not even the Herr to spar with. She returned to the dining room.

Lusita slid a platter of chicken, roasted in olive oil, garlic, and onions with potatoes in front of Blanche. She opened her mouth to ask her if the Schemmers were joining her, but clearly, the girl was not in the mood to chat. Her face was flushed, her mouth set in a tight line. Blanche backed off. She'd already picked at Lusita for information, and lamentably, gotten her into an awkward situation with the Frau. She was gone in a beat.

The beautiful food diverted Blanche's attention. She stared down at the glossy chicken leg, and it got to her. She jiggled her fork and picked up the knife. Suddenly she was starving.

Lusita glided soundlessly into the room and placed a basket of bread on the table. Her face averted, she was as skittish as a cornered kitten. Blanche should help her. As much as she wanted to rescue Emilio and herself—and poor, dead Margarita—they all had to get away from this morbid place.

Blanche guessed Lusita's frame of mind had something to do with her imperious employers. Maybe Blanche could convince her life would be better away from here—away from the Schemmers. The idea needed to simmer. Blanche smiled at Lusita. Somehow, they would have an exchange at Lusita's own pace.

"Thank you, Lusita!" Blanche called after her. "This is so nice." She cut into the chicken. "Please tell the cook thank you, too."

"I will tell him, and thank you for the good words." She was gone before Blanche could put the bite in her mouth. It seemed odd that Lusita hadn't asked about Emilio. But what wasn't odd at La Palma?

Blanche needed to eat. She ate it all, every last potato and bite of chicken, and left the table with a full stomach and renewed resolve. She needed her strength more than ever. There was work to do. She hadn't been eating much, and it had made her lightheaded and dizzy. Anxiety made it worse. Revived, she determined to stay up all night if that's what it took to find him.

She hurried to her room and grabbed a change of clothes. Thankfully, the long pants, jacket, and trainers suited a hike around the property. Sitting on the edge of her bed, hands on her knees, Blanche thought hard about where to search. The main house was an obvious choice, but not with the Schemmers about. She'd do that later, once she found out their shopping and visiting schedule, or whatever else they did, hiding out here in the middle of nowhere. The Herr seemed to spend all his time with the horses and running the farm. But the Frau? She was always puttering about, appearing in the middle of Blanche's interrogations, and abruptly cutting them off. Always in a hurry, these people. Blanche would need to get around those two somehow and do a proper snoop. Drawers and bookcases and such.

Blanche thought of Lusita again. The girl must be a gold mine of information. Unfortunately, so far, digging anything out of her had been pretty hard, except for her suggestion to look in the chapel.

A week into this trip, and here she was, planning a midnight search into these unforgiveable grasslands. The adrenaline pumped like crazy, and her mouth was dry from all the salt and wine. She downed a glass of water from the pitcher next to the bed. Then sniffed it. Too late. Paranoia kicked in. She should be more careful. Surely, she couldn't trust anyone around here, except Emilio. The Schemmers must be leery of her, too, especially with all the questions. They'd be on to them soon. There was no telling what they'd do. It was one more reason to get on the move.

She pocketed the flashlight, and for good measure, her Leatherman knife. She'd become adept at using the tool for fishing and small jobs at home around the cabin, but the knife had also come in handy—for survival. *You never know when you have to cut your way out of a situation.*

The food had leveled her out, calmed her down. She felt strong, and determined, and she was glad it was nighttime. The darkness gave her cover. She had little hope of finding Margarita, but she wouldn't give up. If she did find her, Blanche would have information for the police, including the trail of letters and a pile of complaints from Margarita and Issie. She'd throw in her own sleuthing, which always included a plethora of detail and a lot of extraneous opinion.

The moon was out, gilding the rounded bushes and flowers in soft light. The trees rustled gently as the crickets chirped and night birds fluttered. The dark had settled in around the house in just a few short hours. Blanche melted into her surroundings.

It was peaceful out on the lawn, but as an island girl she was most comfortable on the beach. She was way out of her element here. But the island had taught her to survive. She'd grown up climbing palm trees and swimming, unafraid of sharks and rays. She'd never been afraid of the outdoors or the dark, and she was not about to start now. She crept farther from the main house.

She looked up at the windows in the tower. Second guessing clouded her thoughts. Had she really seen a figure earlier? Or was it a shadow? Or was it the result of too much Malbec and a trick of the late sun? She dismissed these notions. She wasn't seeing things. That black sleeve falling away from the glass was real. Someone had been up there. The question was, how did he, or she, get in?

No light shined in the tower. There was no sign of life there, the night was dead quiet. She shook the latch on the tower door, but it was futile. It was sealed shut.

She stepped back and decided to move on. Emilio would not be in the tower. She crossed it off. *Impossible.*

A few windows blazed at the main house. She'd turned the light off in her bedroom. If it were on, Emilio would have returned. She had a sudden attack of missing him. They'd grown so close, she couldn't imagine being without him. She wanted to see him running across the lawn toward her. She needed those arms around her, the reassurance that he was all right, and that she wasn't alone in this godforsaken place. But he wasn't here. He didn't seem to be anywhere. She sank to the grass, swallowing hard against the welling in her chest. She refused to cry, she wasn't a crier; she was a rager. And patience and plodding along like a turtle were not in her DNA. Doubts and anger pummeled her with such force, but it did nothing but drive her to her feet to go on and *do this*.

The flashlight beamed over the thick grass and onto the path to the chapel. She hadn't gone inside after the discovery of the bullet holes, but now she would. Despite the faint warning going off in her head, she crept toward the squat little building, shuddering to think of those marks on the back wall. The mystery of what had happened here tied into the whole sad, secretive history of this place.

Emilio surely wouldn't be in the chapel, but she'd look. She took out the Leatherman and worked it into the cracks around the door, then put her hand on the latch and gave it a good, hard push. To her surprise, the thick, carved door creaked open. A sweep of light revealed rows of wooden pews on each side of a short aisle leading to a stone altar.

"Emilio!?" No response. The light flickered into corners, but nothing. The place was dusty with neglect and gloom.

The floor was rough plank and the walls were soft pinkish clay. The light revealed the windows, and, despite the dust, the saints in stained glass glowed red and yellow, white and blue. One held a staff and wore a gold crown on his head. *Witnesses to murder?* A wave of revulsion hit her. She sat down hard on a dusty pew. Time had absorbed all this like nothing had ever happened here. " ... the things that went on here during the Dirty War ..." The words that Margarita wrote to Emilio came back to Blanche. She couldn't get away from it.

She filed it away. It couldn't dwell on it now; it was only another distraction to tamp down her determination.

Blanche continued down the aisle and shined the light all around the peeling interior, from the overhead beams set in plaster to the floor and to the small niches with solemn saints. The light wavered over the dusty objects like ripples on a pond. Suddenly, she stopped. Someone had been here. White lilies, on the edge of decay, drooped on a corner pedestal in front of a statue of St. Joseph. She guessed it was him. He held baby Jesus in one hand and a carpenter tool in the other. The pungent scent of the flowers lifted the stale air. She stepped near the figure in his dull brown robe and shined a light on him. The eyes in his plaster face gleamed back at her.

What a place. What did they believe here? She could feel a presence, but it wasn't the Lord.

So. Why the flowers?

She tapped the flashlight against her leg. Lusita had spoken urgently. "Explore the chapel," she'd said. Blanche had cut her off impatiently. *Once again, Blanche.* Now that she thought about it, Lusita had *insisted* that Blanche visit the chapel when she'd pestered the maid about Emilio and Margarita and the Schemmers. *Why?* From where Blanche sat, she didn't see much to explore in this small, dark space. She stood up.

Blanche went over the ceiling to the floor, then each wall, with the flashlight.

I'm going to scour every inch of this place.

Her search yielded nothing but enough dust to cause a sneezing fit.

Her options were limited. She could see that, even in the dark. It was frustrating, but she wouldn't give up. Blanche fanned the light over the pews, the statues, and a stack of hymnals. And then, the light, like a beacon, settled on the large, stone altar.

Fifteen

The Golden Secret

BLANCHE STOOD IN THE CENTER aisle of the dim chapel and stared at the altar. A few blackened candles tilted haphazardly in the pocked brass candleholders. She worked her way toward the front as she flipped a couple of hymnals open, checked the niches and the kneelers. Empty, clean of any clues. She gave St. Joseph a thorough going-over, felt the cool ridges of his brown plaster robe, but her hand only came away with fine dust.

Blanche couldn't look away. She wouldn't, despite a sinking feeling. Her curiosity was overwhelming, but that alone was not going to get her anywhere. She needed a strategy instead of stumbling around in this haunted place. She stared at that altar. *Talk about a stumbling block.*

She gathered her wits and walked slowly around to the back of it and faced the pews. The large stone top and base took up most of the space on the platform. It was the size of a tomb. She swiped her hand over the top to clear the dust. She shined a light on it. It appeared to be made of one single slab. Ornamental scrolls at the corners had no inscriptions. She pushed hard at the top, but it didn't budge. *What a ridiculous attempt.* If it were a tomb, it would take a giant to lift it. Or a couple of determined conspirators.

She felt along the smooth sides of the altar. Solid, all of it. The pieces fitted together tightly. Not a seam, or even a hairline crack. It was possible she'd found a hiding place for a body, but where was the opening?

Crouched on the platform, she checked the base of the altar. Stumped, again. She shined a light on the door and the windows. A beautiful place. Dusty and peeling, but restful. And old. Very old. Her mind didn't linger on the old and peaceful. Surely, shots had been fired at people along the back wall, murdering them all. The chapel had an aspect of beauty all right, and horror. Real serenity in such a place would never exist.

"Well, I can't sit here all night," Blanche said aloud. Lusita had said to look, and so she must. She gave the floor around the altar another lackluster sweep with the flashlight. Then she shined it down the aisle. The flooring appeared to have different patterns, from back to front. The wood slats here on the platform were smaller. Newer? She supposed that were possible, an old building with additions and repairs and such. She made another pass with the flashlight and came back to the spot where she was sitting. There were seams here in the wood, odd seams, that crisscrossed. Forming a large square.

No question about it. A separate cut in the floor.

Her first thought was that it covered a hiding place. Not unusual, really. It had happened before. Her own grandmother had left a treasure under the floorboards of the cabin, and the rest had become family history. That revelation had yielded a stash of cash and a reunion with Irish cousins. Hiding places could be good. So she continued to hope, the excitement pushing away dread.

She tapped the flashlight around the edges of the square. The sound came back with a hollow note. She tap-tapped over the floorboards all the way to the wall. Dull and solid there. Blanche scooted back to the altar, convinced she'd found an opening.

She took out her Leatherman and released the heaviest blade. She thrust it into the cut in the floor. The opening resisted the knife, but she worked it along the groove, clearing the dust and debris. Finally, the blade fit under the slats along the edge. She tried to lift the cover. Nothing. The piece wouldn't budge. She kept at it, working the blade all around the seam again. At some point, surely the thing would give up, but she didn't have enough leverage. A blip, considering her determination. She would get into that floor if it were the last thing she did.

Then it hit her. She dropped the knife, picked up the flashlight, and ran out of the chapel back down toward the gravel path to the tower. She needed a lever, a tool. Even a broken one would do, and she knew just where to find one.

When she reached the tower, she groped her way around the base. *Aha!* A pile of gardening tools she'd seen earlier. She picked out a shovel, and a pick, not sure which was the right tool. She hurried back to the chapel with several pieces of rusty junk.

She positioned the flashlight on the floor. The shovel was in miserable condition, but it seemed sturdy enough. She clunked it on the wood surface. Inserted the tip into the crack and jumped onto the upper rim, wobbled on and off until she got a decent purchase. Her weight was only a hundred pounds or so, but this was a matter of physics, not weight. Little by little, the square beneath the shovel gave up. She jumped and pried, jumped and pried, and finally up came the section of wood. She dragged it aside. The flashlight revealed a deep, dark hole.

Staring into the abyss once again...

Someone had configured this opening for a reason, and she dreaded to think what that could be. Her first thought was of Emilio, and then, of course, Margarita.

"Emilio?" She called, faintly at first. Then she yelled. No response. She was instantly relieved. He couldn't be down in this place. The cover had been sealed over with time. That was good, but maybe bad. She wasn't sure.

Blanche thought hard about what she needed—had—to do. She lay flat on her stomach and leaned over the edge. A rope ladder descended into the hole. *How convenient!* She held the flashlight under her chin and carefully swung a leg onto the first rung and started down. The creep factor was overwhelming as the flimsy ladder wobbled. *What if Emilio—or Margarita—is down here?* She was already wondering how she'd get them out. She'd play hell finding a way.

She put two feet firmly on the dirt floor and aimed the flashlight into the darkness. Nothing but a small room. Dismal, and disheartening. She'd expected *something,* but here was nothing. Just the damp, dead smell of neglect and dirt.

Then one last sweep of the light revealed a wide crack in the seam of the far wall. An opening? She crossed the packed dirt floor and stood before a low cut hidden in the shadow. On the other side, another room, and this one was even smaller. It was full of neatly stacked crates. They looked like boxes her Gran would store and never open again, the things she put away and promptly forgot.

She went in. This was not a typical storage space. These crates were very old, constructed of wood slats that were wired shut, and they were covered in a sooty grit. The initial disappointment turned quickly to intrigue.

She wiped away the grit and looked at the faint markings. The slanted, purple writing on the peeling labels was unintelligible— she could hardly read the scrawl—but the boxes screamed, *I am not your seasonal decorations or your papers and mementos you'll never look at again in a hundred years.*

One crate came down easily off the dusty stack. Blanche blinked in the wavering light. She was surrounded in this packed dirt; it was like a grave. She shivered.

She had to hurry and get out of here. She propped the flashlight, whipped out the handy Leatherman, and went to work on the wire fastenings. Once loosened, they fell away from the lid. Shredded paper crispy with age sprang out.

Eagerly, she dug down into the packing and struck a hard surface covered in more paper. She threw aside the mess and lifted out the heavy, oddly shaped object. Her fingers ripped through it and hit cool metal. *Gold?!* It gleamed bright yellow in the light. Blanche lifted the piece—an exquisitely etched menorah. It shone with a patina of age and craftsmanship. Florid inscription was etched on its curved branches and pedestal. Obviously, this was a piece of well-loved history. She ran a finger over the polished flourishes, hefted the weight of it. She was stunned. This object of timeless importance certainly didn't belong in this dark hole in Argentina. It belonged in a museum, or a temple, or in possession of those who owned it, whoever they were.

Where are they now?

She reverently set the menorah on the stack of crates. One thing struck her. This piece had made a terrible journey.

The open crate yielded another wrapped object. Blanche expected more treasure, and she was right. Carefully she removed the paper. Her mouth dropped open. It was a gold cup, like a chalice. She set it next to the menorah and stared at the other crates. What did they hold? Why was all this treasure hidden away under the noses of her German hosts? Surely these were not Schemmer family heirlooms. The former *Jugend* had not been Jewish. *How did all this end up here?*

She found a list, crinkly with age and hastily but carefully written in old cursive. The writing was in German, but she could make out vague references to the items. She folded the paper neatly into quarters and stuck it in her pocket. She'd study it later. Right now, she couldn't concentrate.

The dusty boxes made her heart sink, but, mostly, they made her want to find out more. She opened another box. A wine cup. A Passover Seder plate. Shabbat candlesticks. Medallions marked with Jewish religious symbols. Some encrusted with jewels and fine marks. The Jewish inscriptions were unmistakable.

She couldn't believe what she was holding in her hands. Though she wasn't particularly religious, she'd studied religions in college as a matter of historical importance, and the significance of this find struck her. Her thoughts turned to the loss, the pain, the horror—of how these objects had come to be here and the grief of those who'd suffered. It was overwhelming. But she needed to move on, add this find to the bullet holes in the chapel, the death of Margarita, and Emilio, still missing. Her mind was spinning. These treasures were tangible proof of ill-gotten gain. Now she had to figure out how to wield this new-found evidence.

She carefully gathered up the mess of paper and the treasured items and packed them up in the boxes. She needed to know more, to make connections here. She wished she were a ghost and could flit in and out of windows and cracks in the doors at La Palma. Get a look in that tower. Listen in on Gerda and Karl and the staff. What other secrets—and lies—were they hiding?

Sixteen

Saddle Up

AS BEST SHE COULD, Blanche stacked the crates full of Jewish treasure back in the order she found them. Would anyone suspect they'd been moved? Too disturbed to care, she just wanted to get out of this awful hole under the chapel. She needed to figure out the next move.

She retraced her steps over the dirt floor, quickly smoothing the ground with the sole of her shoe. The tracks couldn't be eradicated, and the dust could not be put back to the way it was. Her prints were everywhere. It was just as well, she thought, with a burst of anger. It was proof that she'd found their cache of stolen treasure.

She'd left her mark.

Still, she wanted to call authorities, but she couldn't just yet. She needed more background. The Schemmers most likely had smuggled in the crates. Or had the caudillo done this? So unlikely. Someone of the Jewish faith? That, too, was unlikely. It was too important to guess. She'd wait and dig around. At least now she had the list in her pocket, a new piece of evidence.

She cast the light around the underground vault one more time and quickly climbed up the ladder.

The chapel was just as dark and creepy as she'd left it. She moved the wooden cover back over the hole in the floor. She thanked God she was alone. If anyone asked, she was looking for Emilio and praying. It wasn't that far-fetched. Her hosts and staff seemed to tolerate her poking about, but she shouldn't push it. Fat chance. She'd like the opportunity to question the Schemmers directly. Instead, they put her off. Except for Lusita. The girl had come forward and been a valuable source.

Even so, this discovery opened up more questions. How were the treasure, the wars, the Schemmers—and the missing aunt connected? She'd keep her eyes and ears open. Someone had to drop a clue.

Blanche raced back to the house. It was well after midnight, but the lights were on in rooms on the ground floor. In a place such as this, the staff had chores to do at all hours, in fact, they'd probably not finished the business of dinner. Now they were lining up the breakfast things, cleaning sinks and tables and floors. She soundlessly let herself in and scampered up the back stairs to her room.

In the hallway, a light shined under the bedroom door. Blanche threw it open. Emilio paced back and forth—rather staggered, slightly—his shirt untucked and a desperate look on his face.

"Emilio!" She leapt into his arms in two steps.

"*¡Baquita!* Where have you been?"

They wrapped themselves around each other and held on for dear life. He smoothed his hand down her back, and relief coursed through her like a current of warm water. Safe and secure now, with him, in this room.

"Oh, Emilio, where have you been?!" She pulled away from him and slapped her hand against his chest, choking out the words. "You were supposed to be here at six, and you missed dinner! I thought ... I thought ..."

He held her against his chest. "Where have we both been?" He blew out a breath as if he'd been underwater too long. "We have to get out of this place."

"No kidding!" She had so much to tell him, but for now, she laid her cheek on his heart. The sound of it calmed her and gave her reassurance.

He kissed her forehead and lips and lingered there, murmuring. "I am *estupido*."

"Yes, you are. But I don't care. You're here."

He gently ran his hands up and down her arms. "I'm sorry I'm late. It's all crazy."

"Crazier by the minute."

"Come up here." He lifted her easily onto the bed, and they lay back against the pillows. She was so happy, so relieved to be together, but she couldn't think straight. She didn't want to do anything except be with Emilio and get the hell out of La Palma. With or without Margarita.

She curled up next to him. "So, tell me. Where have you been?"

Emilio had set off for the farm buildings around five o'clock, intent on finding clues that would lead to Margarita's disappearance. He'd come to a horse barn first. A laborer was pitching hay into the entrance, another worked at hosing down a ramp that led out to a pasture.

Emilio raised a hand in greeting. "Hola. Taking a walk about the grounds." The fellow with the hose swept an arc of water distractedly along the bordering grass, grunted and turned his back. His leathery face under a tight black cap was not friendly. Emilio decided he'd get no information from him; it did not look promising in these parts.

He sauntered into the barn and checked the rough wood walls and dividers and dirt floor. Nothing here suggested a hiding place or, he shuddered to think, a burial place. He looked back and decided not to linger with the workers nearby.

A group of men talked and joked outside. Emilio stood framed in a wide rear door against the dim light. He guessed they were gauchos, and he'd tread lightly. Two wore wide-brimmed leather hats, baggy pants, and shirts with long puffy sleeves. One of them had bolos tied at his waist. They stopped talking at once. One smiled crookedly. But it was hard to tell in their hard expressions. One of the men stepped forward. *"Bienvenido, flaco. ¿Qué hace por acá?"*

"No hago nada, amigo." He'd keep it short. "Emilio Del Sierra. Taking a walk about." He extended a hand.

The man took it. "Hernan Candela."

"Un placer."

"I am sure." Hernan's lips curled in a wry grin. "You are staying at the big house." It was not a question.

"Yes." Emilio glanced around. He wouldn't find Margarita in this horse barn. It was all wrong. The trail was cold, and he should move on.

Hernan sized him up, a smirk suddenly forming. "Hombre! You ride?"

Emilio didn't hesitate. *"Claro.* I ride."

"I see you around here. Herr Schemmer tells us to show the visitors a good time. I take you on a ride."

The other men stood in a tight knot, murmuring and laughing, their backs to Emilio. He didn't feel right about this, but it was too late now. He knew how to ride a horse. He'd play along.

Feet planted wide apart and determined, circumstances crowded his thoughts. He had no idea how this would help find his aunt, but maybe these rancheros knew things. Blanche was not going to wait around. She wanted to call Issie and press the Schemmers. Get the police involved. Whatever happened, they needed to be in it together. He wished he had her bloodhound instincts. Maybe if he nurtured some of that curiosity and went along now, he could speed things up. He only wanted to get his aunt and his girlfriend and leave.

He took a deep breath. A ride on the pampa? Why not. Emilio walked through the barn following Hernan to the horse stall. This one reared its head, snorting and stomping. It was a fine stallion with an intricate woven blanket on his back and a rather churlish look in his bright but rheumy eyes. He had a white star on his forehead and pranced around like he owned the place. "Should I take this one? That all right with you?"

Hernan shrugged. "You are the visitor. We wish to please."

Emilio patted the horse's hindquarters. "What's his name?"

"Punto. Like the points of the star." Hernan jerked his head in the direction of the horse's mark.

"*Pues, vámanos.*"

Emilio mounted Punto, who reared up with spirit. Hernan rode out on the more placid Canto. Emilio followed the gaucho down a trail that parted the grassland. The sun was low and dusky, gilding the tan stretch of pampa gold. They trotted through a brief patch of forest and came to a wide-open land. Hernan kicked his horse into gear. Emilio took off after him. The hooves pounded the flat surface. At full gallop, Emilio felt the surge of power. Punto charged ahead like he was on fire.

"Eeeeeeeow," yelled Hernan as he made a sharp right turn off the trail and across a stretch of scraggly wood into the pampa.

Emilio pulled up on the reins, but Punto galloped ahead. Then without any warning, the horse stopped, all four legs locked. Emilio lurched forward, frightfully aware that he'd lost control of his ride. He grabbed Punto's mane, but it did no good. He went flying off the saddle, headlong into the unknown. The sky seemed to come up close to his nose, and in the next instant, the flight ended with a crash landing into a clump of bushes. Emilio looked up at the clouds, his mouth full of leaves. He was afraid to move. The horse stood perfectly still at his side, bobbing his head and snorting, as if giving his approval that Emilio was not dead.

Hernan rode up, leading his horse in a circle around Emilio. And laughing.

"What the hell! *Hombre*." Emilio got up, dusted himself off, and raked a hand over his mouth spitting out leaves and dirt. "What was all that about?"

"Electric fence," said Hernan. He jerked his head toward the barrier. "*Lo siento*." He was grinning ear to ear.

"Sorry?" The gaucho didn't seem all that sorry.

"Fences. We do not like them. The government and the foreigners, they try to put fences around us." He was sucking on a reed, eyeing Emilio. He reined in Canto, but, clearly, the horse had liked the run and wanted more.

"*Pues*, I'm not putting any damn fence around you. *Joder*."

Hernan nodded. "That is good."

Emilio stomped out of the bushes and looked up at Hernan, sizing him up. He narrowed his eyes. One stern look deserved another. Emilio waited one more beat. "I am only a visitor to your place."

"Sometimes the visitors have other intentions," said the gaucho.

An understanding passed between them like a charge. Emilio extended his hand and Hernan shook it.

Hernan waved him back up to the saddle, and without another word, they trotted off down another trail.

"Can we not do that again?" Emilio shouted after him.

Hernan shrugged. "Your choice."

Emilio did not feel he had a lot of choices. This ride was a bad idea, but he'd see it through. He patted his horse, who trotted ahead. He was glad the bushes had saved him. Nothing had been hurt, except for his pride. And maybe this experiment was worth it. Maybe he'd found an ally in Hernan with that handshake. He and Blanche needed someone on their side.

When they returned, the other gauchos were still in the barn, brushing the horses, watering them, and pitching hay. One threw his pitchfork down on the floorboards with a clatter.

"Was a good ride?" He grinned. All the others looked up at once and grinned, too. Clearly, they were all in this together.

"*Sí. Terrífico.*" Emilio dismounted and patted Punto, looking from one to the other. "Except for the fence."

"Ahhh." They all laughed. One kicked at the hay, another rubbed his chin. Emilio stuck his hands in his back pockets and slouched against the post of a stall.

"*Escuche,*" Hernan said. "You are a good sport. Is that how you say it in North America?"

Emilio grinned.

"Let us stand you to a whiskey and beer." Hernan clapped Emilio on the back and nearly dislocated his shoulder. "*Buen hombre.* You will come with us. To the village."

The others stepped forward, slapping Emilio on his back.

"Maybe another time. I have to meet someone," Emilio said.

"The *guapita*? Woman can wait."

Blanche was not good at waiting. Patience wasn't one of her virtues.

"Really, another time."

"We promise. We will return you. After we drink. ¡*Ven!*"

At that point, Emilio figured he had little to lose. And he just might get some information with the help of liquor. Casually, he followed them out of the barn. He'd be late to meet Blanche, and she would probably be angry. Then again, she'd be happy if he learned something from the gauchos—especially if it helped find his aunt. They hadn't told Issie about her mother yet, and that nagged Emilio. She should know. *We all need to know more.*

The men climbed into a Jeep, open on the sides and top. Hernan bounded down a dirt road toward the village of San Antonio de Padua as if he were in a race. The bumpy main street was dusty and vacant, except for a few inhabitants meandering past a nondescript block building with one dark window.

The Jeep skidded to a stop in front of a tavern. The old gold lettering on the window read Olga's Inn, a shiny dot on the front of a whole pile of blackened, weather-beaten boards. Inside, the interior was dim with round tables and well-worn captain's chairs scattered around the room. An old woman stood behind the bar. She barely looked up.

"Howza," she said, and without further preamble, lined up half a dozen shot glasses and took down a label-less bottle of brown liquor from a shelf.

Hernan lifted his glass to Emilio: *"Salud, amigo."* In an instant, he'd gone from gruff to warm and hearty.

"I'll drink to that," Emilio said. He sniffed the shot of whiskey, downed it, and clapped the empty glass upside down on the bar. His plans were to pick the brains of these gauchos and, at some point, have a quick look around the town.

"Bueno, the village. You live here? Or on the estancia?"

"We all live here in San Antonio." He shrugged. "It is a living. Barely."

"And you speak English well. How?"

"It is necessary. Many visitors of many types. And the estancia provides lessons." He didn't seem interested in discussing language lessons, but Emilio persisted.

"Who teaches?"

"Frau Gerda, at times. But the first teacher is Margarita Goyez."

At the sound of her name, Emilio stiffened but contained an expression of surprise. "She must be a good teacher."

Again, Hernan shrugged.

"And this Margarita? She lives here in the village?"

Hernan seemed irritated. "Yes, I say, we live here. All the staff live here in San Antonio. Except for some of the little kitchen maids. They sometimes have small rooms at the big house. We had access, but now ... not so much." He smirked. Emilio was at once disgusted.

"So, the women complained?"

"You know women." He stopped and scratched his head. "You know women?"

"No."

Hernan laughed. He was a rough one. Stubbly chin, broad, strong shoulders, and he was clearly concerned about his own neck. Emilio understood this. He'd grown up with it. The Mexican countryside wasn't exactly a gentle way of life. It was hard and challenging and often produced men with their own set of rules, determined to survive, and take what they needed, or wanted, no matter the consequences.

The drink was taking effect. The men were getting rowdy now. The bottle, now empty, disappeared, and Olga set up another. Emilio wasn't counting shots, but time was short, and he needed to take advantage of this little side trip. Soon they'd all be drunk, and he might be left in this forlorn place with nothing to show for it and no way back to the estancia. He had to make a move.

"Hernan! Where does this Margarita live? I want to talk to her, ask a couple of questions. Some of my family lived in Argentina. Years ago. On a farm."

Hernan's eyes opened wide beneath his dark, bushy brows. "*Ché, boludo.* A regular boyo of the pampa."

"No, I'm a Mexican farmer. Working the land, the horses."

"You are no horse rider." Tavi, one of the hands, laughed and threw back a shot. "But you have *cojones*. I drink to that!" Now they all laughed.

Emilio downed another shot. "I need some air. What say I take a walk in the village? I'll be back here shortly." He wasn't sure of the direction he'd take, but he wanted to keep them talking and drinking for a little longer. It was good they'd loosened up. One thing for sure, he'd be the driver on their way back to the ranch. "Do you know where this Margarita lives?"

"You take English lessons now?" one of the gauchos yelled. Another round of drinks, another round of laughter—at his expense. He could feel the heat rising at the back of his neck.

"*Luego.*" Emilio lifted his hand. He was inclined to give them the universal gesture but thought better of it.

"Go look around, you want. Olga has stew, we will eat." Hernan was no longer laughing. "You walk and come back here for a bowl."

Emilio nodded. "*Listo.*" He walked to the door, looked back briefly, and pushed out onto the street. It was getting late, but a soft light still hovered on the buildings and trees. He strolled away from the tavern and took a dusty side street off the plaza. It was hardly a street, more like a semi-paved rough stretch of dirt and rock. The village was small, and the streets were deserted, except for two kids with a soccer ball and a skinny dog. He hoped to find someone who knew Margarita. Surely everyone knew everybody in this place.

A small laundry down the block sent humid puffs of sunshine-scented air through the open door. Despite the hour, two women were industriously stuffing a machine and folding clothes. Emilio stood inside the door.

"*Perdón.*"

The two women looked up in surprise. "*Buenas,*" came the response.

"I am looking for the home of Margarita Goyez. Can you help me? I am a friend."

The short woman at first looked startled. She hurried to the door, smiling warmly, her immaculate apron tucked around her neat little frame. She pointed across the street toward a nut tree and a couple of pin oaks, and not far off, a small yellow stucco cottage nestled in the foliage.

"But I do not think she is there. I have not seen her in many days now."

Emilio smiled, bowed, and casually walked away. He waited and made certain his wandering went undetected, then he hurried across the street toward Margarita's house. The yard was strewn with a carpet of leaves and broken grasses, the front stoop crowded with neglected geraniums struggling for sunlight and water. Still, the house was neat and seemed well cared for. He felt a pang of regret, for not getting here sooner, for missteps that might have hastened Margarita's death. He should have warned her away. Too little, too late. He had no part in her death, but that didn't matter; guilt had a funny way of playing a role, invading the brain like a virus.

The windows were clean and free of drapery. Emilio peeked into a small living room crammed with books, knick-knacks, an overstuffed chair, and a fireplace. Despite the number of items, the room had a spare, empty look. He went around back. The door was locked, but the window next to it was not. He opened it and clambered into a small kitchen. The appliances seemed designed for a small person—a two-burner stove and a three-foot-high refrigerator. Some cheese and a few withered peppers sat on a small table with covered jars and a bunch of dried flowers. Near the window, a rack of laundry laid to dry stood off to the side. No one had been in the house for at least several days. The stale air of the closed space was depressing and reeked of a dead end.

Emilio crossed his arms and looked around, sadness overtaking him. *What am I doing in here? How will this ever help me get to know my Aunt Margarita?*

Papers. There had to be papers, mementos, clues to whom she was and what she'd lived through at La Palma. He poked around, but the cottage was small with little space for cabinets and storage.

He opened a few drawers in a desk in the living room, scoured the one bookshelf. Took out a couple of books and shook them. He went into a bedroom with a single bed made up in white damask and crocheted lace. Like the other rooms, it was stuffy with a vague, dying floral scent that lingered. This, it seemed, was all that he had left of her. "I am so very sorry, Tía Margarita." He picked up a book of Borges poetry on the bedside table. Beneath it was a stack of Jane Austen works. A small dresser held some neatly folded night dresses.

The last of the sunlight shined on the small chintz-covered chair next to the bedroom window. He imagined his aunt's slippered feet on the footstool, the small pillow at her neck. The chair was comfy with a nice view of the backyard. He sat staring at the loopy branches of an old tree, enjoying the view as much as she must have. The stitching on the arm was loose, and his fingers idly twisted it. He shifted and an object poked him in the leg. Another book. Stuck down in the cushion. He pulled it out. It wasn't another book but a leather-bound journal. No larger than his hand. It was filled with pages and pages of legible writing in Spanish on tightly spaced blue lines.

The back door banged open. *"¡Oyez!"*

He tucked the book in the front of his trousers under his shirt and jumped to his feet. No time to run. He'd have to face it. A charge of trespassing.

He started toward the door and ran directly into Hernan.

"Why you in here?" He grinned slyly.

"I could ask you the same thing."

A shrug seemed to be his main mode of communication. The smell of whiskey nearly floored Emilio. The gaucho's eyes were red, and he swayed precariously.

"I need to see her. Do you know where she is?"

"She not here," yelled Hernan.

"I can hear. You don't have to shout."

"Why you looking? You want lessons? I don't think so." He threw his head back and guffawed.

"No, I don't want lessons. She's a friend of my friend."

"Forget it. You tell friend not to look. Not you, not him." He turned to leave and made it clear he wanted Emilio to follow. "We have to get back to the estancia. There's work to finish." He gawked at Emilio. "I think you have a big nose, and that is not good. You put that nose away."

Emilio insisted on driving. The men threatened to beat him up, but all climbed into the Jeep, except Hernan. He started down a gravelly road back to the estancia.

"Hernan! Get in the jeep!" Emilio shouted.

"No bother," one of the men said. "He run off the whiskey."

The gauchos were raucously drunk, but when Emilio drove away, their jovial attitude turned somber and moody. Emilio clenched the wheel, following Tavi's slurred directions, and prayed he could steer over this pocky road through desolation. At least he had the journal. He patted his stomach and felt the outline of it tucked away. Something dear, if he ever made it back alive. Something that might help find his aunt.

Seventeen

Day Two, Reboot

"WE CAN'T GO BACK INTO the chapel now." Blanche had shared her discovery of the treasure beneath the chapel floor. He was full of questions, and she had few answers. Emilio wanted to go down into the room full of crates, but they were going to have to figure a way back without being found out. There were eyes everywhere; she was sure of it. She showed Emilio the list she'd taken out of a crate. "This. Look at this."

He held the brittle paper and his expression paled. "I know enough German to know these things are valuable. It's an inventory, a pretty hasty one. Of items from a temple in Wurzburg."

"And I know enough about Germany to know that Wurzburg is near Schweinfurt. That's Herr Schemmer's hometown."

Emilio shook the paper. "Do you think ... ?"

"All I can come up with is that they stole this stuff from Jewish temples and homes and somehow brought it over here, or, in the very least, were instrumental in moving it here. That list is a piece of evidence."

"*Aye, Dios.*"

"Yes." Blanche folded the paper carefully and stuck it in a book in her bag. She climbed back on the bed next to Emilio. "Let's have a look at that journal you found. Maybe it has a clue to some of the secrets around here."

Blanche had slipped down to the living room and brought up the crystal decanter and two glasses. She and Emilio huddled on the bed, tapped their glasses of whiskey, and read over Margarita's writing.

The days are long. So long.

I need to leave here but Gerda has other plans.

I miss Issie.

I heard them today. A phone call from the United States, but I couldn't understand. A man here in the Capital knows them …

When are they coming … ?

Blanche took a deep breath. "Emilio! Who do you think these people are? Who is coming?"

"That is a good question. The authorities, maybe? Us?" He looked at her quizzically, sat back against the headboard, and paged through the journal. "But most of this goes back. Years. No names; nothing more. She's fearful, I see. It's vague, *mi amor*, but it backs up what *Tía* said in her letters. Which I don't have with me." He held up the journal.

"Seems to relate to that note we found earlier. *No más, por fin.* It is evident that she was sick of these people."

"We don't really know what the note meant." He turned several more pages, a furrow between his eyebrows.

"It's the details," she said. "It's always that. The small details."

He tilted his head and smiled. "Here's one detail. Come here."

He planted a kiss on her lips. Blanche curled up against him and peered at the journal. "She writes about calls from the US and Buenos Aires. 'They are coming.' This must be related to the things she overheard. Don't you think?"

"I guess it's not us. This part goes back a ways, and it could mean anything. *Who's coming?*" He closed the book and carefully stuffed it under his pillow, then scooted lower on the bed, pulling Blanche next to him. He looked exhausted and disheveled—and slightly hungover. "I have to sleep. We are going to figure this out in the morning."

"It is morning."

"It's dark outside, *Baquita*," he murmured. "Sleep."

Immediately, he began snoring. He looked like someone had run him over. Running with the gauchos, surviving Argentina. She sighed.

First thing in the morning, Blanche intended to look into the comings and goings of the Schemmers. Dig around in the library and den. Look through their office. She wasn't sure how she was going to get in there, but there had to be a way—with them out of the way. There had to be records. A paper trail. No one ran an enterprise like this or kept the details of the stash under the chapel without jotting a note or two. Just to keep track of their dirty work and their lies.

Blanche and Emilio slept until after nine o'clock and then went to the sunny patio at the end of the house for breakfast. The table was set with white linen, lilies, and gold-rimmed china. The smell of coffee and baked bread should have lifted Blanche's spirits, but she was too wired.

No one was around, but she whispered, "Ok, what do we have so far?"

"The journal ... and the treasure under the chapel." Emilio held a piece of toast and waved it distractedly. Blanche took it from him and put some jam on it. Handed it back. "Theft? All that gold? Did they steal it, or are they storing it for someone? And still no Margarita."

"We really shouldn't talk here." She leaned closer. "Wonder if Margarita knew something about that chapel business."

They picked up their coffee and moved out onto the lawn to the benches under an acacia tree. The morning light was soft and warm, deceptively peaceful on the beautiful landscape.

"Those phone calls she mentioned. Maybe there were buyers for the loot showing up. People who supported the Schemmers. The government was infiltrated with sympathizers during all those years of war." Emilio squinted against the sun, absently holding the coffee cup at an angle.

"We need to get in that house and look around." Blanche stared fiercely at the far windows in the back of La Palma.

"The look on your face, Blanche. How are we going to do that?"

"I don't know. Yet." She smiled at Emilio, sweetly. "What else did you find out in the village?"

"Not much. My adventure with the gauchos got me the journal." He placed the palm of his hand against his forehead. "And a headache."

Blanche laughed. "Serves you right."

"Margarita's house was a nice little place, well kept, and not much else. It looked like she'd been gone for at least a few days." Now he was glum again.

"That doesn't tell us an awful lot, does it?" She tapped a finger on her lower lip. "Unless ... Lusita knows about those calls, too. She must. She's always around."

"Really? Why do you say that?"

"She's the one who said to give the chapel a good going-over, and lo and behold. She's either got big ears, or something," Blanche whispered. "I don't know if she meant for me to find the gold, but I did. That girl knows things. I'm sure of it."

"I don't like dragging her into this. The Schemmers could make her life miserable."

"More miserable, you mean. That's just it, Emilio, I'd like to help her. Get her out of this place. That is, if she wants to go." Blanche pursed her lips. "In the meantime, I'd like to press her for more info. See if she knows about the treasure. She already offered … kind of."

"Blanche. I don't know. Let's back off Lusita for now. All right?"

"Then what do we do?"

They put their heads together to ward off paranoia, both deep in thought.

Lusita hurried in and out of the patio with fresh linen for the table and vases of flowers. Her head was down, seemingly oblivious to Blanche and Emilio sitting on the lawn. Blanche tried to catch her eye, but Lusita was gone like a wisp.

"Look. I want to poke around here when the Schemmers are out. And there are still plenty of places we should look for Margarita," said Blanche. "Maybe the tower."

Emilio tried to hide his concern at this suggestion, but Blanche could read the lines on his face like she was reading a book. "And then we get caught and end up like Margarita. We have to be careful around these people," he said. "I don't want you putting yourself in any more danger. Bad enough already."

"I'll be very careful. I do ask a lot of questions, but, so far, they seem to dismiss me as nothing more than a super inquisitive, and annoying, tourist."

"I hope so." He took her hand and squeezed, trying earnestly to get her undivided attention. "It's time for the police."

"We will. But not yet." Her wheels went round and round. "I'm thinking we should call Tomás."

"*What?* He's the one who sent us out here with that driver!"

"There has to be some explanation for that. A coincidence? A plan gone wrong? I don't know. The whole thing seems strange. I really think Tomás is a good guy. Basically, and truly."

"What makes you say that?"

"A hunch? I want to talk to him. Not reveal too much but see what he knows about this place. What other contact do we have? Like Lusita, I think he knows a lot."

"I'd rather call a taxi to get us out of here. Or maybe call the hotel for a driver. They'd be able to send someone. I want to get us out of here in one piece."

"I know you do, but we can't go yet, Emilio. You know that," she said gently.

He slumped down on the bench. He looked so lost. Blanche didn't know whether to shake him or kiss him, or both.

She took his fist, clenched on his lap, opened it and laced her fingers in his. "Emilio. I say we scour this place and keep looking for Margarita. One way or another, we have to find her. We need to snoop up a storm."

He ran a hand through his hair. "I give it one more day. Then we call authorities."

"We've only been here a couple of days."

"And look what's happened! Things are not getting better!"

"Heaven knows we need a miracle," she said. And then, it happened. She tore herself from Emilio's sad expression and glanced out across the lawn as the sound of gravel crunched the driveway. A bronze Mercedes rounded the corner of the house and headed for the curve out front. Blanche caught sight of silver hair in the passenger's seat and the large head of Herr Schemmer at the wheel. Just the two of them. Leaving.

"Oh, wow!" Blanche wanted to do jumping jacks, but, for once, she contained herself. "Look Emilio!" She shook his fingers still entwined in hers. Together, they gleefully gazed after the trail of smoke from the Mercedes. "Think we just got ourselves a break. Our miracle."

Eighteen
Ring A Ding Ding

THEY STROLLED AWAY FROM THE HOUSE, hand in hand. The morning was bright, the sun shining on the pink buildings and darkened windows. Blanche felt a strong sense of purpose. A burst of energy and confidence. But she was pulled in different directions. Where to start? They had a lot of ground to cover before the Schemmers' return.

Blanche pointed across the lawn. She folded her arms and stared at the tower. "Remember, I told you I saw someone in that window?"

"Yes, and you couldn't get in."

"Now is a good time for us to investigate."

"That person you saw, it couldn't be Margarita. Could it?"

"Emilio!" she said, as softly as she could, "I found her. Quite … immobile."

"So hard to believe this could happen," he murmured.

They were close to the tower. "There's a door, *Baquita*."

"It hasn't been opened in forever. I can't figure out how someone got in there." She looked up to the third story windows.

"Unless whoever is in there has been there for a long time. Or you're seeing things."

"I'm *not* crazy, Emilio"

Emilio looked at her sideways. "I believe you. I do." He pulled her to his side and scanned this side of the tower. The two of them stood there staring up at the large, round stucco surface. "Now. In case we're being watched. We're just two lovebirds out for a walk. Right?"

"You mean like this?" Blanche reached up on her tiptoes and kissed him.

"Yeah, just like that."

"So, what should we do first? Take a nap?"

"Emilio!" That handsome face, those eyes. He always smelled so good. One more minute and she might take him up on it. "Come on. Be serious! We gotta make good use of the time. Before the Schemmers get back. Maybe we should get inside their office while we have the chance. And I have to show you the chapel treasure. And we have to find a way to get up in this tower."

"Whoa!" He sighed. "All right."

"We've already checked out most of the grounds, and since we can't get in here, we should check out the house."

He didn't fool her for a second with that surprised look. "Look where? Their office? Their bedroom? The library?"

"Exactly."

"OK. I'll meet you in the library," Emilio said. He seemed to perk up now that they were on the move. "After I do a quick hunt of the grounds again."

"Gotcha. I'm going to the kitchen first. To talk to Lusita."

They were still holding hands. "Be careful," he said. "Come and find me."

She peered up at him. His eyebrows drew together in consternation. "Oh, I'll find you all right." Emilio slid his fingers from hers, the warmth gone, and he walked away.

Blanche headed to the kitchen. She didn't want any surprises from staff or from the Schemmers should they return and find her and Emilio poking through drawers and such. She needed to get an idea of their schedules. She might actually have a chance at getting Lusita to open up, now that the Frau wasn't around scaring her silly.

Lusita was seated at the large pine table in the staff dining area. She was drinking tea and working on a jigsaw puzzle. When she saw Blanche, she bolted out of her chair, almost knocking it over.

Blanche raised her hands in greeting. "Hi there."

"*¡Hola,* señorita! Is everything all right?"

"Of course." *Not.* She was a liar, just like the rest of them. "Just wondering when the Schemmers might return. I saw them drive off."

"They have errands and a visit at the Constaneda's estancia. They won't be back for several hours. Maybe half a day or so? Can I help you?"

"Actually, you've already helped me. A lot. Thanks." Stacks of suspicious crates of gold gleamed in Blanche's head.

Lusita opened her mouth, but nothing came out.

Blanche waited for the girl to continue. In vain. Lusita returned to the puzzle.

Gently, Blanche said, "Lusita. I do have a question, which I've asked before, and, forgive me, I must ask again. Can you please tell me about Margarita, the nanny? Did she stay here at the estancia?"

"I told you, Señorita, she is retired. I don't see her. Anymore." She picked at the puzzle with a look of fake concentration.

"And the tower? Is there a way to reach the tower? I'd swear I saw someone in the window of the tower yesterday. Who's up there?"

"*Imposible.* There is no one there." She bent closer to the tabletop and swung away from Blanche's earnest gaze. Her face reddened with the lie.

"For certain. I must be seeing things then," said Blanche in a dry, measured tone. She'd take her time with this. "Seeing things, for example, in the chapel. Thanks for the tip, by the way."

Lusita's fingers shot to her lips. "What did you see there?"

"It was an interesting visit. There'll be more about it. Later. But don't worry. Please. The Schemmers will find out I was there when it's time, and they won't know you advised me to check it out."

The girl deflated, her anxiety escaping in a vapor.

Blanche didn't want to stir Lusita up further. She'd done enough already. She'd wanted information, and she got what she'd come for. For now. The Schemmers were out. She hurried off to snoop and meet Emilio.

Lusita was definitely lying about Margarita and about the tower. She knew far more than she was willing to say, and Blanche was determined to one day wheedle it out of her. It wouldn't do any good to force the issue just yet. At some point, though, Blanche would bring it all together—if they could only find Margarita!

Blanche crossed the house to the library where Emilio said he'd meet her later. The scent of lemon polish emanated from the shiny surfaces and mixed with that of pink lilies in a crystal vase in the hall. In the living room, the sun slanted through the window. It was so lovely, but like so much at La Palma, the luster was skin-deep.

Thankfully, it wasn't noon yet; they had plenty of time. She stood in the doorway to the library.

"Emilio?" He wasn't there or in the adjacent den. She walked through to a game room and an outer room where galoshes and rain gear were lined up in white cubbies and bins. She glanced out the window at a magnificent sweep of grassland ablaze in the brilliant sun. The land shone golden, the tall sheaves swaying in the breeze.

She had to move on. She backtracked to the small office area in the library and went to a mahogany desk in front of a multi-paned window. Books lined one wall, and several leather chairs were arranged around a low glass table. What kind of business happened here? Talk of selling smuggled goods, fast horses, and farm products? Tourist business? It seemed the Schemmers might be very busy in the commerce department.

The drawers to the desk were not locked. Neat ledgers and letters were piled inside. Mostly in German, Italian, and Spanish. Very little English, and all of it in orderly columns and figures. Most of it had to do with running the tourist trade, food and supplies, and payrolls. Nothing looked amiss, but it was hard to tell. Blanche knew from past experience—in Ireland and Mexico, to name two of her destinations of impromptu sleuthing—the good stuff was usually locked away. She poked around for filing cabinets and boxes to break into and for hidden keys. She came up empty.

She roamed around the shelves full of books. Blanche loved books, but in this instance, she was hoping for a different sort of experience. Surely, as in all those mystery shows with bookshelves that opened to secret safes and passages, she'd find something. Where was the dramatic reveal?

She walked over to the window where a bust of the Greek god, Kratos, sat on a pedestal. "Kratos," Blanche said, as she ran her hand over the bust. "God of might and power and sovereign rule." *Right.*

The room was tidy, lovely, and hiding something. Then, as in all things Blanche, irritation took over, and like a hot little ribbon in her gut it burst into flame. *Surely something has to be here!* Her fingers skipped over the top of the desk, picked up the blotter, and flapped it over. Nothing. She yanked the desk drawer open again and felt along the bottom of the interior for keys. Everything, everywhere seemed so orderly, and confounding. So many events, so many lies, and the mystery of this place! *And where the hell did Emilio go off to now?* She peered out the window toward the outbuildings. He always seemed to be disappearing.

"Damn!" She turned and slammed her fist down on the edge of the desk, and instantly, she heard an audible click. A pop. She stared at the panel at the end of the polished mahogany surface. A door opened some four feet away in the wall of bookcases. Blanche nearly whooped. She covered her mouth. That hot, little flame of irritation turned to adrenalin.

She'd been looking for papers, but she'd take this. She went to the secret door and stuck her head into the opening. Just a couple of feet inside was a passage into the dark. Trying to make sense of her find, she came away and peered out the window. Indeed, this side of the house was up against a sloping berm, camouflaged with rose bushes and tall grasses. She looked back toward the bookcase and fetched a penlight she'd come across in a desk drawer. A light would be necessary, for sure. All the better to inspect this hide-away. She also had the Leatherman. Her heart thumped with the discovery of the opening. She shined the light into the darkness.

Then, she stopped. It would not do for her to just disappear. Plenty of that had already happened. She tested the door. It hung on a spring with no lock. She would be able to get back in, she was sure, without someone opening the door from the desk. Well, as sure as she could be. In this case, as in most, curiosity outweighed caution.

The opening was low and narrow. The beam of light illuminated a tunnel of hard packed dirt. Her grandmother's words went off in her head as if she were right there with her. *Keep your wits about you, girl. And another thing, don't go running off half-cocked.* Words of wisdom she had tested many times—finding trouble wherever she went. *I'll just have a quick look around and come right back.*

It was an abrupt descent. The dirt landing gave way to narrow, stone steps wedged into the ground. All the better to access a dungeon. Her heart was in her throat, but she would persevere, gingerly stepping down down down. At the bottom, she landed on a level spit of ground that led straight ahead. The feeble light revealed nothing but dirt. Walls, floor, ceiling. Hard-packed, damp-smelling dirt.

Creeping along underground, she found it difficult to gauge the distance and direction, but all the while she went deeper, it slowly came to her. This passage led away from the main house and almost certainly ended at one of the outbuildings. *The chapel? The tower?*

She kept walking. The tunnel branched off to the left. A beam of light swept over a narrow opening in the wall. Inside, the view was obstructed. She reached in. Crates! And beyond, across the hard-packed ground, was a ladder. Everything was just as she'd left it. In her haste to get out of the chapel yesterday, in confusion and disgust, she'd missed this spot where she now stood.

She straightened up and kept walking through this endless warren of surprises. It was eerie to think she'd been here before, but in another dimension on the other side of this wall and above ground. Her weird sense of place wrapped around her in the darkness. At five feet, Blanche was an easy fit down here, but a tall man would have to stoop. The narrow passage was easily accessible, and, perhaps, easy to fill in and destroy in the event of discovery. Her mind raced with questions over the details of this tomb of secrets. *Why all this?*

Soon she came to another small room. Packed dirt and empty, except for a ladder made of the same rope and slats like that under the chapel floor. The flashlight beam shimmied up the ladder, and sure enough, a square opening overhead suggested a way out.

Without hesitation, she climbed.

Nineteen

The Secret People

IT WAS A SHORT CLIMB to the top of the ladder. The light from above ground gleamed through the cracks around the opening. Blanche put doubts aside that she was up against a barrier. One thing she possessed, besides a fierce determination, was sheer physical strength. Swimming in the Gulf for thirty years had developed muscles in her arms and legs, which often came in handy.

From the top rung, she pushed at the cover. It gave some. She was relieved it was not as tight as the one in the chapel floor. She took out the Leatherman and worked around the edges, then gave the section a couple of whacks with the side of her fist. It resisted but finally came loose. She scooted the cover aside and stuck her head up into a bright—rounded—room.

No mistake about it. She'd arrived in the tower.

It was a slight tussle over the rim of the opening and onto the floor in a heap, but she made it. *Now what?*

It seemed to be decided for her. Footsteps—heavy ones—pounded toward her. Before she could hide, or think what to do, a tall, thin, pale man dressed in tight, black pants and shirt stood in the doorway, hands on hips, with a smirk a mile wide. His narrow face was topped with a thatch of black, wiry hair, and his eyes were the darkest she'd ever seen. No light in them at all. He reminded her of a punk rocker of the most dubious sort. But this guy was not about to sing her a song. He looked pissed and not too surprised to see her at all.

Speechless, she sat on her heels and folded her arms. He spoke first: "It was a matter of time."

"What?"

"Before we met. I am Guli, or Big G, if you wish."

He's been expecting me?

"Hello, G ... I'm in the tower, right?"

"You are right. You are also very nosy. Why you come up out of there like a mole? Why the snooping?"

He was right about her snooping. She still asked, "Why do you say that?"

"Because. I know. Eyes are everywhere. Have you not figured that out by now?"

Now that Blanche thought about it—cameras! They were probably all over the place, but where? Of course, she hadn't really been looking for them, either.

An urge to retreat back down into the hole gripped her, but that wasn't going to happen. The man walked toward her. Her spine straightened. She would not cower. *Do not show fear.* Instead, she'd turn these tremulous doubts inside out like she'd done so many times before. An instinct for survival was strong, and so was her ability to think on her feet. She stood up and nudged the cover back in place with her foot, casually, as if this were an everyday visit. A fine layer of dust coated her arms, and she could feel a sneeze working its way out. She fought it, rubbed her nose, and finally gave up.

"*Gesundheit!*" His expression relaxed, and then he went back to stoney face. An arresting, handsome face.

She extended a hand. "I'm Blanche Murninghan. Nice to meet you, Big G."

He didn't shake hands with her. In fact, he didn't move; she could see the hesitation in his eyes. Maybe deep down he wasn't so scary after all. That assumption, however, might be her first mistake. She stepped back. This guy was far from a soft touch. He did not emanate charm—or weakness—and that steely look was disconcerting. Confusing.

"Why you not be a good tourist and enjoy and go away?" He muttered the last.

"But I am ... a good tourist. Good as gold." She choked on the last word, thinking of the treasure under the chapel.

"Humph." He turned sideways and beckoned her to follow with a jerk of his chin.

She measured the situation. Should she follow him? Actually, she didn't have much choice. Pop the cover off the hole and drop down quickly? He could overpower her before that happened. So, she'd better follow him. The hospitality around here was beginning to stink. And this guy, she was sure, was not about to divulge the location of Margarita and Emilio, nor offer anything helpful.

"After you." Guli waved his arm like a game show host.

They climbed a winding staircase. Windows at odd levels dotted the round wall of the tower and gave the enclosure a stark picture of darkness and light. Outside, nothing but vast green space. What had she gotten herself into now?

She shut off the wandering thoughts and focused on the moment. Was he going to throw her from the roof? Her legs stiffened when she thought about that. It was too late for retreat. Her heart pounded with every footfall of those leaden boots behind her.

They ascended the stairs, and Blanche stopped to glance out a window. The pink house and the tiny figure of a landscaper with a rake stood off in the distance. They had to be twenty feet up. Her thoughts shifted to yesterday, to the figure she'd seen in the tower window. What level would that have been? *And who is up here?* Guli poked a finger in her back, wordlessly.

He stepped past Blanche and opened a door. A woman sat in a straight-back chair, the points of her black shoes sticking out from beneath the folds of her long black dress. She wore a light veil of some sort on her tightly coiffed gray hair. *Whistler's Mother?* She'd once heard that the painter's mother was actually quite lovely and sweet and not as bleak as her son had portrayed. And not as chilly as this lady seemed to be. She stared at Blanche. The woman looked fragile with a sad, penetrating gaze. Her mouth was a slit, and her cheeks were smooth as polished stone. Blanche had no doubt she was related to Guli "Big G." Her eyes were the same dark, impenetrable black as Guli's. She must have been practicing that stare every day. She was very good at it.

"*Buenas dias,*" Blanche said, cheerily. Big G stood at the doorway, his hands behind his back, feet planted wide apart.

"This is the Señora Esmera Leona, the widow of José Bartolo de Losada Iglesias," he said, looking straight ahead.

Bartolo? The Caudillo?

"You are the widow of the Caudillo?" asked Blanche, incredulous. She took a step toward the woman. "The owner of La Palma?" Blanche forgot all reticence and niceties and got right to the point.

The Señora's dark eyes and thin lips didn't change. *Maybe she doesn't speak English.* But then the corners of her mouth turned up. Was that a smile? Blanche would take any form of hospitality. The coldness in the room dissipated some.

"I am," Esmera said, "and you are the curious *norteamericana?*" Her voice was low, like a bass drum, and a little creepy.

"Yes, I am. My name is Blanche. From Florida, actually, and I admit … I am … curious."

"You know the expression? Curiosity kills the *gato?* Yes?"

"Yes, but I hope my attentiveness doesn't end things. I hope." Blanche felt a new, uncomfortable definition for her nosiness. The back of her neck prickled, and she began to sweat. Her stomach was turning flip flops. She was a clueless chihuahua standing up to a formidable lion. However, she was a determined chihuahua, and at the moment, she would have given anything to hightail it out of there. With a glance at Guli, she saw the impossibility of that.

The air was static and dusty in this bare, round space with no color. A mussed, white satin throw lay piled on a day bed with several tasseled pillows. Her eye fell on a table with a tray of china cups and a single white rose in a vase. That was about it. Not exactly the accoutrements of home. But the capper was the attitude of her hosts.

She really needed to get out of there.

She was irritable again, a feeling that came over Blanche like an allergic reaction. "It's been nice meeting you." She took a step as if to leave. Guli stepped forward. No question, she wasn't going anywhere. She'd have to play their little game.

Patience, Blanche.

She steeled herself. Hell, she'd come this far, and she couldn't see another way around it. If she were stuck here, she might as well get what she came for. More information.

She smiled at the two would-be captors and pulled a chair up close to Esmera. Guli made a move, but the old lady put her hand up. "So, Señora? You are the owner of La Palma? And you live up here?" Blanche's tone was warm and friendly and as measured as she could make it.

"*Sí.*"

"I may have seen you before." Blanche was aware she was jiggling her foot. "You weren't, by any chance, standing in the window yesterday afternoon? Looking out at the grounds?"

The Señora raised an eyebrow. "Why would I do that?"

"I'm not sure. Maybe because you wanted to look at this beautiful landscape because ... you are kept here in the tower. Out of the way?"

"No." Señora raised her head in defiance and turned away. "It is complicated."

Why is everything around here complicated?

Blanche threw up her hands but kept it light. "If La Palma is yours, why don't you live in the big house?" She glanced from Esmera to Guli.

"These things ... these are not your business," said Esmera.

Blanche had no intention of backing off. She looked around the small round room. "Seems rather inconvenient living here. I mean, going out for necessities, getting fresh air and such. Through that hole in the floor." She had no idea where she was going with this line of conversation, but it was better than sitting here, dealing with this bottled-up tension. "Bottled-up" was not her forte.

Guli watched silently. He turned and took a step toward Blanche with a sneer. "We do not go through the hole in the floor. It is only for the *moles*."

"Moles?" She was not fond of being called a furry, rat-like creature. Then it occurred to Blanche. "Are there other moles?"

Neither one answered her question.

"The underground life. We do not do that. There is another entrance, of course. For the normal persons," Guli said.

Normal persons? "Really? Another entrance? Besides the tunnel? I took a walk around here yesterday and didn't come across an outside entrance to the tower. The vines are pretty thick, and the day was getting on when I was looking. Kind of ran out of time."

His eyes narrowed. "You must have missed it."

"If you don't mind my asking, where is it?"

"I do mind." He crossed his arms.

Blanche pivoted. "And, by the way, just curious ... What's with the tunnel? Seems a strange addition to a ranch. I mean, estancia."

"Ancient history." His sharp tone startled her.

"Please. Share this with me. I love ancient history."

He leaned back against the wall, one boot crossed over the other. "The pampa is wild. And the family de Losada Iglesias made hiding places. They dug out passages and rooms to escape the renegades while the conquerors and the government exterminated millions of *pueblos indígenas.* Survivors of these exterminations often revolted against authority. It is a sad and confusing history, but what history is not?"

He had a point. The history of Argentina was a long, winding road of individualism, strife, and glory.

"And here? At La Palma?"

"*Sí.*"

Guli held his arms tightly against his middle, his eyes grew even darker and his tone petulant, righteous. "The caudillos ruled. My father was a strong one who employed native Argentinians, and he was good to them. But still ..." His voice trailed off. "There are dozens of tribes here. Often, the families, the descendants, do not get along. They put one against the other, and against authority. Like their ancestors, they will not bow to the government and the conquerors. The killing on all sides went on for centuries. It divided the people. Made them desperate. The fighting isolated families, towns, estancias. Such as this. It was necessary for them to hide from trouble. They fought for their land and rights, and the fight was difficult. Including here at La Palma." His speech was halting, at first, and then he sped to the end as he returned his mother's steady gaze. She set her shoulders and nodded. He looked back at Blanche. "Argentina is a land of troubles."

"Ancient history" had clearly simmered in Guli for some time. Blanche wasn't sorry she'd brought it up, but she was sorry for their pain. Esmera stared past her son, out the window, just the wisp of a smile on her lips. The distance in her eyes told Blanche that the woman may as well have been on the moon. Her mind didn't seem to be with them.

Despite the cold welcome from these two, Blanche could sense a change. With Guli's revelation of history and more perspective on Argentina, she drew closer to understanding him and his country. There was so much here, such a mix of politics, and cultures, and trouble. Blanche was a kin of trouble.

She nodded at Guli. "Thank you."

He tilted his head. "Why?"

"For telling me about your country. Argentina is hard to sort. Your words, your emotion, you've helped me understand it a little better. A very little, given there is so much."

The smile reached his dark eyes. Argentina had suffered and was still suffering, and she could tell that he was, too. She smiled back.

She'd been pacing nervously, then sitting. Up and down, so it went. Now she stood and looked at him earnestly. "Guli, have you ever been down in that tunnel?" She thought of the gold under the chapel.

"No. Why would I? I can leave by the door."

"Is that the only tunnel?"

"Questions. So many questions for a visitor on holiday," Esmera said.

Hmmm. Maybe they don't know. She doubted it. Truly, things were complicated.

"Just wondering." She looked around the room. Spare and clean, but it didn't measure up to the luxurious accommodations at the main house. "Are you comfortable here? The estancia is yours, and the raids have stopped. Can't you move on?" She meant move *out* of here and go to the big house.

Mother and son looked at her with the same expression of incredulity. "Now, why do you ask that?" Guli asked.

"I mean, really, wouldn't you rather have more space? Enjoy those lovely rooms in the main house and the patio?" She took in the spare, round room. Again, she was being nosey, but it was such an easy thing for Blanche to do. She had to push. That was the only way she seemed to get any information and make some headway.

Guli sighed, Esmera turned away. They seemed reticent to answer, so Blanche persisted. "Have you ever heard shooting here? Now, or in the past?"

"Shootings?" He looked genuinely perplexed.

"Oh, say, during the *Proceso*, for instance. It certainly was a bad time. For all things ..."

"I was a child. My father died. The Schemmers have had a hold on La Palma for decades."

None of it added up. None of it except that the Schemmers had been here since after World War Two, and they had slowly increased their power and solidified it, probably with the death of Bartolo.

"Enough of the questions," said Guli. He waved her off and walked over to his mother's side. His hand rested on the back of her chair. Thin fingers patted her son's hand while she smiled at Blanche.

"I suspect you are innocent of deceit, Señorita," said Esmera. "And I admire your ... direct approach. I feel you have pure interests in mind."

That's a first. Nobody had ever accused her of being pure of anything.

"That's a lovely thing to say," Blanche said. "Thank you." The comment was an opening, and Blanche took it. "Can you ... will you tell me what's going on here?" Blanche scooted her chair closer to the Señora and clasped her hands between her knees. She didn't glance at Guli for fear of getting stuck with a reproving glance and a brusque dismissal.

"It is mine." She lifted a gnarled hand and gestured toward the window. A gold band adorned her left ring finger, her skin like old parchment. She waved at the pink house and the extensive grasslands.

"I don't understand."

The Señora chuckled softly. "We are prisoners of the culture ... and of the Schemmers. I am *puebla indígena*. *Toba*. I married a man of Spanish descent, but I had no rights to the land when he died. In 1985, the government passed a law for indigenous rights, and under that law I should have ownership of La Palma. But the officials are slow to implement it, and the Schemmers, they have taken advantage with the help of friends in the Capital. To delay. They maintain a hold on the property." Her words were clear and firm.

Puebla indígena. First people. Argentina counted three dozen indigenous groups. The Mapuche, Diaguita, Guarani, Quechua, Malón, and, yes, the Toba.

Guli said, "I am her son, Juan Guillermo."

Esmera studied Blanche with piercing eyes. To gauge her intentions? It made Blanche uncomfortable, but she accepted it. Esmera was fully present.

"If I leave this place, I will never be able to come back. So, I will not leave. I have come to an accommodation with the Schemmers. I cannot make changes now."

"The Schemmers. They are special ... hosts," Blanche said, carefully. "They have not been open with me and Emilio, and, apparently, not with you, either."

"No, that is not their way. As I said, it's an arrangement. They allow us to stay on, and I do not push them to go away and leave us. They do keep La Palma going ..." Her last words trailed off.

"Do you know where they came from? What they brought with them?" *The gold under the chapel, for example.*

Esmera looked at Blanche, her gaze sharp. "It's been a long time. They came after the war when they were young. They brought nothing but one beaten-up suitcase between them. They worked and took over many duties as Bartolo and I aged, and then, finally, all of it. I remained involved with the kitchen and staff and running the house. Until they moved us here to the tower. I can't tell you much more about the Schemmers, except for that. They are secretive. They always have been that way."

Blanche needed to leave—after a bit more probing. Emilio was probably frantically looking for her, but the history of this place was so compelling she couldn't bring herself to quit questioning them, especially about the one thing that she was determined to find out.

She leaned forward. "I'm wondering if you could tell me about Margarita Goyez? We've come looking for her, but she doesn't seem to be around."

With that, Blanche hit the hot button. Esmera's demeanor changed from warm and accommodating to hot and expressive—akin to a human volcano. Anger shot from her eyes; her fingers clutched the arms of the chair. She tried to get up and fell back with a soft thump. Guli hurried over and held her shoulders, murmuring something in Spanish. He yanked the shawl off the floor and settled it over his mother's knees. Blanche was amazed at the change in him. From hard-rock-scary person to attentive and loving caretaker of his mother. In the space of seconds.

"I'm sorry. Did I say something to upset you?" Blanche knew damn well she'd upset her, and she was glad Guli hadn't thrown her out the window. These people had their lukewarm moments, but there was a dangerous volatility here.

Blanche plowed ahead. At this point, stirring up the tension seemed to be the only way to move things along and find out more, particularly and importantly, about Margarita. Blanche stood up as Guli came toward her and met his gaze head on.

"We do not mention that name," he whispered, his eyes on his mother. His face came closer to Blanche. "You hear me?"

"I hear you. How could I not?" Blanche suppressed her indignation. She was trespassing, she'd admit, and pushing too hard. In a gentler tone, she asked. "Wasn't Margarita your tutor? Teacher? I understand she was a fine teacher."

They ignored her questions. Esmera hadn't settled down; she was apoplectic. Her rage radiated throughout the room. Guli shook his head as his eyes filled with emotion. A guy stuck in the tower but solicitous of his aging mother. His sharp stare shot from Blanche to his mother.

"All right. Fine," Blanche said quietly, "but you must understand, I *need* this information." She backed up a step. Now she was irritated again. "If you're not going to help, I think I'll be on my way."

Guli pushed her back onto the chair. "You'll go when I say."

The big dope. Does he know who he's messing with?

She shot back out of her chair. "Back off. I've had just about enough." She probably shouldn't bring up Margarita again. But once was not enough. Maybe twice would do it. "Look, I'm sorry if I struck a chord here, but I need to know about Margarita. She's Emilio' aunt. You know Emilio?"

"Yes, I know what goes on here."

"How?" But she suspected the staff was informative.

"Then you know she asked for our help. Can you tell me anything about her? How she got on here?" Blanche plopped down in a chair and looked with pleading at the pair.

Guli and Esmera exchanged a look. Blanche couldn't tell if it was in disbelief or understanding. The shift in the air was as if the storm had settled back to a breeze.

Softly, she said, "I'm really sorry if I said something to upset you, but I'd like to know about her. *It's important.*"

She held back from saying Margarita was dead. *Don't tell all ya know.* A Gran-ism popped into her head.

"We cannot help you," Guli said, with finality. Like a lid slammed down on a pot. Esmera shrank back, the stony expression again in place. She seemed smaller and more hopeless with each moment. The silence in the room was suffocating.

Esmera looked up at Guli, her eyes watering and drooping with sadness. "It is time, Guli. Tell her."

"But—"

"Tell her," his mother demanded.

Guli blew out a breath. "I cannot help you with Margarita's whereabouts. That is all." He looked away and collapsed against the wall, bent over and gripped his knees. Then he stood up. "We are prisoners here. No choice in the matter, as long as the Schemmers have the rule. It was the arrangement with Bartolo that Esmera would inherit the property. He'd told them—the Schemmers as much. But they ... the Schemmers suit themselves. They have friends. Government friends. People with land and power. So, we have no choice but to do what they say. For now."

"Wow, that's a freaking bummer," said Blanche.

"Bummer? What is this?"

"Never mind" Blanche waved off an explanation. The injustice toward Esmera and her son was dreadful. "I am very sorry you have been treated this way. I wish we could help." Blanche got up and paced the floor. "I wish we hadn't gotten messed up in all this ..." She stopped and looked at the two desperate people in front of her. "Emilio's aunt begged us to come. To help her. We need to find her." It would surely be a start in cleaning up the whole mess ...

"I can't help you," Guli said, his voice trailing off. Yet again he looked away.

Blanche didn't want to lay out the fearful image of what she'd seen on that bedroom floor. Why dump that on Guli and his mother? What good would it serve? One way or another, she was sure the Schemmers had something to do with Margarita's death and that they were hiding her, maybe buried somewhere.

"So, you haven't seen the Schemmers bring a body here?"

"Body? *What are you saying?* No!" He screeched but then said, levelly, "No. They bring us provisions. They visit. They bring accountants and the priest. They try to pacify us even though we are prisoners in this place." He looked at his mother, who had closed her eyes as if to deny the situation. Guli seemed more resigned than angry. Blanche certainly wasn't afraid of him any longer. More so, she was sorry for him and for Esmera. The obvious pain and confusion in his voice seemed genuine.

"I am so very sorry," Blanche said, "that you are imprisoned here." The injustice of it all was disheartening. *What can I do?*

"I do go to the Capital from time to time. But my mother stays, unable to travel. So, I must always return. I cannot leave her alone. I don't trust the Schemmers." He hesitated, his eyes cast down. "I can hope … that one day …"

"Hope what?" Blanche asked.

"Nothing." His tone was flat. "I will tell you this now. Margarita. She was my father's mistress."

Blanche gasped in disbelief.

Guli lowered his voice and looked at his mother with compassion and sympathy.

"Ah, now I understand the reaction," Blanche said, "and your mother's dislike for Margarita."

He put a finger to his lips. "The Schemmers, though, took a liking to Margarita. They used her. She was good with their children and their language study." He stole another look at his mother. "And with me. She was good to me, too."

"You were only a child, Guli. Nothing is your fault," his mother said.

He clasped his hands behind his back and glared at Blanche.

"Just go away. *Por favor.*"

"I can't go away. Don't you see? Margarita is Emilio's aunt."

"I can't talk about it." He took Blanche by the elbow. "We're stuck. You're stuck. That's the end of it. My mother and I could leave here, but if we do, the Schemmers will take all of La Palma from us, and it will be over." He hustled her out the door.

Blanche wrenched out of his grip. "That's not right."

"On this we agree," said Guli. "Completely."

Twenty

Tango Closer, Darling

BLANCHE WALKED OVER TO ESMERA. She took the Señora's hands, the skin like dusty, dry leaves. The elderly *dueña* of La Palma offered no expression, no farewell, and resumed staring out that window. It was as if she'd sunk into a revery, a place where no one else could go. She nodded off. Blanche glanced at the view the woman had been looking at: the expansive wall of the great house, its lovely garden and patio, the windows reflecting the sparkle of the sun. Esmera's pain was palpable, her isolation a torture of the Schemmers' creation.

They were trapped. And so were Blanche and Emilio. She was convinced now that the prisoners in the tower knew nothing of the whereabouts of Margarita. But then she stopped herself. *Around here, there is no such thing as being convinced of anything.*

"I'll take you back down. It's better if nobody sees you leaving here." Guli threw a concerned look at his mother and waved Blanche out of the room. They descended the stairs and left by a small narrow door choked off in a flowering vine. No wonder she hadn't been able to find it.

They both stepped outside into the sun. Blanche's instinct was to run away from this place as fast as she could, but she turned to Guli. "Is your mother well?"

"As well as can be expected. She sleeps most of the day. Today she was unusually alert, as you could see. I give her medicine to sleep."

"Thanks for telling me about your situation. I'm not going to forget it. And I'm not going to drop it."

He cocked his head. "Why do I believe that is so. But, please, don't worry about us. Worry about getting out of here. You don't want to be around the Schemmers any longer than necessary."

Blanche moved closer to him. She almost put her arms around him, to hug him. He looked like he needed one. But then she stopped.

"Will I see you again?" Blanche genuinely wanted to see him, but his eyes told her he mistook her concern. She was only here for information.

Guli relaxed against the stucco arch of the doorway, his face veiled in shadow. He smiled, a warm, wide smile, and inclined his head. He was so handsome, teeth so white, hair so black. "Do you want to?"

"I'd like to ... help you and your mom. Is there anything we can do? Emilio and I?" She should set the record straight.

He sighed. "I don't think so. I can't leave my mother. We have some connections, but it goes slowly, and it's treacherous." He glanced languidly across the wide lawn to the pink house. "It's beautiful here, but you don't want to stay. Get out as soon as you can. To safety. I'm sorry I can't tell you about the aunt." He made a gallant little nod.

Blanche blocked him from closing the door. "Or you won't? What are you holding back?"

He didn't answer, except to take her hand and tentatively brush

his lips against her fingers and drop them to her side. "Be safe."
Then he shut the door.

What? Blanche stood there, a cauldron of mixed feelings in the
pit of her stomach. She plucked a bougainvillea blossom off the
vine and twirled it in her fingers. Her fist hovered close to the
door. But then she turned and headed toward the main house. Her
attraction to this Argentinian prisoner was dangerous; it made her
light-headed and frustrated at once. He had his issues, and so did
she. But, basically, this was going nowhere. She loved Emilio. She
was eager to finish here and get on with their lives, and, at once,
she feared finding Margarita stuffed in a freezer or shallow grave.
She shivered even as the warm breeze washed over her. She ran
from the tower. It was good to move forward, to get away. As fast
as she could.

Once back at the house, she went to the living room and poured
herself a short whiskey. Was this trip driving her to drink? It was
only early afternoon. She'd have to think about that. Later. She
needed to find Emilio and hope the Schemmers hadn't returned.
She headed to the den where Emilio surely had made a find by now.

He was sitting on the floor against the bookcase, a large green
records book flat open on his lap. A pencil was tucked behind his
ear. The man of her dreams. But then she stopped and tried to still
a mix of emotions. He was tense with concentration and worry
as he bent over the rows of figures, most likely the sum of the
Schemmers' frightening business dealings.

He didn't hear her come in. *I'm getting so good at my creeping skills.*

She planted a kiss on his forehead and spoke softly. "Watcha
looking at?"

"Where have you been? I've been worried." The look of relief on
his face dispelled some of the anxiety in her chest. The trip to the

tower had been disturbing. She struggled with where to begin to tell him about this latest discovery, and Guli. But some things she would hold tightly in a little compartment of her heart.

She whispered, "Emilio, we have to talk." He didn't seem to notice the hitch in her voice.

"Look at this shady stuff. These people are dealing in treasures all over the world, and we know what those valuables are."

"The menorah and plates and goblets I found under the chapel?"

"What else? So far, it looks like they've priced all of them but haven't cashed in on many."

Blanche crouched down very close to him, so close she could read every tense line around his eyes and mouth. He set the book aside, the pencil fell to the floor. "What's going on? What did you want to tell me?"

She mouthed the words. "Cameras, maybe. Listening devices, probably."

"Mmm." He reached for her hand and drew her down to his lap, tenderly. "How's this? Are we far enough away from them and close enough to each other?"

"No." She wrapped her arms around his neck and whispered. "Maybe we could take a walk?"

Emilio didn't move, his head up against the bookcase. He smiled and held her tight. Blanche snuggled next to him and let that scent of lime on his skin carry her away. Out of the stuffy den. "Kiss me."

It was a delicious kiss, full and sensuous, and she gave into him. That's what happened when she was with him. "Why do you have to feel so good?" She ran her fingers down his face and across his chest.

"Because you do," he said.

They scooted to the corner. If there were cameras, she was sure—whoever it was watching—didn't see them on the floor, behind the sofa, wedged next to a bookcase. At that moment, though, she didn't care.

"We have a perfectly good room," Blanche murmured.

"Really?"

Blanche let go. That walk would wait.

Thankfully, the Schemmers hadn't returned. Blanche and Emilio walked hand in hand across the lawn away from the main house. It was a perfect day. The line of palms and poplars separating them from the dense pampa and the lush gardens, and just the two of them together, gave Blanche a sense of peace. But it didn't last. She had to return to the bad news. Emilio had to know.

"Guli and Esmera are prisoners in that tower. Virtually. On their own property," she said.

"They could leave."

"If they do, they'll lose their hold on the estancia. Their home," she said. "I didn't mention the cache in the chapel to them. I got the idea they didn't seem to be aware of it. But I do believe they know about the bullet holes in the chapel wall and how they got there. They've been living here for decades."

"Why do you say that?"

"Surely, gun shots would carry through the pampa to the house. Wouldn't they be aware of the comings and goings of strange people moving around here, and whatever else those revolting people did for the generals?"

"Not necessarily. Guli was a child. If Esmera or Margarita ever asked, the Schemmers could say they were hunting, or they had visitors. Say whatever liars say."

"You're probably right," said Blanche. "But Guli didn't appear to be all that truthful. Like everyone else around here, he sidestepped my questions."

He set his jaw. "Did you bring it up? The Dirty War?"

"Some. But he didn't say much, and there was just so much I could say."

They continued their leisurely progress around the grounds. Blanche stopped suddenly and looked toward the drive for the return of the Schemmers. "We did put the ledgers back, didn't we?"

"How would I know? I was so distracted." He pulled her toward him.

"Oh, you. Be serious. If they come back and find their papers and things all rearranged, it won't be good."

"No problem. I put the ledgers back in the cupboard."

"What exactly did you find? Before I distracted you."

He looked up at the clouds and laughed. "Nice distraction."

She looped her arm in his and tugged. "So, come on. Tell me."

"Inventory. That book has lists of categories and numbers. Words about gold and Hebraic references, some of the things valued at thousands of pesos. My German is not good, but I know enough to know the items don't belong to the Schemmers." They sat down on a bench, hidden in a patch of hydrangea bushes.

"Gotta match what I found under the chapel."

"Yes, but I couldn't understand everything that was written down. They're so damn organized, so precise. They cover their tracks with code words. Latin for gold, abbreviations for countries, no names of interested buyers—numbers only. That's about all I can figure out. I couldn't tell where the items might be going, or where they came from. At least, in these ledgers."

"It's evidence. And I've got that list we could cross reference— for the authorities to sort out. When the time is right."

"I don't know if we should go there, Blanche. International theft and all that. Have to be careful where we step. If we get involved, we could be detained and not be allowed to leave. Who knows? I've got to get you out of here."

She faced him. They were already so deep into this misadventure, she wasn't about to let it go.

"Emilio! It's not our call. These are crimes. Of the worst sort. We have to do something." She spoke softly, looking around quickly. "It might come out anyway, this web of lies. It's really out of our hands. And, don't you see? Margarita was on to them, and now she's gone. We have to find her ... for Issie's sake, and then turn these people in. They're murderers and thieves."

He took her by the shoulders. "Blanche, it's enough already."

She could sense he was giving up, and she was not about to let him.

"We aren't leaving, Emilio. At least not yet. We came for Margarita, and we are going to find her. Were you able to look around in the other rooms. Closets, drawers? Any other places?"

"No." He sounded dejected. He pulled her up. They began walking along a path lined with jasmine and roses near the entrance to the driveway. The scent was enough to take her breath away but gave her no pleasure.

"I've had a creepy feeling before, but then, after my little trip to the tower, it would explain some things. Guli says there are eyes everywhere, so it makes sense cameras are in place to watch anyone who comes to La Palma. I just can't figure out where they are. At least we're safe out here on the lawn."

"What about cameras? What's the proof of that?"

Emilo draped his arm over her shoulder. The predicament they found themselves in—in a matter of days—worried her more by the hour.

"If there are cameras, they know I made it into the tower, and maybe to the chapel. So, they already know I've been snooping."

"And?"

Then realization hit her. She turned and put her hands on Emilio's shoulders. "If those cameras can track others, those cameras ... they can track them, too!"

"Oh, Blanche." Emilio slapped a hand to his forehead.

The crunch of gravel signaled the approach of a vehicle. The Mercedes came slowly around the corner. They were back. Blanche and Emilio ducked behind a tree. Gerda emerged first from the passenger side, slammed the door, and stood rigidly next to the car, her arms taut at her sides. She glanced around the grounds as Blanche pulled back out of her line of sight. Herr Schemmer came around the front of the car. He was loaded down with bags. Clearly, from the look on his face he was irritated, grunting words at his wife, loudly. Blanche couldn't understand his tirade in German. Gerda turned away and waved him off. She stomped toward the house.

Blanche looked up at Emilio. "Lovers' tiff?"

"Seems so. Pretty hot. Not so cold and calculating. Something is going on."

"Murder, theft, deception. Things like that. Eventually it all comes out, one way or another."

"You think they did all that?" His question seemed rhetorical. He was gazing after Herr Schemmer, who retreated into the house. The slamming of the door reverberated across the lawn.

"Well, Emilio, the butler didn't do it."

They were still crouched down behind the tree. "Actually, Blanche, we haven't met a butler yet, so who knows? We don't have enough to go on."

"Don't worry. We will," said Blanche.

She sat on the ground next to Emilio and put her head back against his chest. As long as they were doing this together, she was good. She put her hand on his cheek and looked him in the eye. "Listen. I know this sounds crazy, but I really want to call Tomás."

"Blanche. That's *real* crazy."

"I just want to talk to him."

"I don't think so. Especially him."

She pivoted. "The other thing, Emilio. We can't keep Issie in the dark. It's her mother, and she'd asked us to call her."

"We said we would." Emilio looked glum.

"I have this gut feeling that Tomás can help. I don't know why. He just might give us some idea of how we can pry more information out of these people about Margarita. We can't coast along with nothing. Until they get rid of us, too. Have you ever thought of that?"

He looked away. But she could tell he was considering it.

"It'll be a short chat. I'll draw him out a little. See if it makes sense to somehow get him out here. Maybe it won't. But then again, maybe it will." She raised up and stared at the house. "Something about all that business on the *peotanal* doesn't fit. Besides, I like Tomás. I think he's genuine, and I think there's more here that he can help us with. I want to put it to him, face to face."

"Are you serious, Blanche? Where do you get these ideas?"

"I wish I knew."

"You want to meet him face to face? How are you going to do that?"

"I want him to pay a visit to La Palma. And then, we have to talk to Issie."

Twenty-One
Coming In Hot

FORTUNATELY, BLANCHE HAD PURCHASED a phone at a kiosk in Buenos Aires and filled it with minutes from a purchased card. It was charging, hidden under their bed. She had no idea what she was going to say to Tomás to get him to come to La Palma, but she'd figure it out. He knew a whole lot more about La Palma than he was letting on, and a friendly conversation might draw him out. What choice did she have? At least Emilio had finally agreed to the little plan, albeit reluctantly. She'd make the call. Later.

They went down to the living room and poured themselves a glass of sherry before lunch. Herr Schemmer had been going on about the wonders of a case he'd ordered from Jerez de la Frontera in Spain, and he was right to do so. It was *divino*—the nectar of the gods—a bit tart and not too sweet. She and Emilio clinked glasses. "I feel guilty, this is so good," she said.

"No, *Baquita*. No guilt. Gives us a minute to regroup. That is good, too." They stood by the window, their backs to the room.

Emilio leaned toward Blanche. "What are you going to say to Tomás?"

She kept her face toward the window and whispered, "I should ease into it. Right? Let him know what's going on here, that we have questions." She turned and casually walked along the walls, picked up a few bibelots here and there, while checking for cameras or listening devices. None turned up.

Emilio gulped his sherry and strode over to Blanche who'd made her way to the bar. He leaned in close. His words were clipped, his tone scratchy with frustration. "You're going to accuse him of setting us up on the *peotanal*? Are you going to tell him you found Margarita dead on the floor? Are you going to tell him about the treasures in the chapel?" He tossed off the last of the sherry and poured himself another. She placed her hand on his arm and huddled next to him.

"I have to tell him, Emilio. Some of it. I'll have to see how it goes. But I want to get him out here first. I'm just not sure what I should tell him."

Lusita walked soundlessly into the room with appetizers—spongy little rounds of white bread with caviar on top—and placed the tray carefully on the coffee table. She hurried away before Emilio and Blanche could say "*Boo!*"

They finished their drinks, silently, and then went to the dining room for a lunch of pineapple chicken with a sugary brown sauce and crunchy brown rice. "More delicious regrouping," she said with a sly smile. They each sipped a glass of Viognier and hardly said a word.

"All right," Emilio mumbled, "let's see what he says. "You realize, of course, he's going to think it strange you're asking him to come out here."

"Maybe. He seemed interested that we were going to La Palma. And he certainly knows his way around all of Buenos Aires. More than we do."

Emilio leaned over. "I'd like to know more about the police and how they operate here. Maybe he can tell us. We should call the police, Blanche." There it was again.

"No. Not yet. It's only been two days. We need more time." She sipped the last of the wine. "Of course, we can ask him about the police." The last meant to mollify him.

"If this doesn't work, we're going to get a car sent out from the hotel and get out of here. All right?"

"What about Margarita?"

"She wouldn't want this. She'd want us safe."

Blanche couldn't argue with that but leaving wouldn't solve a thing. She attempted the blandest expression she could manage, which was saying something. Emilio was way ahead of himself. She had to talk to Tomás. Didn't he see that? She wanted Tomás on their side; more than that, she was determined to make a tight ally out of him. They had no one else.

When they'd finished their lunch, they hurried back up to their room, and Blanche retrieved the phone. Emilio stood at the window, rigidly, watching her while she punched in the numbers.

She took a deep breath. "Tomás?" She clutched the phone to her ear and stared out the window. "It's Blanche Murninghan." She glanced quickly at Emilio.

"*¿Señorita Blanche? ¡Qué bueno!*"

"Yes! Hola! Hope you're fine and all, Tomás. It's not so *bueno* out here."

"*¿Qué pasa?*"

"The person we came out here to visit, Emilio's Aunt Margarita—well, she's missing."

"What? Did something happen? Where did she go?"

"That's the problem. Can you come out here?"

"But why? I'm not good at missing persons."

"It's most likely a matter for the police, but I want to talk to you first. See if you can help us figure some things out about what's happening here at La Palma."

"Oh, *Dios*. Don't call the police. *¡Espera, por favor!*"

"*Why?*" Blanche held the phone away from her ear. Tomás's response was oddly frantic. And loud.

"I ... I was planning on coming to La Palma. *De veras.*"

"You were planning to come *here*? *Really?*" She waved the phone at Emilio and hunched her shoulders in surprise.

Emilio mouthed: "*What?!*"

"*Sí,*" said Tomás. "We will practice the tango. The Schemmers ... they like to see the new interpretations of the dance." There was a moment's hesitation. "You might say I've been courting their favor. In the tango, that is."

At this Blanche nearly dropped the phone. "Now I've heard everything," she murmured to herself.

"What's that, Señorita Blanche?"

"Nothing. I just can't believe it. It's so strange ..."

"*Pues*, tango. It is not so strange. It is a way of walking and breathing. And talking."

"But tango? With the Schemmers? They don't seem the type."

"You will be surprised to know they are *aficionados*. Well known at the milongas in Buenos Aires although they don't come into the Capital so much these days. And I must say, the Frau—"

Blanche arched her eyebrows and shook her head at this revelation. Emilio tried to listen in. "She ... they have quite a reputation in Buenos Aires," Tomás said. "Something I have known for some time." He stopped abruptly, cleared his throat before continuing. "But that is for another time. I did not mention the Schemmers and their, ahem, interest in the dance? I'm sure I did."

"No, you didn't," Blanche said under her breath. "I have to say I am surprised. Very. It's one surprise after another around here."

"Then you have arrived in Argentina. It is a place of many twists and turns."

"Which reminds me, Tomás. One of the main reasons I called you. That driver you sent us out here with?"

"*Sí.*"

"I need to talk to you about him."

"We will talk. But not now." He spoke hurriedly. Commotion in the background interrupted the connection.

"When will you be coming? To give dance lessons and such. We're anxious to see you."

"*Mañana.*"

The old car sputtered into the driveway at La Palma. From the bedroom window, Blanche watched Tomás climb out of the dusty old Ford. He walked around the front and opened the passenger door. The glamorous Anna Godoy de Gamoure emerged, slinky as ever.

"Oh, goodie," Blanche mumbled.

Anna patted the top of her glossy black coif, the sun glinting off the gold hoops in her ears. She posed like she was being photographed for a magazine cover and smoothed the long, tight sheath hugging every curve. A patter of rapid Spanish escaped from her plump red lips.

Blanche stood at the window and tightened the towel around her middle, and the one on her head. She'd finished her morning routine of coffee, a shower, and Emilio's back rub. He'd been tense as a board after sneaking out into the night to look for his aunt. He'd returned at four in the morning, disheveled, sweaty and nearly out of his mind with frustration. Blanche had pulled him onto the bed, and they'd fallen into a deep sleep. Emilio was still out cold well after nine o'clock.

Now this. She hadn't expected the glamorous Gamoure. The two tango dancers stood in the driveway, rat-a-tat talking to each other. They laughed, their heads together conspiratorially. Blanche couldn't understand a word they were saying. Tomás wore the same black embroidered jacket and the flat-brimmed hat. The weath-ered lines across his partially covered face settled into a pleasant smile. He always seemed so calm, and she had to admit, she looked forward to chatting with him. If he were reticent, she'd somehow get him to talk. She had a list of questions, and she meant to get some answers. He could help them. Like others they'd met at the La Palma, she was certain he knew more than he was letting on.

He retrieved a beat-up guitar from the back seat. Anna still posed at the rear bumper, one hand primping the shiny bun at her neck. A rose adorned her ear. She wore impossibly high heels that accentuated her shapely legs. She glanced up at the window. Smiled wickedly at Blanche and winked. Blanche shot back into the room, furious.

"Let the dance begin." Blanche clutched the towel around her middle so tight she could hardly breathe and whipped off the one on her head. Emilio, still asleep, was immobile. She went to him and leaned over, kissed him on the temple. "Your girlfriend is here."

In response, one of Emilio's very long arms reached up and pulled her down toward him, damp towel and all, and drew her under the covers. He didn't even open his eyes.

"She is," he murmured.

The window flew open, and the breeze stirred the heavy drapery. Voices carried. Frau Gerda's mellifluous tones filtered up from the driveway. Then the front door to La Palma clunked shut. Blanche couldn't wait for the show to begin.

Well, it could wait. First things first.

Twenty-Two
Eyeball It

THE RAMBLING PINK MANSION pulsed with tango music. At the back of the house, the ballroom was in full swing; the parquet floor glistened and echoed with the heels of boots and dancing shoes. A wall of windows invited the mid-day sun. It dawned on Blanche how small most of the rooms were, except for this one. She'd met Herr Schemmer for drinks in the cozy living room, its size deceptive in relation to the rest of the house. Somehow, she'd missed this grand room, and she hated to miss anything, especially after she and Emilio had put all this time into searching La Palma for Margarita and come up with nothing but more questions. Now she stood in the doorway, rather enjoying a mild case of wonderment.

It was party central with the revelers in full lunge and twirl. They tangoed past the velvet benches lining the walls hung with tapestries. Candelabra tilted haphazardly on small round bar tables, and assorted musical instruments were neatly stacked on shelves and the floor next to a grand piano. Tango music blasted from enormous speakers strategically placed in corners of the room.

Anna's tight yellow dress and strappy heels didn't hamper a single movement as she swung around with the Herr. Tomás was spinning a rigid Frau Gerda in a light blue dress with a full skirt and scoop neck. Her small steps were robotic.

"You must give in, no, *mi amor*, give up to the music," Tomás intoned, his head shifting back and forth, his large hand splayed across her shoulder blades. *This is the accomplished Gerda?* She danced with the plastic movements of a Barbie doll.

"Ah, but you are hardly the Herr." Her comment was frosty, but Tomás didn't seem to give much of a hoot. He was clearly taken with the music.

"*Pues*, is that it? We will work on my *forma* ..." He swept her off her feet even though he was barely taller than she. "The steps, *meine Frau*, the steps. Ah, now we are getting somewhere." She moved in time with the rhythm, but the woman was hopeless. Even Blanche could see that. At the other side of the room, Anna whipped the Herr around like a dirigible in the wind. He was amazingly light on his feet, given his size. Blanche had to hand it to La Gamoure, reluctantly; she could lunge and circle and twist her way with the best of them.

Blanche took a step into the room then held back. She tried to get Tomás's eye, to no avail. The strings and horns hit a frenetic crescendo, and the music stirred her to her toes. They danced as if they didn't have a care in the world. Blanche knew differently. Emilio would be down soon, and she needed to get this done. She needed to get Tomás alone.

Tomás and Gerda spun to a halt in front of Blanche. He bowed. Gerda looked winded, her tight, blond hair-do sprouting wisps. She hardly acknowledged Blanche. "I think I'll get something for us to drink." She hurried out the side door.

"How fortunate." Blanche barely moved her lips, her focus on Tomás. "I am so glad to see you."

"And I, you, Señorita."

"Tomás, we need to talk."

211

"I am at your service." He showed no urgency to leave the ballroom and the music. "Would you care for a turn around the dance floor? Would that be amenable? It is a lovely venue." He spread his arms and threw in a charming smile.

"No!" Oh, she didn't mean to sound like that. She clapped a hand over her mouth, sorry she'd been so abrupt. She'd completely wiped the look of musical bliss from his face. "Tomás, I apologize. I'm just anxious. I really need to talk to you. In private." She gestured toward the patio. "Out there."

The Herr was entertaining Anna in a loud mix of Spanish, English, and German with a great deal of laughter—on his part, not hers. A fixed smile was pasted on her red lips. The strains of Gardel from the speakers kept her feet moving as she nodded at the Herr. Blanche would have given a great number of pesos to know what was in her head, but she bet Gamoure was patiently putting up with his chatter.

Blanche tore herself away. "I mean now, Tomás." She tamped down the desperate tone and linked her arm in Tomás's. "They're busy. Might be a good time."

The dancers didn't look up. The Herr grappled Anna around her waist; she bent backwards, a sinuous curve of silk and sweat. The challenge in her expression matched his inflamed cheeks. Blanche could hardly look away, but then she nearly ran out the door—away from the hypnotic tango.

"Let us adjourn to the grounds." Tomás hurried after her. "I don't think they will mind."

They walked quickly through the small garden enclosed with boxwood and an abundance of wild roses. Blanche chose a bench under a coral tree with cup-like red blossoms. At their feet, yellow flowers carpeted the lawn like tiny buttons in the grass.

Blanche settled in next to Tomás. She was edgy while he

managed a calm expression. She took a deep breath. "It's beautiful here."

"*Pues, si.* And this tree? It holds in its embrace the national flower of Argentina."

"Really? I sure feel like I'm in the hold of Argentina. A stranglehold."

"Oh?" His eyebrows shot up. "I do not think you want to talk about flowers." Gone was any pretense of the light-hearted tango dancer. Concern clouded his dark eyes.

"No, I do not."

"And?"

"First off, please tell me why you sent us out here with the biker who tried to run me down on the *peotanal?*"

He didn't flinch or move a muscle. The hard leathery lines around his mouth and eyes softened a bit. "I'm sorry you believe that. You saw his face? You recognized him?"

"Of course I did, Tomás. We spent hours in the car with him." She spoke sharply. The driver had been secretive about showing himself, now that she recalled. "Was I not supposed to recognize him?"

"I can't think what you mean by that." The same deflection.

"You know exactly what I mean. It's too weird that he tries to flatten me and then you hire him."

Tomás's shoulders collapsed. "Life is full of misunderstandings, Señorita Blanche. You must accept that."

"Well, I don't. Not all of them anyway. I am not getting any answers around here."

He sighed and clasped his hands, looking down to avoid her scrutiny. Blanche was beyond frustrated.

She took a deep breath and looked him straight in the eye. "Okay, Tomás, here's the deal. We came here looking for Emilio's Aunt Margarita, and we're not having much luck."

He jerked his head toward her in surprise. "That is why you came out here?"

"Well, yes." They'd purposely obfuscated their mission. Now it was imperative she confide in him, though, she wouldn't reveal everything. Discretion didn't come easy to Blanche, but she couldn't just plunge ahead. She liked Tomás and wanted to trust him, but she wouldn't until she got the full story out of him. Which didn't seem to be forthcoming.

"The Schemmers won't tell us where Margarita is," she said. "And now I've found ... evidence that these people are not, how should I say it, above board. I believe they are thieves and liars. Profiteers on the backs of war victims."

Tomás jumped to his feet. "You need to leave immediately!"

Blanche stood and faced him, leaning over him fiercely. "What are you talking about?" She lowered her voice, pleading. "Tomás, you need to tell me what's going on here. Now. I'm just about to pop my cork. So, no more games."

"Do not do that, whatever it is, with your cork. You will only make things worse." He looked toward the house. "Trust me, and I will help you, but you must be patient."

"I've been patient. And so has Emilio. You know the Schemmers." Desperation seeped into her tone. "You know how shady they are. So, please, please Tomás, tell me what you know."

He drew himself up to a full five-foot-two inches, his chest out. "We will discuss it later, I promise. But now, we have tango, and a nice lunch, and then all will be fine. You'll see."

He didn't wait for further argument. He took her arm and steered her toward the house. "You must smile. And dance the tango. Trust me. *And be patient.*"

It was all she could do not to rip her arm away, but he'd assuaged her some. His self-assurance had a calming effect. He seemed to be in control—but of what?

"All right," she mumbled, jostling his arm, gently. "But not much longer."

He held on to her and patted her hand. He smiled, a forced smile that barely cracked the lines in his face. "You will see," he said. "*Por favor,* you must wait."

"I don't have much choice, do I?"

"No one does."

They ate lunch—all six of them—on the patio under a canopy of ivy. The afternoon was sunny and bright, belying the doom and gloom that settled in Blanche's mind. She couldn't take her eyes off Tomás. Anna couldn't take her eyes off Emilio. And the Herr and the Frau carried on about the *boeuf a la franca,* a grilled masterpiece from Bruno who had escaped from France without papers, it seemed.

"We are lucky to have him in the kitchen. He is a king when it comes to beef," said the Herr.

"Papers?" Blanche asked. Here was yet another intimation that these people were pulling strings and bucking authority.

"It's a little thing, these papers," said the Frau. "Bruno had some nonsense with the law, but we were able to help him."

Get around the law. "That's so nice," Blanche murmured.

"Yah, we do so like to be helpful." Her knife and fork clacked onto her plate for emphasis.

"Harumph," said the Herr. His cheeks resembled the glistening red beef in front of him—diminishing Blanche's appetite. He turned to Anna. "Would you like some more wine, *meine liebe?*" Blanche nearly choked. Wasn't he getting just so lovey-dovey with his tango partner? Right there in front of icy wifey? Blanche put her napkin over her mouth.

Anna had one long talon poised under her chin, ignoring the big old German, her eyes glued to Emilio. He'd hardly eaten a thing. His hand rested on Blanche's knee. She pressed his fingers, but it didn't lessen the animosity she felt for the witchy tango dancer— and her amazement at all that was being served up for lunch.

Blanche couldn't wait to get away from the table. She had no appetite for *boeuf a la franca* or any of this other nonsense. She nudged Tomás, gently, under the table. She desperately wanted to finish interrogating him. He smiled at no one in particular and resumed cutting his lunch into tiny pieces, savoring each bite. *"¡Delicioso!"* he declared, ignoring Blanche.

Lusita hurried to the table with dessert and dropped plates of flan like they were on fire in front of each guest. They all finished the caramelized custard and the last of several carafes of Malbec. It seemed they'd sat for hours. Finally, Blanche had had enough. She stood up, a bit wobbly, but she managed to steady herself as she backed away from the table. Her frustration doused with Malbec made her slightly disoriented.

"You will excuse me, please," she said. She kept an eye on Tomás. She planned to stick close to him. He nodded graciously to the group, leapt up, and made a bee line for the house without a word. She didn't want to leave Emilio on the patio with that woman, but she had to follow Tomás. Anna sashayed from the table and posed next to a trellis entwined with roses. Provocative as always. Maybe one of the thorns would pierce her heart, and she would faint away in a bloody pool. *Oh. Blanche. Stop.*

Emilio leaned toward Blanche and whispered conspiratorially, "What's going on? You are as skittish as ten *gatitos.*" He led her away from the table out of earshot.

"You bet I am." Blanche looked at Anna, who studied her nails, one hip cocked and one long, lean leg sticking out of the slit in her skirt.

Blanche lowered her voice. "I've got to get to Tomás. To draw him out."

"About? Exactly?"

"We had a chat on the patio earlier. He flipped after mention of the driver, and Margarita, and the weird Schemmers. He says to be patient about all this crazy business. I can't anymore."

He drew close to her ear. "Look. No one else is leaving yet. Let's go along, see where this leads. I understand you're inclined to trust Tomás. Then, trust him. Maybe we should do as he suggests. Wait."

Emilio did not even look at Anna. Blanche had a sense she had nothing to worry about. She kissed him and enjoyed every second of it. Emilio smiled down into her eyes. "All right, I trust you to get it right. Who knows what you may get out of him."

Anna came up behind Emilio and put one long pointy finger on his shoulder. "*Guapo*, how about a dance? It is good for the digestion."

Blanche froze. "I bet," she mumbled. Her temperature threatened to spike, her mouth geared up for a gigantic rejoinder. She pressed her lips together before she said anything she'd regret. "No, he doesn't want to dance." She turned to Emilio. "Do you?"

"Well ..." he stammered. Blanche frowned at his lame response. But something in her brain clicked. He did look lost and forlorn. Why hadn't she tuned into this more? He hovered over Blanche, his hand warm on her arm, caressing and sure. *What's more important here? This stupid flirtation, which Emilio clearly is not encouraging, or the hunt to right the wrongs at La Palma?* It was plain and simple. She gave him a peck on the cheek, squeezed his hand, and stood on tip-toe next to his ear: "*Momentito*. I'll be back soon." She turned without a glance at Gamoure and hurried off, glad to get moving after a stupefying afternoon.

"Blanche!" Emilio called after her, but she was already across the patio in search of Tomás.

Blanche ended up in the back hall where she ducked into an alcove. The sound of angry male voices clashed loudly in the den. Then a shriek erupted. She hung back in the shadows to make sure no one came her way. She crept silently toward the yelling. The Herr and Tomás were having at it. She concealed herself near the doorway and listened in.

"What is this?" the Herr bellowed.

"What do you think it is?" Tomás was the master of obfuscation. He never seemed to give a straight answer. Always answered a question with a question.

"It looks like a *device* of some kind."

"*Pues*, I suppose you could call it that?" Tomás was not shouting anymore. His tone was remarkably calm.

Blanche crouched down and poked her head around the door frame. The Herr was holding a small, black gadget that looked like an eyeball. He shook it at Tomás, who reared back but didn't give the big German any ground.

"I'd call it suspicious, that's what I'd call it," said the Herr. "It looks like a device for spying. I want to know what you are doing with it. Tell me, or I will wring the head off your shoulders." He slammed the thing down on his desk. "I may do that anyway." The man was a bull about to charge.

Tomás backed up. One step, then two, ready to flee, but the avenue of escape was limited. "I'm not doing anything with it. You're the one holding it, Herr Schemmer." The Herr grabbed his arm, but Tomás remained firm. He stood still as a post.

"Don't be *estupido*. I saw you taking it out of the bookcase," said the Herr.

"I was just looking at it," he said, casually. "Nothing more."

"Nonsense! You were placing this, or, perhaps checking it, weren't you? And now I've caught you at your game!"

Tomás folded his arms. "What? I can't tell you anything as I do not know what you are talking about. Curious as to what it was, I simply picked the thing up."

Exasperated, the Herr grabbed a letter opener off the coffee table. The threat of physical violence sent a shiver through Blanche. She eyed the meanness in the Herr's expression and the defiance in the little tango dancer. She was about to leap onto the old sack of German bones. But then Tomás planted his feet wide apart. He advanced toward the Herr, waggling a finger in his red face. "Prove it, you big fool. *Tonterías.* I won't be accused of nonsense." In a flash, he knocked the letter opener out of the Herr's grip, and it clattered across the fireplace tile.

Oddly enough, given the bluster, the Herr backed off as if he were having second thoughts. He clamped his mouth shut, but his eyes narrowed. Blanche remembered something Gran had told her about bullies: "You must stand up to them and call them out. Or else, they will take advantage of you." Tomás's strong stance actually worked to cut the legs out from under the Herr.

Way to go, Tomás! Blanche pinned herself against the wall and lifted her eyes toward heaven. *Oh, Gran!*

She held her breath, tense at how this confrontation would end. No one came into the room to interrupt the arguing. She leaned closer for a peek. Tomás carried on with his stocky resistance, and the Herr sputtered, the Malbec, no doubt, having fogged his brain.

Tomás didn't fool Blanche. Not for a moment. He had a strength in him, and he had secrets he wasn't about to let go of. For whatever reason, he had his eye on the Schemmers.

Twenty-Three

Into The Dark

BLANCHE WAS ABOUT TO INTERRUPT this little *mano a mano* between Tomás and the Herr when Anna de Gamoure swept into the room from the opposite doorway as if life were one long tango. *"Querido, tenemos que salir,"* she said, oblivious to the drama. She swung an enormous red patent leather bag from one arm to the other and licked her lips.

Blanche held back, crouching in the hallway.

Tomás took one look at Anna and relaxed. *"Divina mia. Momentito."* He moved toward the Herr then stopped short.

The old German was puffed up like a dragon ready to spit fire. "This is not the end of it," he boomed.

Tomás raised his eyebrows and pulled at the lapels of his jacket. Anna looked from one to the other and shrugged. *"¿Qué pasa, Tomasito?"*

"Nada. Vámonos." The two sailed out the door. Blanche rested her head on the wall and sat still. Next thing, car doors slammed, and the vehicle revved with a sputter of gravel as Tomás and Anna departed from La Palma.

Tomás! *No!* Blanche was newly distraught. He was gone and

with him the opportunity for more information. She slumped in the dark, her mind wandering morosely.

Blanche snuck a look. She perked up as the Frau hurried into the room and stood directly in front of the Herr. "We need to have a word, *mein* darling."

The Herr deflated and threw himself into a small upholstered chair that nearly tipped over. His wife perched on the footstool in front of him and leaned forward. "Those gauchos. They're supposed to be security, but I haven't seen much of them lately. I'm getting quite nervous."

"No, no. They're about," the Herr snapped. "Hernan is seeing to it. Your little plan to eliminate Margarita went well enough."

"A mere pest. Should have gotten rid of her long ago."

"Then why didn't you?" His tone was imperious.

"You know why. She'd been talking to Tomás, and I needed to find out what she was talking about. If she'd involved the authorities, she'd have mixed things up, badly, and I'm telling you we couldn't let that happen. We're close to getting rid of the gold and getting out of here. If anyone asks her whereabouts, I can say she went to Catamarca on a visit."

"And we never did learn more about those two. Why didn't we eliminate Tomás?"

He's whining? The sight of this large blubbering person cowering to his wife was ludicrous. Blanche even stifled a chuckle.

"And what? La Gamoure, too? Where does it end? We can't risk more killing," the Frau insisted.

"Oh, Gerda, I don't want to leave."

"We must make plans to leave, *dear* husband."

The man's demeanor changed. "Relax, dear wife."

She stood up, her voice a strangled hiss. "What's wrong with you? Our connections, our support system in the Capital is gone. Dead. Defunct. Arrested. Deported. I do not want to join them."

She stomped to the window and gazed outside, her hands clasped behind her back, her shoulders squared. The Herr sat, pensively. Somber.

Blanche had heard enough. She crawled backwards, stood up, but before she could skitter away, heavy steps came closer. She changed it up, stomped along in the dark and whistled a bit, like she was just arriving from the adjoining room. The Herr stormed into the hallway and loomed over her. "What are you doing out here?"

"Nothing." She straightened up and looked at him, wide-eyed. "Something? I was going to come in and look for a book to read."

"These books are all in Spanish and German. You know that, I am sure."

"I need to expand my horizons." She wanted to expand herself right out of there, but before she could move a muscle or say another word, the Herr turned to his wife.

"Were you listening to the nonsense going on in here?" The Frau's tone was demanding, her arms crossed.

"Nonsense? I hear a lot of that lately," said Blanche, pleasantly.

"What's that supposed to mean?"

"Oh, nothing. Really. I was looking for a book … and Emilio."

"Seems you're always looking for him. Or something or someone," the Frau huffed.

"Oh, he's off again. I've been on a wild goose chase … outside and about." She let out a strained laugh. "But, you know, he's probably here or there. We're all here! One big happy group! I want to thank you for the lovely luncheon! You certainly know how to put on the dog." *Another Gran-ism.*

"Dog! Why, that's the finest Argentine beef!" the Frau hissed.

"I only meant …"

For answer, the Herr marched off, mumbling. Blanche stared after him, studiously avoiding the Frau's expression. "You are very strange, and you do seem to be everywhere," she said, suddenly impassive and distant. She turned around and followed her husband out the door.

Blanche made sure they were gone, and she threw herself into a chair. She needed to digest these revelations—all of them—about Tomás and the Schemmers and Margarita. The tangle of involvement in murder and cover-up was stupefying, including the revelation of the "device" during the heated exchange between the Herr and Tomás. The Herr had pocketed the eyeball. So, she surmised, if there was one eyeball, there had to be another: *Eyeballs come in pairs.* And more. The Schemmers, as the Frau had admitted, were guilty as hell.

Blanche hurried off to find Emilio. It seemed more imperative than ever, if that were possible, that they needed to move *quickly*.

"Emilio!" Blanche kicked the door closed and leapt across the bedroom. Emilio stood by the window, arms crossed. He went to her. "Where have you been? What's going on?"

Blanche didn't answer. She was at a loss for where to begin, but her snooping skills were in high gear. She scurried about the room looking in the corners, under furniture, and on shelves for cameras or listening devices. The memory of the "eyeball" in the Herr's fist was fresh in her mind. Were both the Schemmers and Tomás bugging the place?

"What are you doing, *Baquita?*"

She stopped inspecting a light fixture and said, "At least, it seems, they have a shred of decency. I don't see any spying apparatus in our room."

"What? Oh, those damn cameras."

Blanche nodded. "And get this. I overheard the Schemmers. They were fighting. The Frau *admitted* she killed Margarita, and now, they're running scared. She said, too, that their support system is crumbling. They want to dump the gold and get out of here."

He looked at her like she'd smacked him on the head. "¡Aye, Dios! You were right."

"Right doesn't do much good right now, does it? There is still so much *wrong*." She paced about with a new case of nerves. "It gets weirder by the minute around here. After lunch, I followed Tomás and then happened upon him and Karl arguing. We have to figure out what to do with all this information. These people need to be in jail."

"The Frau came to the patio, and she was out of sorts. Must have been after the argument."

"Their plan to get away with it is falling apart," Blanche said.

Emilio deflected. "She wants to see us in the living room … for a drink. Later."

"Hmmm. Maybe we should give up drinking."

"Do you think she knows what we've been up to?" He threw himself into an armchair next to the window.

"We should put on a front. Be as evasive as she is. And we better watch what we drink around here."

Emilio sighed. "So, what exactly did you overhear?"

She went over the entire conversation between Tomás and the Herr and the "device" and the argument between the Schemmers.

"This device looked like some sort of thing for spying—a camera—for sure. The Herr accused Tomás, who didn't own up to it, and then he and Anna stormed out of the house. I didn't get to talk with him. The Herr was not happy with him, or me."

"You? You didn't get involved in it, I hope." He gripped the arms of the chair and raised up. His forehead turned a vivid *rosado*.

"Not really. I made it appear that I was looking for a book."

"Oh, *Baquita!*" he scowled. "Will you never learn?"

"I covered it pretty well. Made a clatter in the hallway like I was just walking up."

"I hope so." He sat back with a thump. "You are pretty good at the dissimulation business."

"Oh, really. What am I dissimulating now?"

"Nothing. Come over here and do not leave me again."

"Oh, Emilio. What happened after I left you on the patio?" She thought of the slithery Anna and wanted to choke on her words.

"That woman, Anna. She was nervous, and short-tempered. Kept poking around in the corners when she thought no one was looking. And then she ran off to find Tomás."

"She found him, but earlier, she sure was looking at you." Blanche nudged his foot, gently.

"I was a diversion."

"That you are." Blanche started to pace. "What do you mean, she was poking around?"

"She was looking for something," he said.

"It sounds like Tomás found it. That device." She touched his arm. "I put Tomás on the spot about that driver on the *peotanal*. He would not answer me directly, or about the business with Margarita. He freaked out when I accused the Schemmers and said I was going to get to the bottom of things. He told me to be patient, but he didn't explain."

Emilio stood and put his hands on her shoulders. "Explain what?"

"I didn't get the chance, I told you. And, I'm telling you, he's more than meets the eye, that one. Spyware and excuses. He knows things about the Schemmers." Blanche stared up at Emilio. Patted his hands and took off pacing again. "I told him Margarita is missing, but I didn't tell him she was dead."

"Blanche, it's time. We need to call the police. The fact is, you found Margarita. Dead. We have to report it."

"Yes, we will, for sure. But first, I want you to meet someone."
She had a new sense about the hunt, and now it was time. She took
his hand and tugged.

"Why don't we lay low for a while? The Schemmers are heated
up and we need to think this new information through." He didn't
budge, his expression a stoney resolution. "We need to call a driver
and get out of here. Now."

Blanche slipped her arms around his waist. "We will. But you
need to come with me. First."

He looked at her askance. "Never a dull moment."

"It'd be nice if we had at least one," she said, smiling up at
those dark eyes. "Maybe someday."

The house was quiet. Not even a sound from the kitchen. Together,
they snuck down the stairs toward the library. Blanche put a finger
to her lips, and Emilio rolled his eyes. The shadows of the oncom-
ing evening sheltered them as they crept across the house. *So much
better for my little plan.* He still resisted but followed her. "Trust me,"
she said.

"What are we doing, Blanche?" Emilio croaked. He looked
around the small library nervously and moved into a niche near the
bookcase. "They might catch us in here."

"They won't. Not where we're going." At least she hoped not.
Unsure of where all the cameras were placed, or if someone were
listening, she had to do this. She moved quickly to the desk by the
window and thumped the end panel. The bookcase creaked open.
Only a crack, but it was enough. "Look at that!" She took Emilio's
hand. "I'll go first."

Emilio peered into the dark space. "Wait, Blanche. What is this?
What if we can't get back in?"

"Door's on a spring. I tested it. It doesn't lock." She took a penlight from her pocket and pointed the way. He followed Blanche into the musty darkness, mumbling. "You're sure this is a good idea?" Ever the meticulous, careful doctor.

"Sure, don't worry." She crept down into the tunnel.

The smell of dirt and neglect engulfed them, along with the dead quiet. Emilio was unnerved, but Blanche walked confidently. She was glad to have Emilio close even though she could feel his resistance.

They eventually came to a narrow opening in the tunnel wall that led to the cavern under the chapel. She shined a light on the boxes. Emilio gasped. "All that? The gold menorahs and plates and things?"

"Yup. You're looking at it. We can't do anything about it now, but take my word for it. It's glorious, and appalling."

"What should we do? Have you thought this through?"

"Remember, I have that list. More proof. For when the time comes," she whispered, and then looked around. Who would hear them down here?

"Blanche, we've got more than enough to call the police. Let's go back—"

"Not yet! Come on!" She pulled him forward.

They groped along. The penlight illuminated the next room where a rope ladder appeared in a triangle of yellow light. "See? We climb."

"*Por Dios, Baquita.* To where?"

"You'll see."

"At least we can get out of this ... hole."

Twenty-Four

Twist In The Tower

EMILIO WENT UP THE LADDER FIRST. Blanche watched him give the cover at the top a good whack, and then he shoved it aside. He pulled himself up into the light. Blanche was right behind him scrambling up the rope. She popped up over the rim, and the two sat on the floor, staring at each other like they'd climbed Mount Everest.

"The tower," he murmured.

"You bet."

"Now what?" he asked, dusting off his hands. "This is a great idea." But she could tell he didn't think so.

Blanche eyed the steps framed in the doorway. If her hunch was right, the tall, dark Argentinian would appear any minute. She was sure he'd known they'd arrived. He certainly had when she'd dropped in, or rather, climbed up, before.

Sure enough, boots pounded down the staircase. Slow and even, like he wasn't in any hurry. Guli's expression was sluggish, sleepy. His hair was spikey, and he was half dressed. But then he came around instantly. He fixed eyes on Blanche with an intensity that was unsettling. *"Muy buenos tardes."*

Blanche and Emilio jumped to their feet. He stepped in front of

Blanche and stuck one arm out in front of her. She slipped around him and extended her hand to Guli. His smile crept slowly from his lips to his eyes.

He was one handsome dude with those sharp shoulders and dark eyes. She detected a faint scent of musk and citrus. *What is it about Latin men?* He took her hand with both of his, his skin rough and warm. Emilio didn't budge.

"This is Emilio."

"I know." Guli offered his hand, and Emilio took it reluctantly.

"Guli was once Margarita's student. In her care."

"*What?*" Emilio made no effort to contain the edge in his tone. "And you know something? All this time?"

Oh, boy. Blanche began to doubt the gamble of this venture. But she couldn't stop now. Margarita had been Guli's teacher. He couldn't be totally oblivious and uncaring as to her welfare and whereabouts. Could he?

Guli crossed his arms and leaned against the wall like he had all the time in the world. "Let's just say I *know*." He pointed at Blanche with his chin. "We've met, and news travels."

"Is that so." Emilio's irritation scorched his words. He rarely had a hot temper, but when it flared, it blew up quicker than a dry grass fire.

"Look, Guli, we just want to talk," said Blanche. She stepped closer. His scent was strong. She hoped she didn't swoon. Emilio wouldn't understand. She shook her head to chase her thoughts away. The shadow under his chin, the whiteness of his teeth when he opened his mouth. ... What could she say?

"We talked," he said. "Remember? And I told you to be a good tourist and *leave*. I didn't mean later, I meant *now*." His words were biting, but he looked down at her with the ghost of a smile.

"Well, that was not going to happen," she said, quietly. "I mean, we're all good here. Together at La Palma. But, like I said before, we have to find Emilio's aunt, and there are other things that need sorting." She could sense Emilio's impatience without even looking at him. He was tense as a taut wire.

I have to be quick about this.

Guli seemed mildly amused. His eyes lingered on one then the other. He hunched his shoulders.

Emilio took a step closer to Blanche. "This isn't working!" he yelled. "Let's get out of here and go to plan B." Blanche shot him a look. *What is plan B?* But his eyes were directed at Guli.

Guli's eyebrows shot up. "You have plan A? Don't know what that is. Except you are looking for someone, and I don't know why you think I know about that person."

"Tell us something!" He shouted. "My aunt! What do you do know about her?"

The air changed as the tension ratcheted up. The small, round entry at the base of the tower stairs seemed to expand. Blanche was desperate to get on with it and get out of there. It was getting late, and they had run into a brick wall: Guli. The men were immoveable, staring at each other, arms crossed as if they would come to blows.

Blanche sighed and sat down on the floor. They ignored her. She didn't expect them to join her there and discuss the situation, but she didn't care. Deflated, she needed to concentrate, and there she sat, in a heap, arms wrapped around her knees. Ruminating. If there was one thing clear to her in all her adventures, it was to follow her nose and force herself to be patient, if possible. Be in the moment. Listen. *From without and from within.* It had worked before, and it might work again, if nothing else, to cool off these two so they could hatch a plan. Together.

Then she heard it. At first, the sound was faint, but eventually it grew louder. She saw it in Guli's eyes, the way they spiked with alarm and then softened with resignation. Emilio seemed oblivious.

He was still seething and poised to start yelling again, his face red with frustration. He clutched Blanche's hand and pulled her to her feet. Gently at first and then with urgency. "Let's go. Enough."

Blanche stood close to him, but she was not about to go anywhere. She squeezed Emilio's hand, hard, and put a finger to her lips: "Listen!"

Guli had not moved an inch, not a hair. He glanced around with the look of a wild animal.

"Emilio! Is that you?" The sound of a voice was strong now, and insistent. It came from high up in the tower.

"Oh, my God, *Baquita*. Do you hear that?" He held her hand and headed toward the stairs.

Guli blocked their way. "Where you going?"

"You know exactly where we're going." Emilio shoved Guli aside. Blanche winced. They didn't have time for an all-out brawl. She could hardly breathe, but they had a clear advantage. She scampered up the stairs with Emilio, the two of them clinging to each other. Two at a time they raced toward the sound, spiraling up and around.

The small woman stood in the doorway, rimmed in the light, her arms outstretched. *"¡Mijo!"*

Emilio hesitated, trying to make sense of it all. Then with a whoop he jumped over the top step and lifted her off the floor, hugging her for dear life.

Margarita! In the flesh!

Guli clambered up the stairs and hung back at the top landing, his shoulders slumped. Emilio set Margarita back on her feet and rounded on Guli, but Blanche stepped in between them. She couldn't stand to see this moment end in violence.

"Wait!" Margarita shouted. "You don't know, Emilio."

"No, I don't."

"It's a long story," Guli said, his voice just above a whisper, his eyes red-rimmed—with relief?

"Oh, this ought to be a good one," murmured Blanche, recovering from the sight of Emilio's aunt. Upright and smiling. Wisps of gray hair framing her lovely face. And very much alive.

Guli sat on a bench in Margarita's tower room, elbows on his knees, hands clasped. He didn't look up. Blanche wanted to give him a good poke in the ribs. Rattle him, so he'd explain and be quick about it. But clearly, he wasn't in the mood to talk. Once again, she reminded herself to be patient. The late sun fell on Guli's hair and shoulders, transfixing him like a statue.

Margarita went to Guli and gently put a hand on his back. "You can tell them, *mijo*."

Emilio's confusion was paralyzing, but overall, Blanche saw relief in his eyes. This secret was out and no longer a burden, for at least some of them. What followed the reveal might be complicated. She would add that to the never-ending list of complications.

"How? Why? What is going on here?" Emilio clenched his hands into fists. He seemed on the verge of wringing Guli's neck. *"You kidnapped my aunt?!"*

"*Ah, mijo. Ahorita, calmate*," said Margarita. She returned to Emilio and placed her hands on his shoulders, gently pushing him into a chair. She was a small woman but forceful. "I was brought here for a reason, and now we will talk about it."

Guli shook his head.

"We need to tell them, Guli." Margarita folded her hands, straightening her back, and looked at Emilio and Blanche. "I was poisoned. On purpose. For my own good."

"What?!" Emilio bounded out of his chair.

His aunt gestured for him to sit back down.

"This place just can't get any weirder," Blanche said, shaking her head. She sank down on a small wooden stool, her eyes intent on Margarita. Guli still hadn't looked up. "Do tell."

"What do you mean, Tía?" Emilio spoke quietly.

"I know things about the Schemmers, as I've already told you, and they wanted me out of the way. They told Guli to poison me. Do me in. Kill me. If he didn't, they threatened to get rid of him, and his mother—and my Issie. In unspeakable ways. They have bullies and cronies, and the Lord knows what they could have done. If he didn't go through with it, they said, there would be much suffering." She put her hands over her face and then gave Guli a tender look. "But he couldn't do it. He couldn't kill me."

"I made it look like I did." Guli's expression wavered between anger and relief. "I'm glad it's over with. They didn't win."

"But how did you do this, Guli? The timing is so strange," Blanche said. "Margarita looked dead as can be, half under that day bed, her skin a dull, grayish tone. And I didn't feel a pulse. She was cold and immoveable."

Guli started to speak, but Margarita put her hand up. "After we talked the last time, and I knew you were coming, I went to my cottage to wait for you, Emilio. But Frau Schemmer made me come back on the pretext of a retirement settlement and to say goodbye. I played along. I met her in the drawing room upstairs. I didn't know you were arriving that day."

"But Frau Schemmer did," Emilio said.

"She forced Guli. Harangued him, told him they were at the end of their limit. He needed to do this. No matter the consequences," said Margarita in a level tone.

"He gave me chloral hydrate. It lowered my blood pressure and made me look quite dead. Laced the herbal tea with it. Believe me, I was willing to do it. So, I drank it and went off to sleep. The sherry helped. The Frau met us upstairs in that bedroom."

Guli looked up then. "Timing was everything, and the Frau was the timekeeper, the director of this plan to get rid of Margarita, and sadly, I went along with it. To a point. The Frau set out the tea things in that sitting area in the bedroom, and I took over. She looked in to see Margarita face down on the floor, presumably dead. She thought I'd given her jimsonweed, or an overdose of barbiturates. Then I got your Tía, my nanny, out of there." He shook his head.

"I can't believe this. I was sure … !" Blanche tried to go back to that scene in her mind's eye, but it was all a blur.

Guli gave her a level look. "When people are shocked, and upset, they don't see things clearly. I had to go with that."

Guli was right. Blanche prided herself on the details, but this time she'd missed. *Big time.*

"You weren't supposed to be there. At that moment," Guli said.

"We were upstairs!"

"Asleep. You were supposed to be sleeping. When the Frau saw Margarita in that room, on the floor, she trusted me. As if she would know anything about trust." Guli's mouth twisted in contempt. "I was just about to carry Margarita off when I heard you coming, Blanche. I hid in a closet. Fortunately, you didn't hang around. Try to move the body or anything. You ran. Gave me time to move her. And revive her."

"You sure fooled me," Blanche said, "thank you very much."

"I couldn't do it. Of course, I couldn't …" said Guli, turning his eyes to Margarita. "All those years, Margarita, an *abuela* to me. My teacher and nurse. The Frau thought she could turn me with her threats. She thought she had us." He smiled at Margarita. "But no. We got them."

Blanche stood up. "Well, maybe so. Up 'til now. But how is this going to end? Margarita's here, and she's still in danger if they find her."

234

"They don't know Margarita is here," said Guli. "I dug a grave and then filled it back up so they could see I'd buried her." Guli stood up.

Blanche had not moved, hands on hips. "And you didn't hear me come into the tower before this, Margarita?"

"Oh, I heard you, but Guli told me to wait, be patient. Now is the time."

"Tonight, rather, very early in the morning, I will call for the car," said Guli. "You three are going to leave here. It's all set up. I knew this would happen, sooner or later. This escape."

"And, how are we supposed to go without the Schemmers' knowing?" Emilio was still seething.

"Believe me. I'll cover you. They've seen tourists come and go for years and years. I'll tell them something," Guli said earnestly. Then he added, "Why wouldn't they believe what I tell them? I am their faithful servant." But the bitter look on his face left plenty of doubt.

Twenty-Five
A Light

BLANCHE AND EMILIO LEFT Margarita in her tower room, a place similar to Esmera's, this one equally spare with lacey pillows and books that Guli had retrieved from Margarita's cottage. He'd made her feel at home. Now she was leaving. Along with Blanche and Emilio. Margarita was safe—and so were Blanche and Emilio. They were all anxious to get to the Capital and be with Issie.

Guli led Blanche and Emilio back down to the hidden door to the tower. He opened it and the three stood in the shadows of the vines and setting sun. "*Escuche.* You are to come back here to the horse barn at the far end of the property at two in the morning. Hernan will be waiting there to take you to the village in a small cart to meet your driver to the Capital."

"Hernan! The gaucho?" Emilio blurted out in surprise. The gruff leader of that bunch had been less than warm and friendly during their trip to the tavern, yet he was going to help them leave.

"You heard me right. Hernan is no admirer of the Schemmers. Many of us are not."

"Who else is in on this?" Blanche was intrigued at the web of secrets that held this place together.

"Not going to get into that now. You need to go."

But Blanche wouldn't be hurried off. "And, by the way, how did

236

you know we came up through the tower floor? You didn't see us from the windows, but there you were. Right there, like you were expecting us."

"Wouldn't you like to know." He had a sly grin, and now he turned it on. Blanche was susceptible—to a point.

"Yes, I'd like to know," she said.

Emilio was barely holding it together, but Blanche couldn't resist trying to get more out of Guli. He sighed with exasperation. "Since you're here, since you're Margarita's family, I'll tell you this much. Cameras."

"You?!" Blanche laughed. "Tomás and the Herr were fighting over one."

"Perhaps. But the last time you were snooping about—did you notice the shiny eyes of St. Joseph in the chapel—the patron of La Palma, El Caudillo José?"

Blanche stepped back and put her hands on her hips. "You're kidding! I thought there was something funny about that statue. And the flowers and all in that dusty place."

"You'd be surprised at who, and what, has eyes on you in this place," said Guli.

"La Palma. Don't think I'll be sad to say goodbye," Blanche murmured.

Emilio took that cue. "Come on, *Baquita*. Time to go."

"*¡Baquita!*" Guli mused. "*Vaquita*—little dolphin. Yes. You do have a … certain quality."

"Yes, she has many qualities." Emilio's tone was surly. Blanche put her head down. She didn't think it would be the right moment to burst out laughing, which is what she almost did.

"I like to swim," she said, smiling at Guli, then Emilio.

"That you do," said Emilio, taking her elbow, firmly but gently, and steering her away from the tower.

But she turned to Guli. "I'd like to thank you for all you did. For taking the risks. And for taking care of Margarita," she said. "Such a strange kind of care, but it worked. Brilliant."

"Quite," said Emilio. "And, yes, *muchas gracias*. Now we must go." The brusqueness returned.

"Be my guest." Guli's tone was hard, his eyes narrowed. "But do not forget. Be there. At the horse barn. The three of you will go back to the Capital. You should make it in two hours." He turned toward the door without another word.

"Wait!" Blanche had plenty more on her mind before they went off to Buenos Aires. "Guli, are you aware of what is beneath the altar in the chapel? And the bullet holes on the back wall? Do you know about all the shady dealings of the Schemmers? They are criminals, those two."

"Yes, they are criminals. But right now, there is no remedy. You need to leave. For your safety. And Margarita's, of course." He disappeared into the tower, leaving Emilio and Blanche to head back across the lawn to the pink house.

Blanche stared after him but then followed Emilio. He held tightly to her arm. She could feel his irritation, but she was still basking in the knowledge that Margarita was alive! And they had a plan to get away. Together! Issie would be thrilled!

Emilio drew Blanche close. "Why do you keep at it, Blanche?"

"What? With the questions?"

"Can't we just move on? Take my aunt and get out of here? Why do you have to push on with this Schemmer business?"

"Because it's right."

"You're right and the world's all wrong?"

She'd never seen him so riled up. "Something like that."

"*Mira, Baquita.* Little Dolphin." He said the last with a bite. "It's not safe to dig into this. We could walk into real trouble with these Nazis."

She stopped, stock still. "Are you condoning what they did?

Dismissing it?" She checked herself. It wouldn't do any good to argue.

Emilio persisted. "Of course not. But do you understand how I feel?"

"Oh, Emilio. Yes, I understand how you feel." She gauged his expression and sensed his love and concern and complete shock at finding his aunt. It manifested as anger and a whole lot of confusion.

"Emilio, we need to finish it off. You know?" She had to make things right, or try to, or she'd be looking back at La Palma for the rest of her life, wondering with regret. She was less a wonderer and more of a doer.

Emilio remained silent as they ambled across the lawn. They reached the main house and crept back to the library. The wall in the bookcase was intact. All quiet. They were alone.

"To thine ownself be true," Blanche murmured, her eyes wandering over the shelves full of books. Gran's words came into her head.

"What's Shakespeare got to do with it?"

"Who said Shakespeare?"

It was late now, and they didn't want to miss dinner. They needed to appear as the happy tourists, hungry and eager to enjoy all the loveliness of La Palma. If they ran into the Schemmers, Blanche meant to smooth over their past meeting as best she could. These remaining hours must pass without further drama.

They hurried back to their room, showered, and changed. Together, they stared out the bedroom window at the purple sky and the myriad stars that popped out here in the pampa, so vivid and sparkling away from the city lights. Blanche pushed open the window and breathed in the verdant air. A sense of freedom from worry about Margarita rushed over her. At least they had this wonderful outcome. It was the loose ends that nagged at her.

"I'm so happy," said Emilio.

"Now you tell me." She teased.

"I am. And relieved. Margarita is safe, and you are, and now we can get on with it." He smiled at her. "And if the ... other ... comes along, the righting of wrongs that you talk about, we'll do something about that, too."

Blanche smiled and squeezed his hand. She had no idea how this would all end, but if she followed her nose, it would lead her to the resolution. She was sure of it. She leaned her head against his shoulder. "It's good. We'll get into the Capital, and Issie will be so pleased. And then we'll see, won't we?"

Blanche set the matter aside. In her mind. She had no idea how she'd circle back to exposing the Schemmers for their crimes—not the least of which was attempted murder. But she couldn't let it go. There had to be a way. Again, she thought of Guli. He'd been working on ways to free himself and his mother from the Schemmers, and it seemed he was on the right path with authorities. She wondered how she could help things along.

They packed all their things, what little they'd brought, and headed down to dinner. The candles were lit in the dining room. A tureen of soup sat steaming on the sideboard next to a silver basket of bread, and on the table, carafes of Malbec. The scent of roses from the open window filled the room. Emilio whistled softly. "Hard to leave it and go back to normal."

"Uh-huh. Sure." They laughed.

Lusita glided silently into the room with a platter of *milanesa* and a bowl of salad. "*Buenas*, Lusita," Emilio said.

She didn't lift her eyes as she industriously arranged dishes. "*Sí. A vos, a gustar, por favor, Señor y Señorita.*" Then she was gone.

"So strange," said Blanche, tearing a piece of bread into bits.

She pulled her chair closer to Emilio and whispered, "This is what I'm talking about. We have to do something about this, Emilio."

"Blanche, she can decide for herself." His lips barely moved except to chew.

"Like Margarita? These people have a hold on Lusita, just like they had on Margarita. And Guli and his mother."

"You found Margarita. I couldn't have done it without you." He smiled and lifted a glass. "Let's celebrate that."

"We did it together, Emilio. Please."

He gave her a sideways glance and sighed. She looked at the clock on the mantel. It was after eleven o'clock. "Only a few more hours, and then we bolt," she murmured.

And then what?

Twenty-Six
Coffee Clutch

GULI WAS GOOD ON HIS PROMISE. At two in the morning, he stood in the shadow of the horse barn with Hernan. As Blanche and Emilio approached, they stopped whispering. Blanche's heart was pounding so loudly she was afraid she'd wake up all of La Palma. She should have been tired, spent, but instead she was excited, marveling at this turn of events, that they were safe and on their way to Buenos Aires. The moon threw light over the landscape, but it left them with a sufficient cover of darkness.

Margarita sat in the front of a small, open-sided cart, bundled in a fringed shawl, her hair pulled back neat and tight. Like a queen in her chariot. She smiled at them in the shadows and waved. Hernan grunted a goodbye at Guli and climbed in. Emilio came around to Margarita's side and fussed over her, tucking her into the cart and murmuring in Spanish.

"*Vaya con Dios,*" Guli said, hustling Blanche into the back seat of the cart. "*Rápido.*" Blanche had no words—what words simmered wouldn't come out. He caught her hands in his as he stood silhouetted in the lantern light. He leaned into the cart, and his eyes glowed.

"I won't forget," she murmured.

242

He held her arms, and for one frantic instant, Blanche thought he might kiss her. He said nothing. The caress of his hands on hers said it all.

"¿Qué?" Emilio turned from Margarita.

"Nada," Blanche murmured. Guli had already stepped back from the cart.

The wheels crunched over the back road to the village, not a sound except for bumping along on the dirt track—and the sound of her heart. It beat with relief, with exhilaration. She wouldn't look back; she would move forward to possibilities. The clouds obliterated the moon and stars as if they were in on the escape.

They turned onto the narrow road to Margarita's cottage. A green sedan was parked behind the house in the bushes. The battered, dusty car looked familiar. Tomás! He opened the door slowly and emerged, dressed in a baseball cap and tight dark clothing. He would have disappeared into the surroundings had he not given a whispered, hearty greeting.

They piled out of the cart and huddled near the sedan. Margarita took Hernan's face in her hands. "Buen hombre. Cuidado. Te veo … en el cielo." The stout, gruff gaucho wrapped his arms around the tiny woman and lifted her off the ground in a hug. "Por eterno," he said, then gently loaded her into the car. He climbed into his little four-wheeler and took off down the road in a plume of dust. He didn't look back.

Blanche watched him go. So many chapters ending. Margarita wiped a tear. "He was my bébé, my estudiante, and my helper for many years. As much as I am eager to leave this place, there are those I will miss."

"He kept you safe?" Blanche spoke wistfully as she touched Margarita's arm.

"When he could."

Blanche held the questions for now though she itched to know more. *What were they mixed up in? What does Tomás know?* She stared at the back of his head, his eyes intent on the road. These people were in it together and helped each other. Blanche was grateful they all seemed like such a tight, happy group. But how? And why?

The awesome silence of the pampa swallowed them, the tall grasses, taller than the car, thick and impenetrable. Blanche breathed deeply and held onto Emilio. The worry and concern were unsettling, but their commitment to be in this together was solid. They needed this reunion with Issie and a resolution to this venture. She fought sleep, clinging to Emilio whose head bobbed off his chest. The car hit every bump and managed to rocket forcefully into the dark. *I hope Issie has coffee.* Her brain was an idle stew of thoughts and emotions.

Tomás drove at a steady pace, his hands ten and two on the wheel, never wavering. Margarita sat bolt upright next to him, occasionally glancing around with a smile. It was so good to see her happy. Blanche focused on that happiness and prayed it would last.

Soon the humming of the engine lulled Blanche toward sleep, and she gave up. She was bone tired. The business of escaping under the noses of the Schemmers had wrung her out. Emilio held her even tighter, smoothing away the tension. She went off to dreamland before she could think of one more question.

Blanche startled awake as they rounded a plaza in Buenos Aires near Issie's apartment. She'd fallen asleep to the rumble of the wheels and Margarita's whispered encouragement to Tomás. Now the faint light settled on the sleepy old buildings and filtered through the car window and roused her. Traffic was sparse with the Capital on the edge of coming to life. Blanche looked forward to the end of this drive, anticipating the look of joy on Issie's face when they arrived at her door. Guli had promised to call ahead and tell her they were on their way.

Issie's window was open, the white curtains fluttering in the gray dawn. She stuck her head out and leaned dangerously over the sill, both arms waving frantically. Blanche could hear her hooting as she disappeared from view and came flapping down the stairs toward the car. She yanked open the front door where Margarita sat and fell into her mother's arms. Margarita wrapped her daughter in the shawl like a newborn baby.

"¡Completa, todo!" Margarita's voice choked with emotion as the two rocked back and forth.

Issie cried and looked around at the passengers—the smiling Tomás, Blanche, and Emilio.

"Qué bueno, primo mio. How good to see you again." When Emilio got out of the car, he hugged Issie, lost in the folds of her tie-dyed caftan.

"You've done it! Come up! We celebrate!" Issie pulled them toward the door and up the stairs.

Her apartment smelled of spices and herbs, bread and coffee. The room seemed brighter, even at daybreak, and less cluttered. Issie had assembled all the makings of a great reunion. She placed a tray of buns, butter and jam, and bowls of grapes, plums, and peaches on a low table as they all settled on the worn purple and red cushions and chairs. Blanche flopped into the bean bag, her appetite on hold for now as she watched Tomás and tried to make sense of the scene. It was like a party in the middle of a beloved second-hand shop. Emilio and Margarita, finally at a safe place together, tore into the bread and chattered away. Not a care in the world.

But Blanche had questions. She was itching to clear up some details. She stole a quick glance at Emilio and sat down next to Tomás.

"Tomás, please tell me, what's the connection here—among you all? Besides tango with the Schemmers, how do you know La Palma and Guli, and Margarita?" She was bursting. *"How did all this happen?"*

Tomás put his coffee down on the table with a firm click. He spun his cap around and placed his elbows on his knee. The morning sun fell harshly on his lined face and slicked-back hair and beat-up leather jacket. He showed his age. Now that he was away from the dancing and music, he seemed to be tense and sad. A different person. "Well, Señorita ..." He didn't seem eager to talk.

Maybe this was a bad time to bring it up. She sat back and focused on the contents of her coffee cup. She should let the man have his breakfast and some relief. But then he touched her arm and smiled openly.

Blanche took this as permission. "What's the story, Tomás?"

Issie hovered with the French press and stopped pouring into the cups on the tray.

"Oh, he has a story, all right. As if the situation isn't complicated enough."

He looked up and nodded, ruefully. "I should tell it. Yes, I will. I've known Margarita for a long time. And I know her history with the Schemmers. Our connection began in the seventies ... .

He stopped, but every eye was on him, hanging on his words. Blanche read determination in his expression. "I was a boy back then. Small for a teenager. But that didn't matter at the time, how big you were or how old. I guess I was lucky I escaped the fate of the Dirty War. They took the young ones, and the old against their will, and the pregnant women. They gave away their babies. Those who didn't agree with the generals, they disappeared. Like that." He snapped his fingers. "My brother Eduardo was one of them. He was a student at the university." Each word came with deep sadness. Blanche held her breath.

"I remember the day. The details, the color of everything. The smells. A metallic scent of fumes and dust in the air. The heat made it all much, much worse. The day he disappeared, four men in uniform drove up to our house in a green Ford Falcon with no license plate. Antennae stuck out all over the car. Looked like a beetle, or the Sputnik." He shook his head. "Something foreign in it. So unreal. I could only stare.

"The doors on the car flew open at once, like the men had done many times. Like it was natural. A horrible kind of normal. They marched up the walk. Quiet and serious. I didn't know what they wanted at first, but I had a feeling. I'd heard the rumors. They rushed through the door past me and straight on through the other rooms in the house looking for Eduardo." Tomás buried his head in his hands.

"*Y por la gracia del diablo*, they found him. They took him to a detention center in the Capital. They stripped him and put wires on him, forced him to say things about the monsters running the government. Then they took him, and others, out to the pampa. *Out to La Palma*. And then they shot my brother. Killed them all."

Blanche put her hand over her mouth, and it was a good thing. She shouldn't talk. She couldn't move.

Tomás delivered this awful memory without inflection, his shoulders slumped. The tango dancer gone, the devastated brother in his place.

"Oh my God. The chapel wall!" Blanche blurted. When he looked up, his eyes were filled with tears. "I am so sorry, Tomás," she said.

"We're all sorry, Señorita Blanche," he said. "That we let this happen. It started well. A revolution and a call for change, with flag waving and patriotism. The people wanted a return to a better way of life. Then the arrests of protestors, 'the enemies,' and the opening of the detention centers. At first we looked the other way. We said, these people must have done something wrong to be taken away. To be punished. But, no. The killing and torture were random with no trial or explanation. Protest of any kind—in the newspaper, the theater, in class—surely led to disappearance. Innuendo was enough to destroy an entire family. Hundreds and thousands of people, disappeared. In a few years' time ...

"We must never forget this happened, and we need to remember the disappeared. I say my brother's name. Eduardo. It is the only way he is alive to me. In my heart and memory." Tomás looked around the room. "You never knew him, but say his name. So we never forget. So that he's here with us."

"Eduardo," they said.

The lines in his face relaxed. The room was silent, breakfast forgotten. A car honked and broke the stillness down in the plaza. A dog barked. Below, someone yelled, *"¡Ya voy!"* The world spun on, away from history, but not away from the memory.

"The mothers and grandmothers, the ones who wear the white scarves, marching with the signs and names ... ?" Blanche had seen them in the plaza on a Thursday, and now she understood. "This is 2005, and they walk. With the pictures of the missing. Twenty-five years later?"

"Wouldn't you?" His tone was bitter. "As long as they march, the disappeared are in this life. At least in this way."

"Tomás, how did you learn about what happened to Eduardo?" Blanche drew closer to him.

"There were eleven people taken from the detention center and driven out to the pampa. One man got away. He'd been sent on an errand to the truck under armed guard, but he eluded the captors and ran into the woods. He climbed a tree and watched."

"Did they ever recover ... Eduardo?"

"No," said Tomás. "Not yet."

"Why, Tomás? Why did this happen?" Blanche could barely speak.

"Evil, and desperation. And fear—those with power wanted more, and they were afraid of losing it."

"But *how?*" she said.

"The country was in desperate shape. Economic and political. For decades. Farm production was down, inflation was up. Groups such as the Montaneros and others fought for change, and the military began to resist with force. Even the United States, who feared the threat of communism in Latin America, backed the military—despite the knowledge of the brutality and injustice going on here." He lifted his palms and shrugged.

"Fear rules," she said.

"If we let it."

They drank the coffee and ate the croissants with little enthusiasm. What he'd told them was too devastating to take in all at once. Blanche looked over at Margarita, her expression sad and wistful. She knew. She'd lived through it.

What happened to Eduardo? That was the question. What awful secrets went along with that? *La Palma.* Blanche studied Tomás's face. The cigarette burned down in his yellowed fingers. She waited for him to speak, but he remained silent.

The silence broke. Suddenly. Boots clomped on the stairs and stopped outside the apartment. Fists pounded on the door, threatening to break it apart.

They jumped, coffee cups clattering. Feet hit the ground.

"You expecting *more* company, Issie?" Blanche asked. "They don't sound too ... genial."

"No. I do not know who it is." Issie said, and not happily.

An uneasy tension swept the room. They were all standing when the door burst open. Bruno, the cook, stood framed in the doorway, a venomous look on his face, his pallor like the underbelly of a fish. He wore a tight, black skull cap emblazoned with a swastika, but that was not the most arresting feature. He leveled the gun and pointed it from one to the other.

"*Raus*. All of you. Move over there together."

Then his expression changed from hard and mean to shock as his eyes lit on Margarita.

He didn't know.

A wiry fellow with a face like a rat stood behind Bruno, slapping a small bat against his palm. He nodded at the sight of Margarita, very much alive and well in Buenos Aires.

"Oh great," Blanche murmured. Bruno waved the gun back and forth over the group as if deciding who to shoot first. "Not this again." They were rooted to the spot, afraid to move even though they'd been ordered to do so. The coffee roiled in her stomach.

Blanche did a quick calculation: *There're five of us and only two of them.* But the guns changed the equation.

Tomás stepped forward but didn't say a word. Bruno planted his feet and pointed to the corner with the gun. "Go there, *hombre*. *Todos*."

"You don't need to do this, Bruno," Tomás said.

"What do you know? I am ordered to bring you back to La Palma. I came for you, but now I want Margarita … and the girl."

"I don't think so," said Tomás. He took another step toward Bruno.

"Tomás! Wait!" Blanche yelled.

Too late. The gun exploded. The shot ripped a hole in Tomás's chest, lifting him off the ground. He landed against the bean bag, spread-eagle on his back. His eyes rolled up in his head.

"Tomás!" Blanche dropped down next to him. Emilio reached for Blanche and pulled her flat on the floor. He felt Tomás for a pulse.

Bruno snarled and advanced into the room. "What did you expect? He came at me."

"No. He did not!" Blanche's temper rose. The heat of anger burst out her. Emilio held her down. "You didn't have to do this!" she screamed, hysteria choking her words.

A red blotch below Tomás's shoulder leaked and spread like an evil bloom under him. Emilio urged Blanche: "Stay down."

He yanked at the curtain on the window and the whole rod clattered to the floor. With one eye on Tomás, he tore the fabric and wadded it against the wound in one sweeping move.

Bruno moved quickly. He grabbed Margarita's arm and turned toward Issie.

Issie was quicker. What appeared to be a toy gun was not. She raised the weapon and fired at Bruno. The gun in Bruno's hand clunked onto the floor, and he started to go for it. She fired again. He fell against the door jamb, regained his footing, barely. His partner already was running down the stairs.

"The next one goes right into the middle of your goddam head," she yelled, but Bruno, bent over, unarmed and bleeding, was frantically clutching his middle. He backed into the hallway and stumbled down the stairs.

Issie stood on the low futon, her elbows out and feet planted apart. One combat boot came out from under her caftan. She still clutched the gun in both hands and aimed it directly at the door, her tiny knuckles white. No one moved. The air was heavy and rank with the smell of gun powder. The hot morning sun burned through the room.

Voices and shouting rose from the street below. A vehicle backfired. Blanche crept over to the window and looked down at the curb. The rat-face accomplice was gone. Bruno leaned into a van, his body limp and bleeding. The van sped off down the street and disappeared into traffic.

Twenty-Seven
Rally

EMILIO HELD THE BALLED-UP curtain against Tomás's chest. His breathing shallow, the bleeding seemed to stop. "We need to call an ambulance," Emilio said. Blanche looked around for Issie. She'd left her burner phone at La Palma.

"No! No hospital." Together, Issie and Margarita protested. "I have a neighbor, a doctor," Issie said. "I'll get him."

"What's going on? Why can't we get him to a hospital?" Margarita and Issie's blank expressions said nothing. Blanche choked back the worry and emotion, overwhelmed that their effort to save Margarita had come to this.

Emilio worked on Tomás, loosening his clothing and checking the bullet hole. Blanche could hardly see the rise and fall of his chest as his breathing evened out. She hoped Emilio's medical training kicked in, but this was hardly a place to treat a gunshot wound. "He can't lose more blood. He needs treatment. Now." He looked around desperately. Issie was gone.

Tomás opened his eyes and fumbled at his pocket. His lids flickered, desperately, as he jerked his head up at Emilio.

"Lie still, Tomás." Blanche pleaded. "Help's on the way." *I pray.*

He grimaced but persisted. His fingers clutched at his clothing until a slim wallet fell out of a pocket. Blanche picked it up.

"The card," he said. His head fell back. An unhealthy pallor spread across his face, the rims of his eyes and mouth white.

"Relax now, Tomás," said Margarita. Blanche had not seen her hovering, but now she rested a hand on his forehead. He suddenly reached up and grabbed it. "*Cuidado, Señora,*" he mumbled.

Blanche read the card. Javier Ochoa-Villafranca, Esquire. A phone number. In gold lettering. His office was nearby on Reconquista off the Plaza de Mayo.

"We will finish this. I promise," said Margarita, still close to Tomás's ear, but he'd lost consciousness. Her tone was hollow and remote as she turned and patted Blanche's hand.

Blanche was about to launch into a whole new set of questions when Issie appeared in the doorway with a stooped, elderly man. He smoothed back the wisps of white hair, his eyes twinkled with the depth of deep blue water.

"Doctor Irigoyen here." He didn't hesitate but went straight to Tomás and bent over him crookedly. He nodded at Emilio. "Let us get him to my apartment," the doctor said. His sure hands were old, like well-washed linen, but swift.

Emilio and the doctor lifted Tomás and gently carried him out the door.

Margarita still sat crouched on the floor. Blanche joined her. "This is not how it is supposed to be," Margarita murmured.

"I couldn't agree more," said Blanche, eyeing Margarita, remarkably calm and poised. "So, we'll tell *who* what happened?" She still held the card, snapping it between her fingers.

Margarita pointed to the card. "We're going to see him. Soon."

"Maybe right now?! For some answers. And really, we should get out of here." Blanche was thinking a one-way ticket to Florida the best option, but there were a lot of pesky details, such as passports—and Tomás's condition and this lawyer. "Bruno might come back even though I think Issie plugged him. I don't think that accomplice would have anything to do with us now."

"Bruno! That *estupido*! The Schemmers' bully and lackey," said Margarita. She sat down hard on the edge of the sofa, her shoulders pulled back in disgust. "The farther we get from all of them, the better."

Blanche persisted. "Margarita, you certainly can't stay here. Does Issie have a place far away from here for you two? She said she was looking into it."

Issie bounded back into the room, her forehead lined with worry.

"How is he?" Blanche asked.

"He's out cold, and it'll be a while before we know anything. He's lost a lot of blood."

"We should get him to the hospital, Issie."

"No, we can't get the authorities involved." She shot her mother a look and then began to move frantically around the apartment, gathering coffee cups and plates.

"*Why is it that no one wants to involve the authorities?*"

"Other matters." Margarita spoke gently as she began to straighten the apartment with restless energy. "Everything will be resolved soon."

Blanche had to go with that. For now. She eyed the pool of blood and dashed to the kitchen for towels. The three were a whirlwind of cleaning, but it didn't wipe away her concern. Blanche threw the dirty towels in a bucket. Her mild reserve of patience dribbled away. "OK, I hope Emilio and the doctor can handle it, and if not we're going to have to call—"

Issie stopped flitting around the room. "Doctor Irigoyen has seen it all. And fixed it all."

Blanche was right on Issie's heels. "What about the gun? What's up with *that?*"

Issie relaxed some. "I had to be ready. You can figure why. And that caftan hid it pretty well, don't you think?" Blanche didn't know what to say. Issie looked away. "I didn't want to take any chances." She dropped the tray with a clatter and held out the voluminous folds of the bright red and purple robe. Like she would fly. She pulled it over her head and stood there, hands on hips, in her skinny jeans, combat boots, and T-Shirt that read: *"Nunca Más."*

Never more. "How familiar ... The rally against terrorism. During the Dirty War," Blanche murmured.

"Exactly. And *no more* from those yahoos at La Palma," Issie said. She scooped up the broken curtain rod and marched off to the back of the apartment. "You are right, Blanche, we have to get out of here." Her voice trailed off as the door to the kitchen flapped shut behind her.

Margarita smiled. "Chica hasn't changed since she was a toddler. *Mi chiquita bonita.*" Her eyes sparkled with love and happiness, seemingly putting aside the imminent threat brewing at La Palma and all the catastrophe at breakfast. Blanche wanted more distance between them and the estancia and its inhabitants, but Margarita looked lovingly after Issie with a contentment that her daughter had all in hand. She turned to Blanche. "I am glad to meet you, Señorita Blanche, and, finally, my Emilio. You've done much to bring us all together."

"Margarita, I don't think it's done," she said, trying to keep the angst out of her voice.

"I know, but it's a fine start. To get away from them."

"You don't know how relieved we are." She smiled at Margarita. The near misses and the loose ends were troublesome, especially with that ghoul, Bruno, on the loose. She hoped Issie had put him out of commission.

"Margarita," said Blanche. "Upstairs in the big house ... after I found you on the floor ... there was a crumpled note that had been left near a table. *'No más, por fin.'* What was that about?"

"Finally, no more terrorism. Of any kind. I was writing to Gerda, but then Guli came in with the tea," she said, "so, I couldn't finish the note. I knew you and Emilio were on the way. I just wasn't sure when."

"And Guli saved you. From Gerda."

"*Sí*. Gerda Schemmer wanted me dead," she said. "That woman." But then Margarita smiled. "We fooled them, though, didn't we? Guli and I. And the Frau was none the wiser." Margarita's expression hardened at the memory of this victory over the Schemmers. "The evil they do."

"I guess I pre-empted Guli's plan. Stepped right into the middle of it," said Blanche. "I'm good at that."

Margarita laughed and patted Blanche's knee. "You are good. A very good person." The strength of this small woman warmed Blanche's heart. She figured it must be a family gene.

"You've known Tomás for a long time?"

"Many, many years. After the Dirty War, he came out to La Palma looking for a trace of his brother Eduardo. That's when Tomás planted himself in the Schemmers' lives. Acting the tango dancer to their *milongas*." Margarita rolled her eyes. "Tomás is *muy listo*. He'd suspected the Schemmers were complicit during the war, and so he found a way in. The generals had long reach, sharp claws. They ruined so many, but justice is coming."

"Did he find anything?"

"Pieces of information are coming together. The witness identified La Palma as the site of the murders, and that was a turning point. But investigations move slowly. It was not the priority for many years to expose these horrors and punish the criminals." Margarita sighed. "But Tomás does not give up. He must not now."

Tomás *must* recover. She'd never forget the sight of that chapel wall.

Margarita shook her head. "I wasn't any help when Tomás first came out to La Palma. I was in the village. But that all changed."

"What do you mean?"

Margarita pointed to the business card. "We met, Tomás and I, with the authorities. Ochoa has been helpful in putting this together. We're close now. The Schemmers are going to pay."

Blanche looked down at the card she still held in her hand and nodded. Tomás had taken a precious breath and made an impossible effort to get that card into her hands. *Are we thinking the same thing?* They were definitely rounding a corner. This man Ochoa had to be a ticket to solving this horrendous mess. Blanche bet on it. And already an idea was brewing.

Twenty-Eight
Stunner

ISSIE HADN'T WASTED ANY time calling Javier Ochoa-Villafranca, Esquire. He was available. Tomás was left in Doctor Irigoyen's hands, and Margarita, Emilio, and Blanche headed over to meet the lawyer.

"I will stay here and be ready," Issie said. She waved her gun in the air.

"Issie, you need to be ready to *leave*," said Blanche.

"Yes, that, too," she said, grinning.

The three hurried down the sidewalk under a row of plano trees. The day had opened bright and promising. Blanche felt hopeful. Margarita took quick little steps, looking over her shoulder.

"What is it, Tía?" Emilio asked gently. She looked up at her nephew. "I want to be done with this. For good."

"We all do," said Emilio, wrapping his arm around her protectively. Blanche squeezed Margarita's hand and beamed at Emilio for his tenderness and concern. It made her steps—and her heart—light. Finally, together, and they were so close to fixing things. It wasn't done yet, and she knew she had to throw down one last big move …

As they walked quickly down Reconquista, Blanche kept a

look-out for the unsavory team of Bruno and company—she was pretty sure that team had folded—but it still made her nervous they were out there. *Somewhere.* The crowd blended into a panoply of faces with flat, citified expressions. She was still wary. Blanche never wished anyone dead, but under the circumstances she'd make an exception for someone who shot Tomás.

The packed, hot concrete city was so far away from home and Blanche's reality; the canyon of gray classically-styled buildings gave her claustrophobia. Blanche longed to get back to Santa Maria Island, the openness of the Gulf, and her log cabin in the pines. It would be soon now.

They dodged workers in hard hats and those in blue suits, and women hurrying from the market with bundles of produce. The aroma of *asado* from a *parilla* wafted down the street, but Argentina hardly tempted her. She had no appetite. She wanted resolve. And she staked all on the lawyer they were about to visit. Tomás—in what looked like his dying breath—insisted they see him.

Señor Ochoa-Villafranca was looking out his office window, his hands clasped behind his back, presumably staring down into the small pocket park below. He turned then. He had an arresting presence, a serene expression, and probing dark eyes. His tall, thin stature and ascetic look reminded Blanche of an El Greco painting. A slow smile showed all-white teeth beneath a trim mustache. He went directly to Margarita in a couple of strides, took her hands, and pumped them up and down, then drew her into an embrace of air kisses. "You're here. Margarita."

One tight bunch. Somehow, this affectionate association, so like a family, did bode well. *The family that stays together gets stuff done.*

Ochoa greeted Blanche and Emilio and invited them to sit in the leather arm chairs in front of an enormous desk. "I'm sorry to hear about Tomás, but I have much confidence in Doctor Irigoyen. He has treated much … trauma. I trust Tomás will recover."

"You know about Tomás? Already? And obviously you know Margarita." Blanche leaned forward, rather eagerly.

Emilio put his hand on Blanche's arm and murmured, "*Baquita.*" She held his hand, but he couldn't calm her eagerness.

"I know Doctor Irigoyen, and I know them all very well, including the Señorita Issie." He smiled at Margarita. "We have a good team." A soccer reference? Blanche's gaze drifted to a photo of the lawyer towering over soccer legend Maradona, their smiling heads inclined toward each other. It sat prominently on his desk. Trophies, balls, and photos on bookcases, typical of the rabid Argentinian aficionado, lined the walls. She hoped Ochoa had the same level of enthusiasm for restoring order—and peace—for those who suffered from evil.

He picked up the photo on his desk. "The famous Diego Maradona. 'The hand of God.' Brilliant, and troubled. Like many things."

Blanche agreed with the lawyer's veiled assessment of Argentina. "You do have an interesting and unsettling history."

He sat down and folded his hands on the green blotter. "That is why we're here. Righting some of it. That is *right*, Margarita?"

She nodded; her expression inscrutable. "We are close to getting justice for what the Schemmers have done." Margarita's voice echoed a new confidence.

"It couldn't happen without you, and Tomás, of course," said Ochoa.

"How?" Blanche couldn't resist the interruption. All the events seemed to collide like a massive train wreck—what the Schemmers had done to so many, what Margarita and Tomás had suffered at their hands.

The lawyer smiled. "Tomás went looking for the place of his brother's disappearance in 1978, and his search led him to La Palma—and to Margarita. They teamed up. Margarita eventually brought us information about the Schemmers. We've been gathering journals, conversations, a record of what has gone on at La Palma for many years now. And you, Señorita Blanche and Señor Emilio, of late, have helped."

"Really?" Blanche croaked. The list of items she'd found in the treasure under the chapel burned a hole in her backpack. But she didn't think Ochoa was referring to that.

He focused on Blanche. "First, let me apologize for the incident on the *peotanal*. I hope it didn't cause you distress, but Tomás is a canny one. I do not condone the stunt, but ..." His clasped hands tightened. He leaned forward toward her earnestly. "It was part of a plan, more or less, the business with the biker and Tomás. We needed another connection to the estancia, and your visit was a fortunate opportunity."

Blanche jumped out of her chair. "I knew it!" She'd always suspected there was a story behind the episode on the *peotanal*, and her hunch was right. She glanced at Emilio and looked away. *I told you so!* His expression was a mix of irritation and surprise.

"What are you talking about, Señor?" said Emilio. "Nearly running down Blanche was a 'fortunate opportunity'? What if she'd been killed?!"

"Señor Emilio." The lawyer's knuckles were white, his head tilted at an uncomfortable angle. "You told your aunt you would help, and you'd spoken of the skills and talents of your *querida*, Blanche Murninghan. This knowledge was exceedingly helpful. We trusted her abilities to stay alive. So, it encouraged Tomás to go ahead with the, shall we say, maneuver? I was reluctant to agree to such a plan, and I must say, tacitly, I did not. But as I said, Tomás is canny. Relentless. He'll stop at nothing, and he has been instrumental in our pursuit of these people at La Palma, which has dragged on for years."

"Yes, and I am partially, and unwittingly, responsible. I'd

confided in Tomás about your arrival. He took it from there."
Margarita sighed and shook her head. "Oh, so much happened, and
so fast."

"*¡Por Dios!*" Emilio shouted.

Blanche put a hand on his arm. "It's okay. You see I am fine."
Yet she didn't feel fine.

Ochoa raised slim fingers. "Tomás planned to engage you,
and that happened. He's become fond of you both. Completely
enthralled, I'd say."

Emilio was hardly mollified. He reared back, hard against the
chair, his eyes blazing at the lawyer. Blanche was intrigued but
not surprised. And for all the drama, it looked like it was going to
be worth it. The *hit and run. Meeting Tomás. The poisoning.* And now,
they were about to expose the Schemmers. A welcome storm was
brewing.

"The biker? You must know it's Ramón Garcia, Tomás's driver,"
said Ochoa. "Remember when he drove you out to La Palma? He
left you and the car in the driveway and ran off around the house?
It was then that he delivered spying devices to Lusita. She is, how
you say, a very fine *mole*. We've been watching."

"Lusita?! Wow, this gets better and better. Or worse?" Blanche
was suddenly horrified that Lusita could be in terrible danger.
"Lusita! We have to help her!"

He nodded. "We can get to Lusita, and she is completely safe,
but for now, let me tell you we need discretion, and we are in the
throes of the last efforts to get to the Schemmers. Your skills,
Señorita Blanche, while at times more than enthusiastic, have
delivered much information."

Blanche gave him a wry smile. "That's me. All gung ho. I did
sort of blast away at them." The alcohol-fueled meetings in the
living room came to mind.

"You got them to talk. And thanks to you, we have a lot of the conversations recorded, which will help for comparison to the information we have on file. And, in the long run, for support in incrimination."

Blanche didn't recall any major confessions on the Schemmers' part, but they had spilled context to their nefarious deeds. And she was a witness to their post-tango argument. *Well, goodie for us. And goodie for them!* All the same, she couldn't help feeling a bit heated over the news they'd been watched. Watched—and set up.

"So. You've spied on us?" She didn't check her annoyance. In fact, she liked the feel of it, the righteous weight of it. It was a cudgel, and she always liked to have one at the ready.

"Señorita Blanche, if you hadn't done what you did, I mean, your curiosity, your questions, your *tenacity*, it would have taken much longer to complete the investigation. And time was—is—running out.

"You brought things to a head with your visit to the tower. You have remarkable instincts." His tone was level, his hands clenching and unclenching as if to help make his point. His gold cuff links twinkled. His manicure added extra polish. His eyes followed Blanche as she paced about the room.

He was buttering her like a roll. She stopped and stared back at him, aware she had to let the indignation go. Better yet, use it.

"Please, Señorita, sit," he said.

"There have been things we had to do." Margarita spoke up, firmly but gently.

Like being drugged and playing dead. Blanche shook her head and sighed, loudly.

"Your safety was always first," Margarita continued, "and at the same time, we needed your help. I knew I'd be safe with Guli, and you and Emilio would be safe with Tomás. Although that *peotanal* business ..." Margarita patted Emilio's hand, still tightly fisted. "We need to finish this."

Blanche couldn't shake her distress, her feeling of being violated. Ochoa let the conversation rest, for what it was worth. In her mind, she worked through the parts she and Emilio had played in bringing everything to light. Mostly, they—she—had stirred things up. But, like Gran used to say, *Sometimes the best ingredients settle to the bottom of the pot and need a little stirring.*

"Why didn't you tell us? We would have been discreet." Blanche looked from Ochoa to Margarita for answers. "Why have we been dragged through all this until now?"

"Geez, *Baquita*, we've only been here days." Emilio stood and lifted his arms. "They've been doing this for *years!*"

The voice of reason. Always the voice of reason. She didn't look at Emilio but gazed at the lawyer. Eventually, the tenseness in her shoulders eased. "You're right. Of course."

"In short." The lawyer resumed a stern expression, after seemingly mollifying Blanche. She stood peacefully, all ears. "This investigation has taken decades. Since Tomás traced his brother's disappearance to La Palma. Since he met Margarita, and they teamed up to expose the Schemmers. They tipped their hand during the *Proceso* when they assisted the generals in their murders. That is when the background of the Schemmers began to emerge. They've tried to keep a low profile since, but the truth has finally outed them.

"We had every intention of telling you. When the time was right," Ochoa added.

"And now, the time is right?" Her frustration began to melt. She lifted that cudgel; she was beginning to see how she'd swing it.

"Oh, yes," said Margarita in tandem with the lawyer.

Blanche put her hands on her hips. "Okay, so what's the rest of the story?"

The lawyer clenched his fingers. "Please sit down, Señorita."

Blanche sank into the chair, and Emilio pulled his close to her.

"Do you know of your Office of Special Investigations in the Department of Justice? It was created some twenty-five years ago to hunt Nazi collaborators living in your country. We have something analogous here, and I am part of that so-called group of Argentinian hunters. There are lawyers, investigators, and historians who work worldwide to help in the investigation. It doesn't stop. In your country alone, there have been hundreds of investigations and dozens of prosecutions that have come out of the work."

"I've heard." Actually, she had no idea the scope of it, but Blanche could feel all the pieces coming together, forming a fuzzy landscape of history. The aftermath of war.

"This sounds like something out of a novel, full of intrigue, secret meetings, murder ... Outcomes too good to be true," she said.

"Nothing of the sort. It's real. A lot of paperwork and tedious phone calls and visits to foreign countries. And searching in our own back yard, so to speak. At La Palma."

"So, what do you plan to do? In your own backyard?" she said.

"The US has given us some information on the Schemmers." Ochoa's stony expression didn't waver. "They're accused of fleeing Germany for the war crimes they committed. They were young, but they participated in the extermination of many Jewish people in the camps. In addition, we've found they were complicit with the generals during the *Proceso*, and they have been withholding rightful ownership of La Palma from Esmera and Guillermo, the descendants of Bartolo, the deceased owner of the estancia. You might as well know. It will be a matter of public record soon enough."

Blanche leaned forward in her chair. "You have proof of all that?"

"Grinding proof."

"But the *Proceso*? The Dirty War of the seventies, early eighties? The Schemmers were part of *that*, too?"

"The dissidents, the activists, the clergy, students, those who disagreed with the military regime. Some were brought to La Palma, shot and buried. A new law in 2003 has enabled the government to have another look at the collaborators, find them, and punish them. It's been slow, but justice moves at a snail's pace, as we all know."

"Tomás's brother," she said. "Eduardo."

"Yes. Eduardo. And José, Jorge, Matilde, Francesco, Xavier ... and others that night."

Blanche rummaged in her backpack and produced the yellowed list she'd taken from the crates under the chapel. "Maybe this will help. Add it to the pile of grievances. The theft of crates upon crates of precious artifacts I found at La Palma in a small storeroom under the chapel. These things were no doubt stolen from their rightful owners."

Margarita clutched the front of her dress with a look of stunned disbelief, her mouth open. Ochoa was on his feet now. He took the list and scanned the paper, shaking slightly. He looked up at Blanche. "You've seen these things?"

"Oh, yes."

He sat down. "Gold. What is this? The Nazis and gold. Stores of it stolen from the Czechs and laundered through the British and German banks. Even the removal of gold from teeth at the time of extermination ... They were fascinated with gold."

"Yes, well, that's great to be fascinated with it when it's yours. This cache at La Palma clearly does not belong to the Schemmers. All of it, I can just bet, came from temples and museums, sacred spots, and from families. Stolen. Taken for the benefit of the Schemmers. Disgusting."

Margarita was incredulous. "How did you find it?"

Emilio spoke up. "*Mi Baquita*, as I say, she is the small blood hound."

"I couldn't sit still. I had to look for you, Margarita. Lusita was a help. She encouraged me to look in the chapel but said nothing of going underground. I found the crates under the chapel. God knows what else is down there."

"I have never seen this, did not know of it," she said. "But Guli said there were tunnels. I don't think he knew about the gold."

Ochoa raised his eyebrows. "It's a fine piece of evidence. We need to have a look."

"May I make a suggestion?" Blanche leaned forward again and put the tips of her fingers on the edge of his desk. Her earnest expression had his full attention. The cudgel was about to drop with a *Bang*.

"Please do," said Ochoa.

It was a hard sell, especially to Emilio, but Blanche talked them into backing her return to La Palma. The lawyer agreed to bring one of the inspectors investigating the Schemmers into his office. They all met within the hour.

"I have a plan," Blanche told them. They heard her out.

Twenty-Nine
Guli: Meanwhile, Back At The Ranch

GULI PACED IN THE THIRD story room of the tower. He was anxious, but he should have been relieved. He would have been, if he could have thought more clearly. The girl had come and jumbled up everything, especially his emotions. She'd sped up the process of getting Margarita to safety with her snooping; in fact, everything about Blanche was like holding back a tornado and then the release of it. But finally, after years of this torture, the plan was coming to a head. Ochoa had called and gotten him up to speed. They were going to rid themselves of the Schemmers. He and his mother had been patient. They knew they would beat the Schemmers at their game, but they'd had to wait it out.

The Schemmers never had legal ownership of La Palma, and this was public knowledge now—Guli had made sure of that with the authorities, Lawyer Ochoa among them. The couple could have gotten rid of Guli and Esmera. But where would it stop? They couldn't root out the truth, not when it had taken hold of everyone who knew about La Palma—and everyone Guli had contacted. He'd

visited lawyers and government officials and quietly and relentless-
ly dug around, going about securing what was rightfully his mother's property under the land grants to the Indigenous.

Guli felt secure, for now. At least, the Schemmers were at arm's
length, and they certainly couldn't afford to come under scrutiny.
Their past was too disturbing, and they risked deportation in the
event of an inquiry.

They'd all bided their time. And now, the Schemmers' time had
run out.

Guli pulled the phone from his pocket. The girl, the American.
She didn't stop. Now, here she was calling him again, surely with
another update.

"Guli, we have good news," Blanche said. "We have more to do
to put the Schemmers away. *For good.* But I am going to need your
help."

He listened. If he weren't so intrigued—and slightly in love with
her—he would have hung up. But he couldn't do that. He needed
more, and this could be the final push. She'd just promised. She
would tell him more. Soon.

They were on the verge of something big. He'd been chasing
the Ministry of Justice and Human Rights and a law passed in
1985 that meant to return confiscated or unlawfully retained land
back to the Indigenous people. Esmera, as widow of Bartolo and
a member of the Toba, was eligible under provisions of the law.
Guli had been caring for his mother and juggling the demands of
the Schemmers, trying to keep his head up, while the government
plodded along for twenty years, sorting claims. Guli's had been
among them. It was going to happen.

He sat in that tower, his mother's needs taken care of for the
day, and he waited for Blanche to call him back.

"Guli? Blanche."

He clutched the phone, wishing it were she he had in his hands.

The feel of her small bones, soft skin. She smelled like jasmine that curled around the palms at the edge of the lawn ...

"I am here."

"Treasures, there is gold under the chapel. Crates of it. And I have a list of the items for authorities."

"What are you talking about?"

"The Schemmers. They have stores of artifacts stolen from the Jewish people." She unraveled the strange story of her discovery. "Have you never been in those tunnels? Under the chapel?"

"It is not a place I linger. I never saw any Nazi treasure."

"I am coming back, and we are going to get them. You will wait there in the tower? Be ready to help me? We are going to coordinate with Lusita ..."

The last he'd thought about the tunnels was when he'd smuggled Margarita up into the tower. He'd considered using the underground passage, but then decided it would be easier to dress like a gardener, bundle up his nanny, and escape through the side door of the big house. The plan had worked.

What Guli couldn't understand was how Gerda thought he could kill Margarita. Cold blooded, the German woman had no soul. Of course, he would do what he could to implicate both the Schemmers for all their crimes. This new twist was intriguing. He waited to see the girl.

Thirty

The Final Solution

BLANCHE STOOD AT OCHOA'S DESK, the phone trembling slightly in her hand, but her voice was firm.

"Frau Schemmer, this is Blanche. I hope everyone is well. You? Herr Schemmer? The staff?" Her tone was the sweetest, the warmest, under the circumstances.

The woman's voice was stiff. Frosty. "Yes, we are doing well." She paused for several seconds too long. "I am surprised you have called. Guli explained some about your sudden departure."

Blanche hesitated. They measured each other. *She must not know about Margarita and the details of our departure or I'm walking into a trap.* It was a gamble she had to take. "I am sorry that we left unexpectedly and couldn't say goodbye in person, but Tomás only advised us late that the driver was available that night. Did you get my note?"

"Yah," she said.

Blanche plunged in. "I was wondering ... if Emilio and I might return for a short visit? We can arrange payment when we get there, if that would be okay with you and the Herr. Maybe stay a couple of days? Do some hiking and horse riding? We love the city but our hearts are really in the country."

Frau Schemmer's voice softened. "Yes, we can arrange that."

Blanche prayed Bruno hadn't surfaced. Maybe Issie had finished him off. Blanche could hear Gran's words running through her head. *The bloom is off the rose, and the chickens are coming home to roost.*

Emilio, of course, would stay back in Buenos Aires, but the Schemmers didn't need to know that. Over a barrage of his pleading and protest, Blanche would go ahead without him. The police had reassured him she wouldn't be alone. They'd be nearby if the slightest hitch occurred, and they planned to swoop in at the last. Blanche had Guli for back-up. Emilio still balked at the plan, but Blanche intended to go, with or without his agreement.

"It's a chance to get them, to end this," she'd argued to Emilio. "And the injustice Guli and Esmera suffered needs to be rectified. Throw that in with the theft of the gold—and crimes against humanity."

Reluctantly, Emilio had agreed. He stayed with Margarita and Issie in hiding near Tomás who was recuperating slowly at Dr. Irigoyen's apartment.

Two policemen drove Blanche out to La Palma in an unmarked car. They dropped her off near the house and headed to an out-of-the-way post. To wait, and listen in. Other forces were on the way.

Blanche wore a wire.

She walked over the gravel drive, crunching the last of her nerve with each step. She would see this through. The great imposing fortress of lies loomed up in front of her, all quiet except for the rustle of poplars and the call of birds. So beautiful, and so deceptive.

She hoped the technology did its job, and that she could retrieve what was needed. But that worry was not imminent. First, she had to face the Schemmers.

She knocked on the door. There was Lusita, her face a pale mask of incredulity. "Señorita Blanche! *Bienvenido!* I hear you are coming but ..." She looked over her shoulder and then back at Blanche. "Guli will be watching," she whispered.

Frau Schemmer came clicking down the hall out of the dim interior. She was dressed formally in a white blouse with a soft ruff and a gray pencil skirt. Her hair was pulled back in a tight bun, and the smile didn't reach her ice-blue eyes. Blanche was at once aware of her own travel-weary outfit, a faded linen skirt and a loose cotton top (the wire and tape slightly irritating her middle).

"So nice to see you again, Señorita Blanche. Please." She pivoted on her heel, and Blanche stepped into the hall, distracted by the cloying sweetness of lilies on the hall table. The Frau looked out the door. "Señor Emilio?"

"Oh, he'll be here soon. A delay. Something to do with some calls to his department chair and his studies." She lied so easily.

Blanche looked sideways at the retreating maid. "How is everyone? You and Herr Schemmer?" Blanche was dying to know if the Frau had an update from Bruno. After all, the Frau supposedly assumed Margarita was dead. If she had other news, Blanche would be in big trouble. That detail could surely complicate matters if not tank the plan.

"Very well, I suppose," said the Frau. "No word from Tomás? You didn't see him?"

"Why no. Did you have some business with him? More tango?"

The Frau ignored Blanche's question, mincing quickly toward the living room. She'd been pleasant enough but now seemed agitated and brusque. Blanche didn't find that unusual. The Frau had an odd personality that seemed to shift at will. She pointed to a sofa and smiled, wanly. "How was the sightseeing?"

"Good, yes, the Capital was fine," Blanche said. "We had a great time!" She averted her eyes.

Herr Schemmer sat in a sunny spot near a living room window, a wreath of smoke from his pipe above his head and a crinkled newspaper in his hands. He rose when he saw Blanche. "Ah, the little *americaine*." Now she had a French soubriquet. She'd had many iterations "down life's path," as Gran used to say, but this was a new one. She was prepared to be, or do anything, to get these people arrested. "And your handsome beau? Is he here?"

"He'll be here soon." She'd come alone, and she would remain alone, praying she could pull this off and get back to Emilio. "So nice to see you again, Herr Schemmer. And you, Frau Schemmer."

"I think you can call us Gerda and Karl. I'm sorry not to see Emilio." Her clipped tone indicated a lack of interest in that department. It was clear the Frau was intent on dispatching Blanche, one way or the other.

"Yes. Gerda and Karl." Blanche clutched her backpack and put on her best smile, given the fluttering in her stomach. She took a seat on the edge of a leather armchair.

"What brings you back, Señorita?" the Herr asked. "You and your beau settled up with us though I do think your departure was rather abrupt." His eyebrows shot up in question.

"I'm sorry about that. We had an early drive back, but we love it here. Would *love* to stay on a bit. So gracious of you to accept these whimsical plans."

Oh, boy, have we got a plan.

"Yes, whimsical," said the Frau. She positioned herself at the window, the light obliterating her features. Her posture was ramrod straight and her tone offhand.

Enough with all the fake pleasantries. Blanche steeled herself.

"And, so, you might guess, that we would come back. Since there is some unfinished *business*. Besides settling up for a couple of more days here, that is" She struck a soft note, toned down her impatience. She shouldn't rush it.

"Oh, we'll worry about that later. I'd imagine you're good for a few more pesos." He had such a hearty way about him.

Blanche eyed the silver tray with the heavy crystal glasses and decanters of brown booze, the perfect grease for this wheel. She glanced from one to the other and waited for them to pick up on her comment about unfinished business, but they didn't. Their expressions were impenetrable.

Blanche held her tongue, trying not to bite it. Finally, the Herr asked, "What unfinished *business* would that be?"

Blanche adjusted her backpack next to the chair and crossed her leg, resisting the urge to start twiddling her foot. Her head was down, her emotions were doing somersaults. "Let's chat a bit first, if that's okay. Why don't we have a drink? Wouldn't that be nice?"

"I am so remiss. I should have offered you refreshment. You do look a bit peaked." The Herr stood up, headed for the tray, and poured drinks for the three of them. The Frau didn't seem inclined. She hadn't moved from the window, arms crossed, and the vibe she sent was one of irritation. "Not for me, *danke*."

Blanche leapt at the word. "German! I hardly hear you speak it, and you are German, after all."

"That's true," said the Frau. "A pity. This English and Spanish, only."

"You clearly miss the homeland?"

"Wouldn't you? Cut off from all you know, out in the middle of nowhere? With these ... savages?"

"Now, Gerda. It's been some time," said the Herr. "We've made adjustments."

The statue came to life, her arms flew out to her sides. "I think I will have that drink." She moved swiftly to the tray, picked up the glass, and took a healthy swig.

"Well. Cheers!" Blanche raised her glass and leaned back, her most nonchalant pose while her stomach did flip flops. "Please, tell me what you miss. What was life like? In the homeland ..."

She looked away. "It's been a long time. One would think I might get used to this place, but, really, no. I remember Schweinfurt like it was yesterday." Her nostalgic tone was sad, and bitter.

"Gerda," he said.

"Oh, why not?" She shot him a look. "Every young one was with us. In the *Jugend*. We were leaders. Young and strong. We had power."

"Over whom? Or what?" Blanche spoke softly, but she meant to hit the mark.

The Frau looked right through her. "We were at *war*. We had the solution in sight."

"*Meine liebe.*"

"Karl! It *was* a long time ago. We did important work, and what difference does it make now? All we have are the memories— wonderful memories of Germany." She clapped a hand to her chest and gazed at him.

"What memories are those?" Blanche asked.

"Of the camaraderie and the discipline and our work."

"Work?"

"Yes." The Frau stood up straighter. "The final solution."

"Of the Jewish people?" Blanche managed to choke it out, knowing the answer. The churning in her stomach made her sick at the thought.

"Yes, exactly," she said, all pretenses gone.

The Herr made a loud hiccupping sound. He gulped his whis- key. "Don't, Gerda."

Her eyes, the ice gone. Her words flamed. "Don't what? Don't talk about it? Talking about it, remembering it, it all comes alive again."

"How's that? Does it make millions of Jews come alive again?" Blanche was on her feet, clearly asking for it. Too late to back down, but it never crossed her mind to ever do such a thing.

If looks could kill, Blanche would have been dead. The Frau

shriveled into herself. She waved a hand dismissively and headed to the tray of liquor. She sloshed whiskey into her glass. "It does not matter. We did our jobs. Of guarding, of marching them off, of loading the cars." She turned to Blanche with a hard, empty look. "And so young, vee were."

"Some would say that was abetting murder."

"Murder isn't a word used in war. But the war is over. Who is to blame *us*?" She lifted the glass.

Blanche reached for her drink and nearly knocked it over. She fought off being physically sick, but she had to keep going. She hoped those at the end of the wire picked up every word.

"I have to tell you. I've done a little exploring," said Blanche, coolly. "In the chapel. *Under* the chapel."

"*Ach!*" The Herr put the newspaper down with a whap. "You are a curious young lady and becoming something of a conundrum." The Frau's cheeks puffed out in her narrow face. Blanche thought about moving closer toward the door. The air in the room had clearly shifted. *Might as well be hung for a sheep as a lamb.* All her life, her grandmother's expressions steered so many of her decisions. She wished divine intervention went along with it.

"That I am. Curious as a cat." Blanche couldn't stop now. "I'm wondering about your storage unit. You know the one I mean, the one under the chapel? Seems like an awful lot of gold down there. What are you saving it for?" Her tone was a studious mix of naiveté and ditz, which wasn't much of a stretch for Blanche.

The Frau shouted at Blanche. "That belongs to us!"

"Really?" Now she couldn't help herself. "By chance, the spoils of war?"

"Why do you want to know?" The Herr was on his feet, and his tone was hard and demanding.

"Just curious." Both feet were planted. She moved to the edge of her seat. The urge to flee suddenly took over. She turned then. "I apologize for snooping. But this place is so fascinating. I couldn't help but stumble across the entrance to those tiny rooms in the tunnel."

"I think that's about enough," the Frau said.

"I agree," said The Herr. He picked up the letter opener on the coffee table.

That was it. Her cue. She threw her glass at the Herr and leapt over the coffee table. She was out the door before the seventy-something Schemmers could move. Even an adept tango dancer couldn't have caught her. She ran. One thing Blanche was exceptionally good at was running. High school and college track had stood her in good stead. The malevolent look of hate on their faces was one that would be a lasting remembrance, and she was glad to leave it behind.

She raced to the back of the house, and miraculously, Lusita was in the kitchen waving her through. The door was wide open, and from there, it was a clear shot to the tower. Blanche bolted past Lusita like her feet were on fire.

Guli stepped out of the shadows at the door to the tower. She fell against him. "Hurry," he said. "Up. The police are on the way."

From the third floor in the tower, Blanche and Guli watched a van pull around and the authorities jump out. The police who had driven her to La Palma were there, too. The plan had been that they would carry warrants and directions to the tunnels. A sense of relief flooded through her as the many threads of a tangled web tied tightly around the Schemmers. Blanche stood close to Guli, so close she could feel the tension leave him and sense the calm rhythm of his breathing. His gaze was riveted on the parade of authorities back and forth at the entrances to La Palma, the vehicles crunching over the gravel, the saga rolling inevitably toward conclusion. She'd lived a lifetime in a very short time, and the lives of many would change forever. Including hers and Emilio's. And Guli's. She looked up at him.

"I'd like to be a mouse running through those rooms right now. What do you think the Schemmers are doing?" she murmured.

"Denying? Pleading? Lying? More of the same. But they can't hide anymore." Guli's hard stare at the big house didn't waver. "I talked to Señor Ochoa. I hope the police got what they need on that wire. You are *loca*."

"Maybe. But it was worth it. Right? After what they've done to you and Esmera—and Margarita? And I don't know how many others. I keep wondering about Tomás's brother, Eduardo."

"There'll be excavations, I'm sure, in many places throughout La Palma."

Disgust shook her. She focused on the relief and success of the moment and the thought of seeing Emilio soon, but her heart tugged for Guli. He'd put up with these tyrants his whole life. "It's been real," she said.

"Yes, it has been real. A real pleasure." Guli looked away from the view to the big house and smiled at Blanche. He draped one arm casually around her shoulders. His taut body and genuine warmth were hard to resist. "One I'll never forget. You'll never know what you did. The extent of it. *Muchas gracias, chica rica. Qué tenga buen vida y el tiempo para gastarla.*" He leaned down and hesitated one second and kissed her forehead.

She smiled up at him, her eyes on his lips. "What a very fine wish."

If that policeman hadn't been walking across the lawn to the tower, she would have done something unforgettable. And unforgiveable? But it didn't end like that. The uniform pounded on the old door below, and Guli was gone to answer.

Thirty-One

Home

THE PALMS PLAYED UP and down the scale in the wind, a high scratchy sound against the window for the small scrubby fronds and low and heavy for the old sabals. Blanche took a deep breath and sank back on the pillow. The empty bottle of Veuve Clicquot clunked over on the uneven cabin floor and rolled across the bedroom.

"I think this is where we started," Emilo murmured and threw an arm over Blanche. "Can it be three months?" Emilio was on a short break from studies in Gainesville.

"Just don't bring me any more dire letters from an estranged aunt." She laughed and snuggled in next to him, so relieved they'd gone and done it all.

"No, I won't! But Tía Margarita is fine and happy. She and Issie. And you and me, *Baquita*." He pulled her closer and squeezed tightly. "I'd say that was one hot tango."

"What a way to meet the family!"

"Sorry about that." He sat up and threw a pillow behind his head. "It was an adventure, no?"

"Yes. With you?" Blanche smiled. "Always."

"The Schemmers are out. And Margarita is free. She can visit

La Palma if she wants—and Esmera's all right with that. Can you believe it?"

"What else did Margarita say?"

"Some you know. Issie is Bartolo's child by Margarita, and they are celebrating the truth of it, to be honest. Margarita's made amends with Esmera. They have known each other for so many years, and grudgingly, they've come together. For the sake of their children. For the sake of family. And, I guess, for the sake of La Palma. Margarita and Issie are settled in Buenos Aires for now. In Issie's apartment. But they'll go out to the pampa. They love it out there."

"You do, too. Don't you?"

"Well ..."

"And Margarita and Issie are coming to visit! That's so fun," said Blanche. "And what about Tomás? Oh, Emilio. I got a letter from him."

"Is he coming up?"

"Don't think so. But he sounds good."

Blanche leaned over to the bedside table and opened a lacquered box covered in coquina shells. It contained a lock of her mother's hair, her father's dog tags—and Tomás's letter.

"Dr. Irigoyen did a good job on Tomás," she said.

"Yes ..."

"But this." Blanche unfolded a letter written on tissue-thin stationery in a spidery hand. "Listen ..."

Estimada, y querida, Blanche Murninghan,

It is with full heart and many thanks that I write this letter. You and the honorable doctor, Emilio Del Sierra, accomplish much in your visit. Your generous spirit does great service to your family and to us. Gracias a Dios, I met you. Many things happen since I write you last.

Here is latest news.

The Schemmers will go to Germany to face conse-quences of World War II. Many factors enter here. Anna

Gamoure, you must remember, is good tango dancer, and she is also witness to Herr Schemmer's war stories and anecdotes to take over La Palma. Lusita is invaluable in the plan to expose the Germans. She provides assistance with cameras and good hearing. Y, no puedo olvidar— Hernan! He gives much background to the Schemmers' plan to murder Margarita. He does not like fences and the boundaries of bad intentions. Por fin, the treasure under the chapel belongs to the Jewish people, and there is provision now to return it.

But the damage is done. We look forward to new times and rebuilding. I hope repair is imminent.

La Palma, respectfully, belongs to the viuda Esmera. She and her son, Guillermo, are rightful owners under the law, and they now take over the grand pink house. They cooperate with authorities in the excavation of the land around the estancia, and soon, the bones rise out of the ground. My brother, Eduardo and the others of the Disappeared are recovered. The team who works to restore our lost loved ones gives to me the blue and white box containing my brother. Something I hold close and often shake. The dull sound of bone and ash is nothing like his singing and jokes, but it is a kind of music to me.

I remember the day they came and took him away. More than twenty-five years ago. I was a boy. Eyenda, the maid, crying in horror, the curtains moving like ghosts. All that is gone, but I have my box of memories and relief and gratitude that I have him back to me, such as he is.

We go full circle, Señorita Blanche, and we come back to one another. I hope one day to see you and the doctor, Emilio, here or wherever Dios may take us. Do not forget to say my name and the name of my brother, Eduardo— and I do the same, the names of Blanche Murninghan and Emilio Del Sierra, who live in my heart and soul.

Hasta siempre,
Con mucho cariño,
Tomás

Thank You!

Thank you for reading! If you enjoyed this book, please leave a review on Amazon, Goodreads, BookBub, The Story Graph, or anywhere else you like to track your recent reads. Alternatively, you could post online or tell a friend about it. This helps our authors more than you may know.

- The Team at Torchflame Books

Acknowledgements

In 2005, I lived in San Juan, Argentina, at the foot of the Andes and worked for a gold mine. I taught English to the children of expats and to the locals at St. Paul Colegio in town. It was an indelible experience because of the gracious hospitality of those I worked for, the children, my fellow teachers, and the Argentinians of San Juan. I flew to Buenos Aires many times for book business, to sit in Café Tortoni and watch people, to drink Voignier and eat steak and frites, to walk for miles and miles around this fascinating city. Thank you to all I met in this beautiful country, and to my five children, Jim, Mick and his wife Mary, Amos, Miles, and Frances, who joined me in Argentina for many an asado and a song. I remember Miles sitting in the stairwell of a hotel in Buenos Aires writing, "Argentina." His band, The Pistols at Dawn, later sang it at many venues in Chicago and recorded it with a flourish of trumpets and strings. Thanks, Miles, for the epigraph.

Thank you to my fantastic reader, Judith Anne Horner, and to my editor, Donna Essner. To Bill Murphy, an Irishman with an extraordinary eye and no nonsense about him, and to Teri Rider, Jori Hanna, and the team at Torchflame Books.

And my most heartfelt thanks to my cousin Charles "Carlitos" Nau who passed away during the writing of this book. He always asked me how it was coming along as he added one more improbable circumstance for Blanche to deal with, which made us laugh. He sent me many books for my research, and always more books to lift me up. It was like Christmas to see that brown box on my doorstep; he loved Christmas. I love you, Chuck. Miss you.

About the Author

NANCY NAU SULLIVAN is the author of memoir, mystery, and a novel. She began writing in high school and college for the newspapers. Later, she worked as an editorial assistant at New York magazines and as a print journalist throughout the Midwest.

Nancy was born in San Francisco, grew up outside Chicago, but often visited Anna Maria Island, Florida. She returned to the island with her family and wrote an award-winning memoir, The Last Cadillac, about the years she cared for her father while her children were still at home—a harrowing adventure of travel, health issues, adolescent angst, with a hurricane thrown in for good measure. She kept the Florida setting for her first cozy mystery, Saving Tuna Street, creating the fictional Santa Maria Island for the Blanche Murninghan mystery series, now in its fifth installment with Hot Tango in Argentina. Blanche's other adventures have taken her to Mexico City, Vietnam, and Ireland. Nancy also wrote a suspense novel, The Boys of Alpha Block, based on her experience teaching in a boys' prison near Tampa.

Nancy lives near the Florida Gulf Beaches. She is a graduate of the University of San Francisco (San Francisco College for Women, Lone Mountain) with a double major in Spanish and political science and holds a master's degree in journalism from Marquette University. She later attended the University of Florida in English and education. Find Nancy at nancynausullivan.com.

More from Nancy Nav Sullivan

Saving Tuna Street

When her dear friend is found murdered in the parking lot of the marina, Blanche Murninghan begins digging into his death. With her friends Liza and Hassi by her side, she stumbles into a pit of greed, murder, drug running, and kidnapping. Blanche has survived her fair share of storms on Santa Maria Island, but this one might just be her last.

Trouble Down Mexico Way

When Blanche "Bang" Murninghan visits an exhibit of ancient Mayan ruins in Mexico City with her cousin, she sees that all is not ancient. One of the mummies has a pink hair clip embedded in its hay-like do, and the texture of the skin is not quite right. Seeking the truth proves more dangerous than either of them expected.

Mission Improbable: Vietnam

Against her better judgment, Blanche travels to Vietnam with her new friend to beat down the doors of the past. She is looking for Jean's mother and following her father's trail. He left without a trace. Or did he? Does anyone?

A Deathly Irish Secret

While visiting her newly inherited castle, Blanche Murninghan investigates two mysterious deaths. Soon she fears she may have uncovered too much for the many secrets to send her home unscathed.

www.ingramcontent.com/pod-product-compliance
Lightning Source LLC
Chambersburg PA
CBHW020542020726
47494CB00006B/1883